— AN **ASSASSIN'S CREED**® SERIES —

EDGINTON • WIJNGAARD • FARRELL

LAST
DESCENDANTS
LOCUS

D1147405

LONDON BOROUGH OF BARNET

An Assassin's Creed Series: Last Descendants - Locus
9781782763130

Published by Titan Comics
A division of Titan Publishing Group Ltd.
144 Southwark St.
London
SE1 0UP

Assassin's Creed is trademark™ and copyright © 2017 Ubisoft Entertainment.
All Rights Reserved. *Assassin's Creed*, Ubisoft, and the Ubisoft logo are trademarks of Ubisoft
Entertainment in the U.S. and/or other countries.

No part of this publication may be reproduced, stored in a retrieval system, or transmitted, in any
form or by any means, without the prior written permission of the publisher. Names, characters,
places and incidents featured in this publication are either the product of the author's imagination
or used fictitiously. Any resemblance to actual persons, living or dead (except for satirical
purposes), is entirely coincidental.

A CIP catalogue record for this title is available from the British Library

First edition: April 2017

10 9 8 7 6 5 4 3 2 1

Printed in China.
Titan Comics. 0739

TITAN COMICS

EDITOR: TOM WILLIAMS
DESIGNER: RUSS SEAL

Senior Comics Editor: Andrew James
Titan Comics Editorial: Jessica Burton, Amoona Saohin, Lauren McPhee
Production Supervisions: Jackie Flook, Maria Pearson
Production Assistant: Peter James
Production Manager: Obi Onuora
Art Director: Oz Browne
Senior Sales Manager: Steve Tothill
Press Officer: Will O'Mullane
Direct Sales & Marketing Manager: Ricky Claydon
Head of Rights: Jenny Boyce
Publishing Manager: Darryl Tothill
Publishing Director: Chris Teather
Operations Director: Leigh Baulch
Executive Director: Vivian Cheung
Publisher: Nick Landau

WWW.TITAN-COMICS.COM

Follow us on Twitter @ComicsTitan

Visit us at facebook.com/comicstitan

ACKNOWLEDGEMENTS:
Many thanks to Aymar Azaïzia, Anouk Bachman, Richard Farrese,
Raphaël Lacoste, Caroline Lamache and Clémence Deleuze.

© 2017 Ubisoft Entertainment. All Rights Reserved. Assassin's Creed, Ubisoft,
and the Ubisoft logo are trademarks of Ubisoft Entertainment in the U.S. and/or other countries.

CHAPTER
1

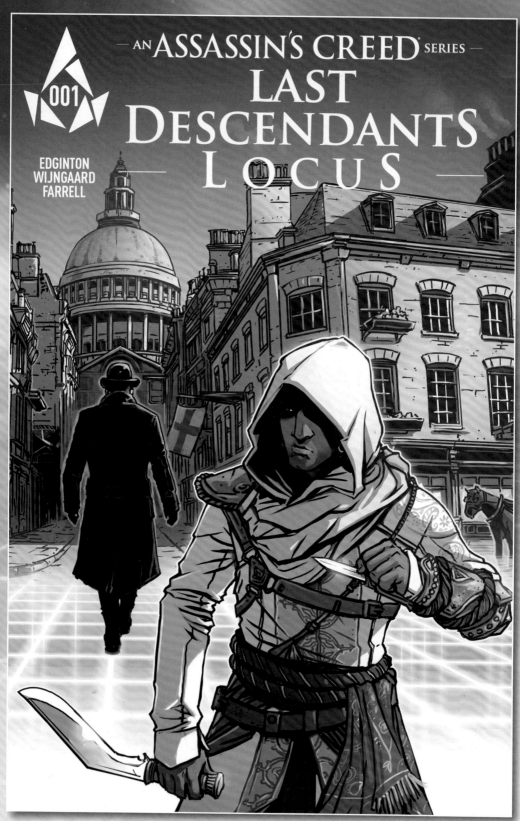

AN ASSASSIN'S CREED SERIES
LAST DESCENDANTS
LOCUS

001

EDGINTON
WIJNGAARD
FARRELL

COVER A: CASPAR WIJNGAARD

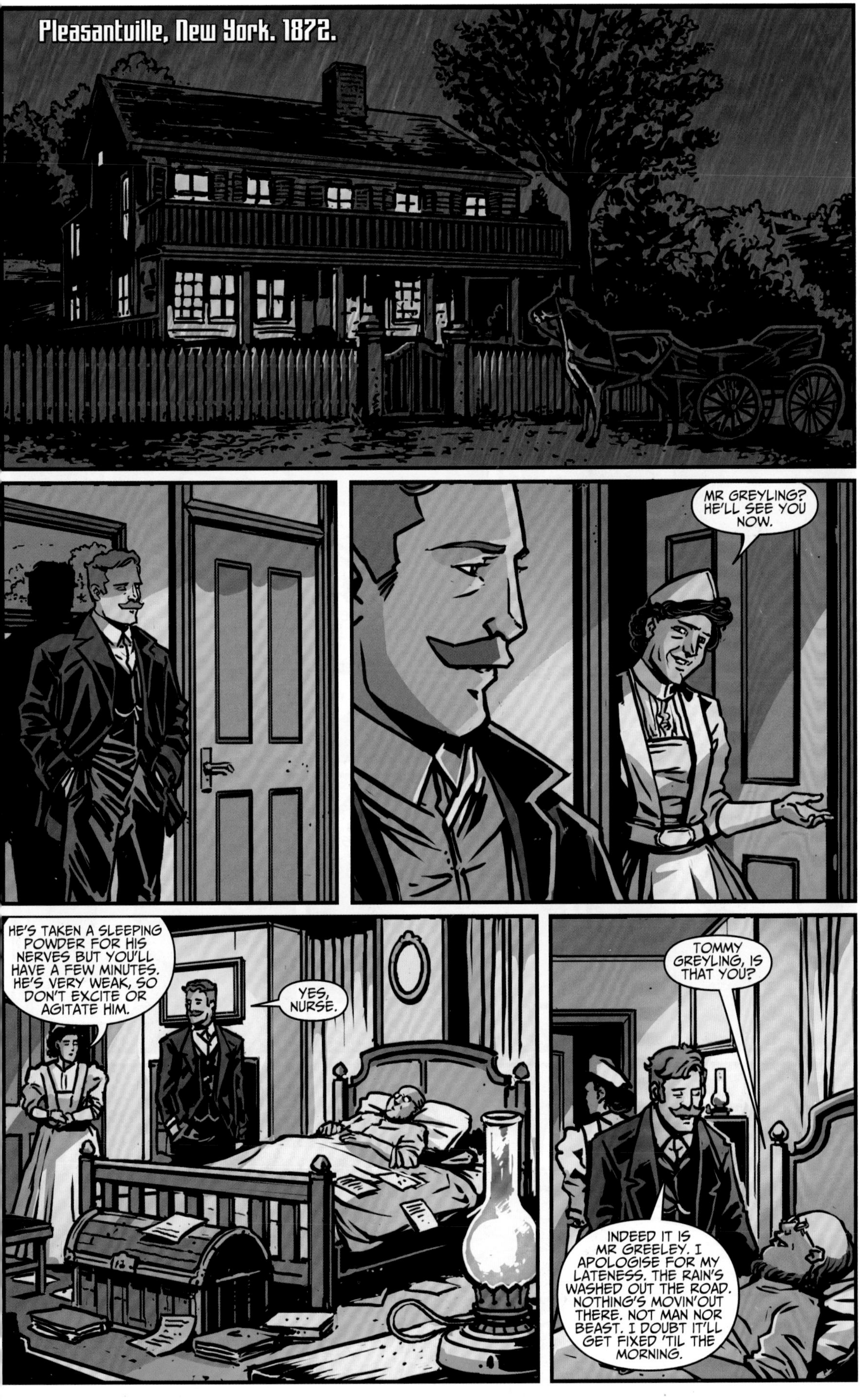
Pleasantville, New York. 1872.
MR GREYLING? HE'LL SEE YOU NOW.
HE'S TAKEN A SLEEPING POWDER FOR HIS NERVES BUT YOU'LL HAVE A FEW MINUTES. HE'S VERY WEAK, SO DON'T EXCITE OR AGITATE HIM.
YES, NURSE.
TOMMY GREYLING, IS THAT YOU?
INDEED IT IS MR GREELEY. I APOLOGISE FOR MY LATENESS. THE RAIN'S WASHED OUT THE ROAD. NOTHING'S MOVIN'OUT THERE. NOT MAN NOR BEAST. I DOUBT IT'LL GET FIXED 'TIL THE MORNING.

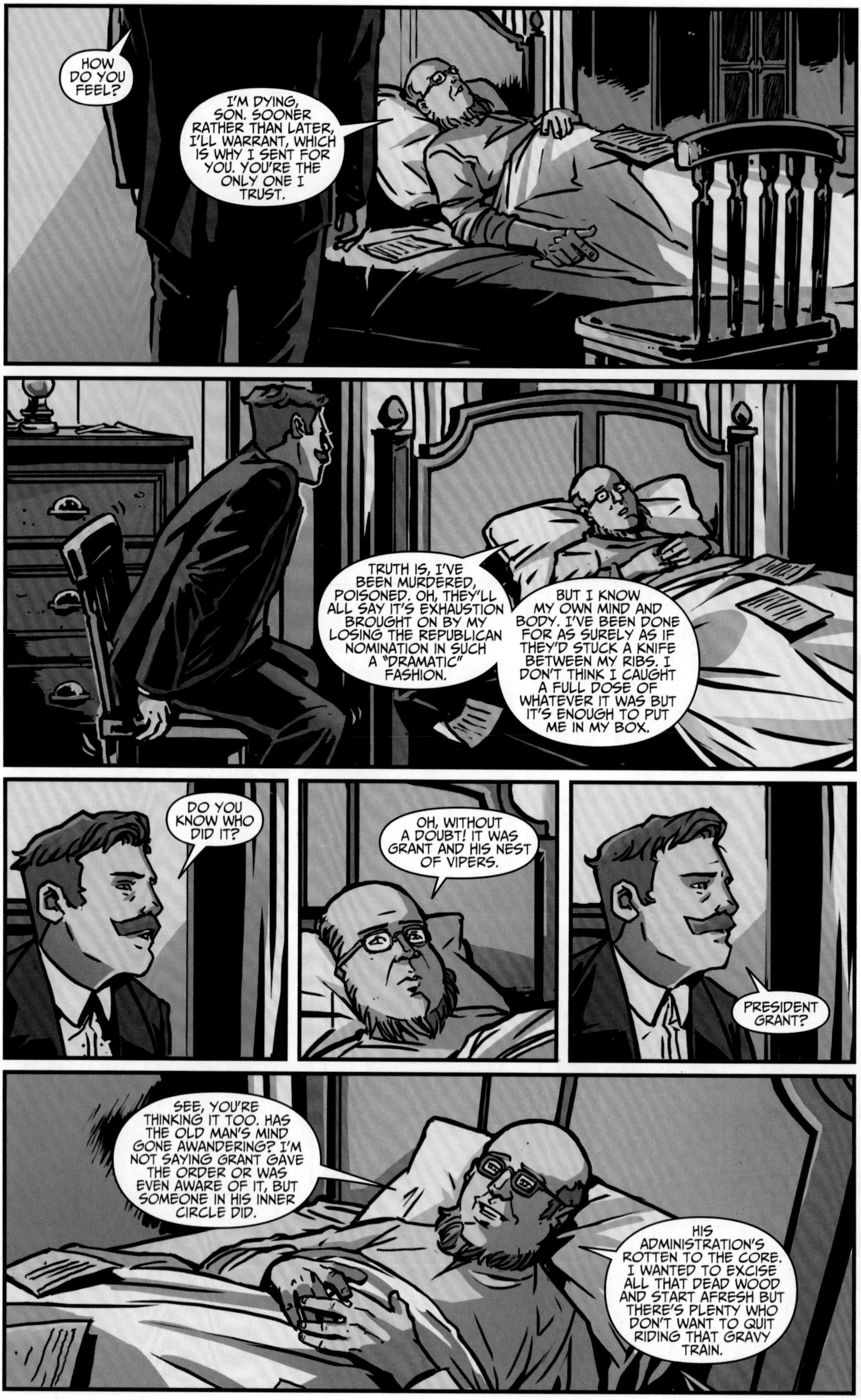
HOW DO YOU FEEL?
I'M DYING, SON. SOONER RATHER THAN LATER, I'LL WARRANT, WHICH IS WHY I SENT FOR YOU. YOU'RE THE ONLY ONE I TRUST.
TRUTH IS, I'VE BEEN MURDERED, POISONED. OH, THEY'LL ALL SAY IT'S EXHAUSTION BROUGHT ON BY MY LOSING THE REPUBLICAN NOMINATION IN SUCH A "DRAMATIC" FASHION.
BUT I KNOW MY OWN MIND AND BODY. I'VE BEEN DONE FOR AS SURELY AS IF THEY'D STUCK A KNIFE BETWEEN MY RIBS. I DON'T THINK I CAUGHT A FULL DOSE OF WHATEVER IT WAS BUT IT'S ENOUGH TO PUT ME IN MY BOX.
DO YOU KNOW WHO DID IT?
OH, WITHOUT A DOUBT! IT WAS GRANT AND HIS NEST OF VIPERS.
PRESIDENT GRANT?
SEE, YOU'RE THINKING IT TOO. HAS THE OLD MAN'S MIND GONE AWANDERING? I'M NOT SAYING GRANT GAVE THE ORDER OR WAS EVEN AWARE OF IT, BUT SOMEONE IN HIS INNER CIRCLE DID.
HIS ADMINISTRATION'S ROTTEN TO THE CORE. I WANTED TO EXCISE ALL THAT DEAD WOOD AND START AFRESH BUT THERE'S PLENTY WHO DON'T WANT TO QUIT RIDING THAT GRAVY TRAIN.

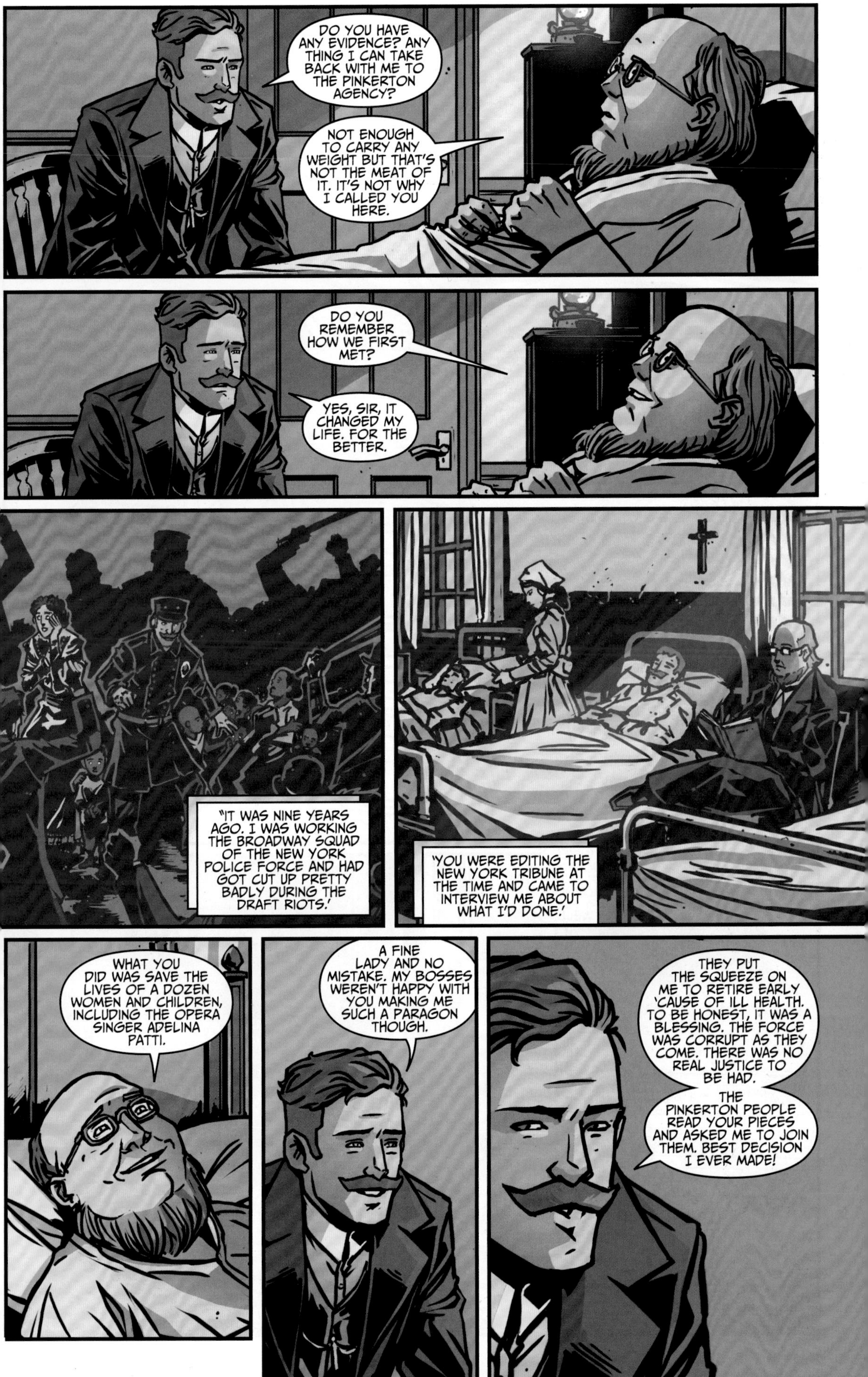
DO YOU HAVE ANY EVIDENCE? ANY THING I CAN TAKE BACK WITH ME TO THE PINKERTON AGENCY?
NOT ENOUGH TO CARRY ANY WEIGHT BUT THAT'S NOT THE MEAT OF IT. IT'S NOT WHY I CALLED YOU HERE.
DO YOU REMEMBER HOW WE FIRST MET?
YES, SIR, IT CHANGED MY LIFE. FOR THE BETTER.
"IT WAS NINE YEARS AGO. I WAS WORKING THE BROADWAY SQUAD OF THE NEW YORK POLICE FORCE AND HAD GOT CUT UP PRETTY BADLY DURING THE DRAFT RIOTS.'
'YOU WERE EDITING THE NEW YORK TRIBUNE AT THE TIME AND CAME TO INTERVIEW ME ABOUT WHAT I'D DONE.'
WHAT YOU DID WAS SAVE THE LIVES OF A DOZEN WOMEN AND CHILDREN, INCLUDING THE OPERA SINGER ADELINA PATTI.
A FINE LADY AND NO MISTAKE. MY BOSSES WEREN'T HAPPY WITH YOU MAKING ME SUCH A PARAGON THOUGH.
THEY PUT THE SQUEEZE ON ME TO RETIRE EARLY 'CAUSE OF ILL HEALTH. TO BE HONEST, IT WAS A BLESSING. THE FORCE WAS CORRUPT AS THEY COME. THERE WAS NO REAL JUSTICE TO BE HAD.
THE PINKERTON PEOPLE READ YOUR PIECES AND ASKED ME TO JOIN THEM. BEST DECISION I EVER MADE!

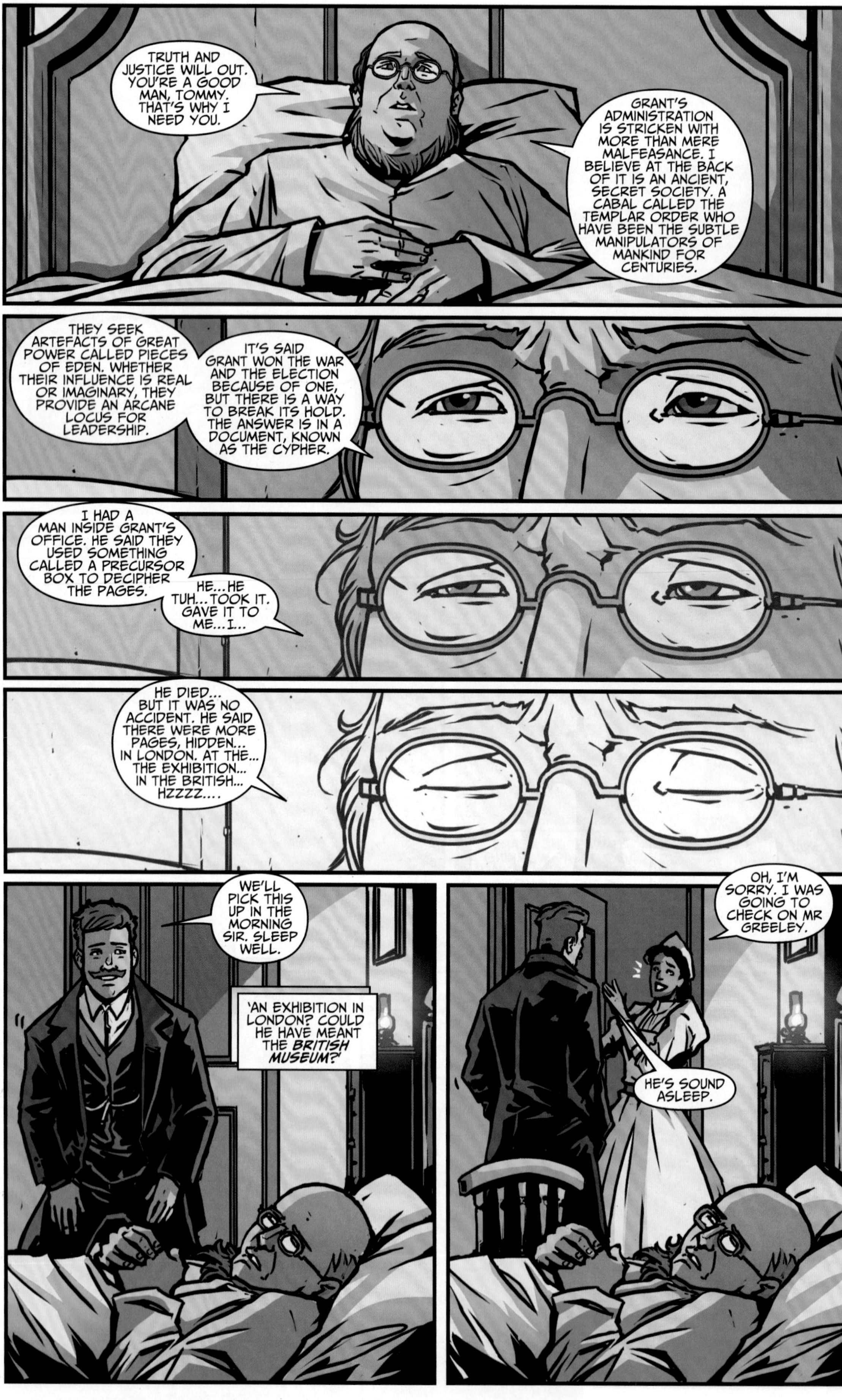
TRUTH AND JUSTICE WILL OUT. YOU'RE A GOOD MAN, TOMMY. THAT'S WHY I NEED YOU.
GRANT'S ADMINISTRATION IS STRICKEN WITH MORE THAN MERE MALFEASANCE. I BELIEVE AT THE BACK OF IT IS AN ANCIENT, SECRET SOCIETY. A CABAL CALLED THE TEMPLAR ORDER WHO HAVE BEEN THE SUBTLE MANIPULATORS OF MANKIND FOR CENTURIES.
THEY SEEK ARTEFACTS OF GREAT POWER CALLED PIECES OF EDEN. WHETHER THEIR INFLUENCE IS REAL OR IMAGINARY, THEY PROVIDE AN ARCANE LOCUS FOR LEADERSHIP.
IT'S SAID GRANT WON THE WAR AND THE ELECTION BECAUSE OF ONE, BUT THERE IS A WAY TO BREAK ITS HOLD. THE ANSWER IS IN A DOCUMENT, KNOWN AS THE CYPHER.
I HAD A MAN INSIDE GRANT'S OFFICE. HE SAID THEY USED SOMETHING CALLED A PRECURSOR BOX TO DECIPHER THE PAGES.
HE...HE TUH...TOOK IT. GAVE IT TO ME...I...
HE DIED... BUT IT WAS NO ACCIDENT. HE SAID THERE WERE MORE PAGES, HIDDEN... IN LONDON. AT THE... THE EXHIBITION... IN THE BRITISH... HZZZZ....
WE'LL PICK THIS UP IN THE MORNING SIR. SLEEP WELL.
'AN EXHIBITION IN LONDON? COULD HE HAVE MEANT THE *BRITISH MUSEUM*?'
OH, I'M SORRY. I WAS GOING TO CHECK ON MR GREELEY.
HE'S SOUND ASLEEP.

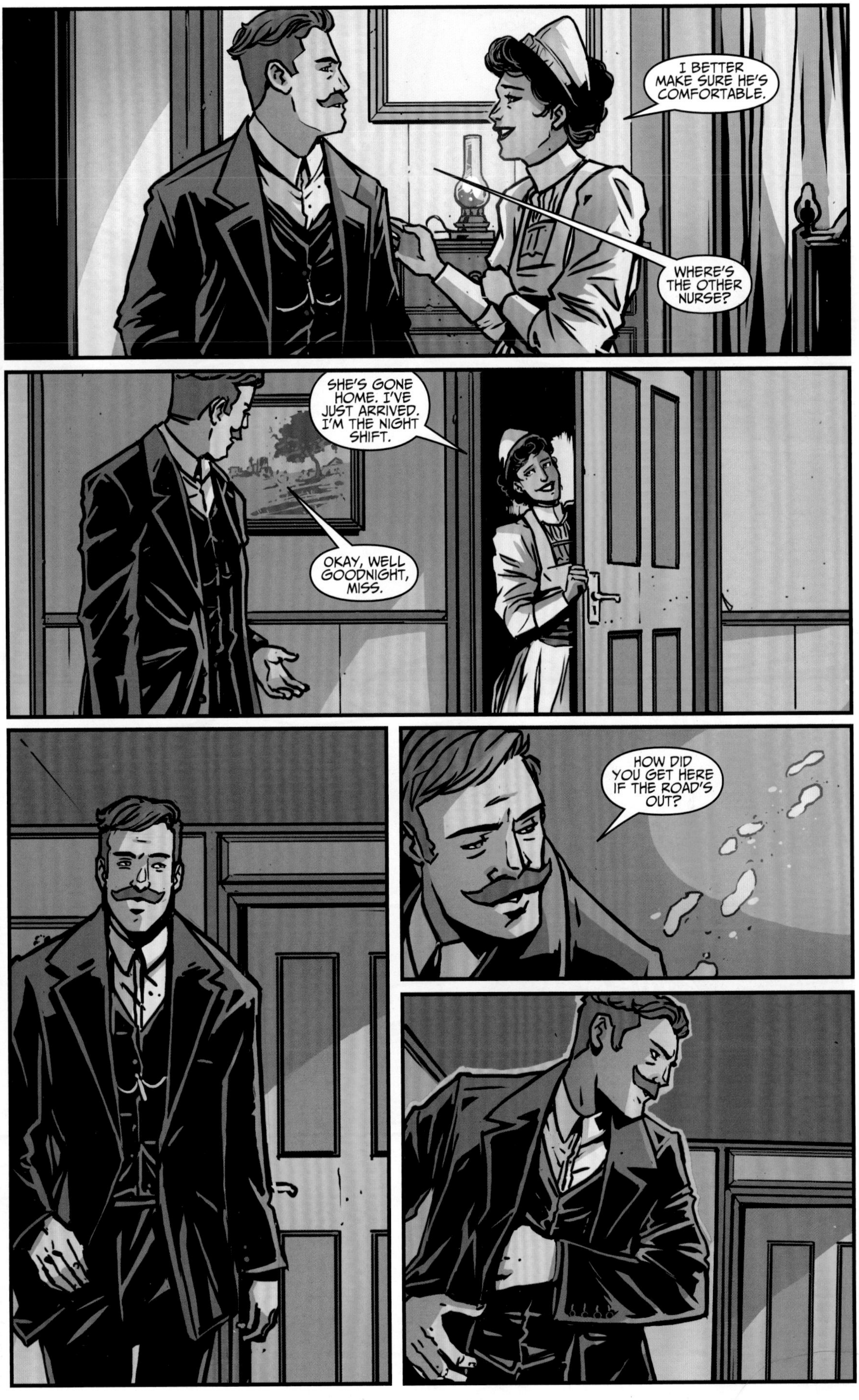
I BETTER MAKE SURE HE'S COMFORTABLE.
WHERE'S THE OTHER NURSE?
SHE'S GONE HOME. I'VE JUST ARRIVED. I'M THE NIGHT SHIFT.
OKAY, WELL GOODNIGHT, MISS.
HOW DID YOU GET HERE IF THE ROAD'S OUT?

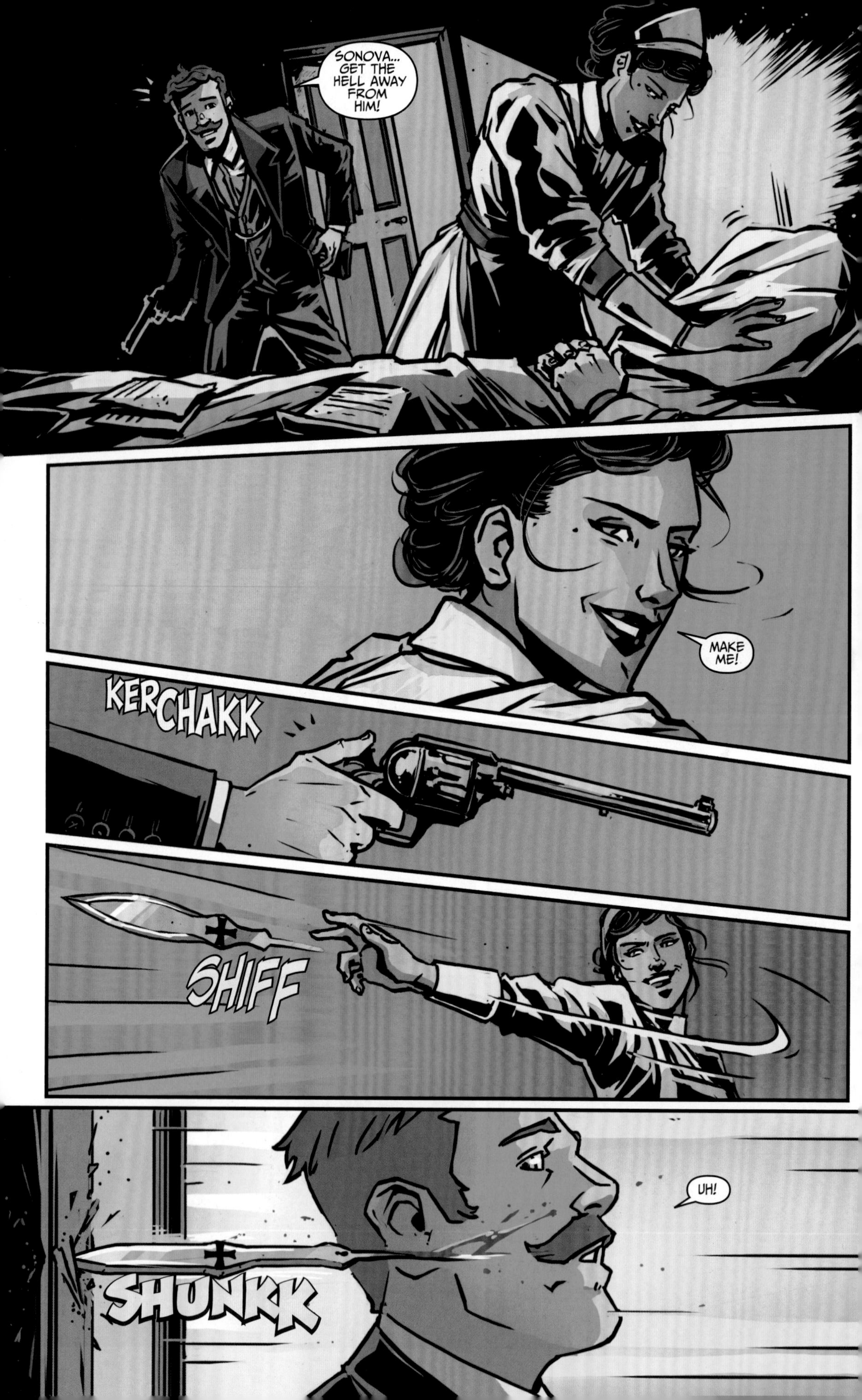
SONOVA... GET THE HELL AWAY FROM HIM!
MAKE ME!
KERCHAKK
SHIFF
UH!
SHUNKK

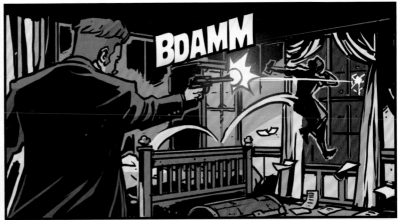

BDAMM

BDAMM

SKISHH

WHAT ON EARTH IS GOING ON IN HERE!

THE STORM, IT BLEW THE WINDOW IN.

HMM. THAT LOOKS NASTY BUT YOU'LL LIVE.

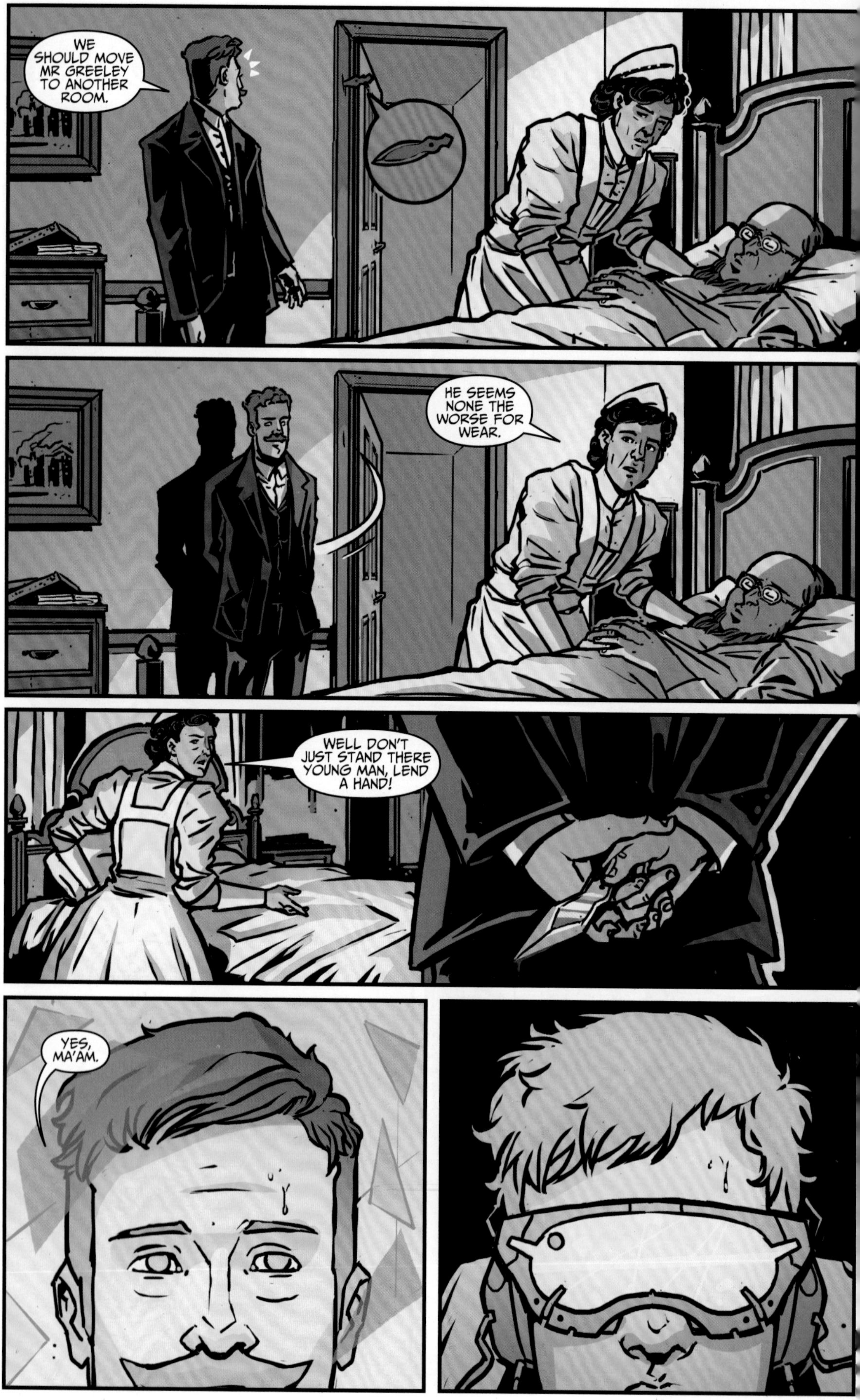
WE SHOULD MOVE MR GREELEY TO ANOTHER ROOM.
HE SEEMS NONE THE WORSE FOR WEAR.
WELL DON'T JUST STAND THERE YOUNG MAN, LEND A HAND!
YES, MA'AM.

HOW DID IT GO?

YOU WERE RIGHT! IT SEEMS LIKE PRESIDENT GRANT'S NOMINATION AND ELECTION WAS THANKS TO THE INFLUENCE OF ONE OF THE PIECES OF EDEN.

AT LEAST, THAT'S WHAT, HORACE GREELEY, THINKS. HE DID SOME DIGGING AROUND AND SEEMS TO HAVE FOUND OUT KINDA A LOT...

SUCH AS?

HERE, LET ME...

I CAN MANAGE... THANK YOU!

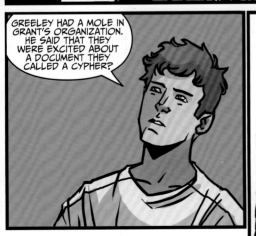

GREELEY HAD A MOLE IN GRANT'S ORGANIZATION. HE SAID THAT THEY WERE EXCITED ABOUT A DOCUMENT THEY CALLED A CYPHER?

WHAT ELSE DID HE SAY?

WELL, GREELEY WAS SICK AND ON MEDICATION. HE SUSPECTED HE'D BEEN POISONED...

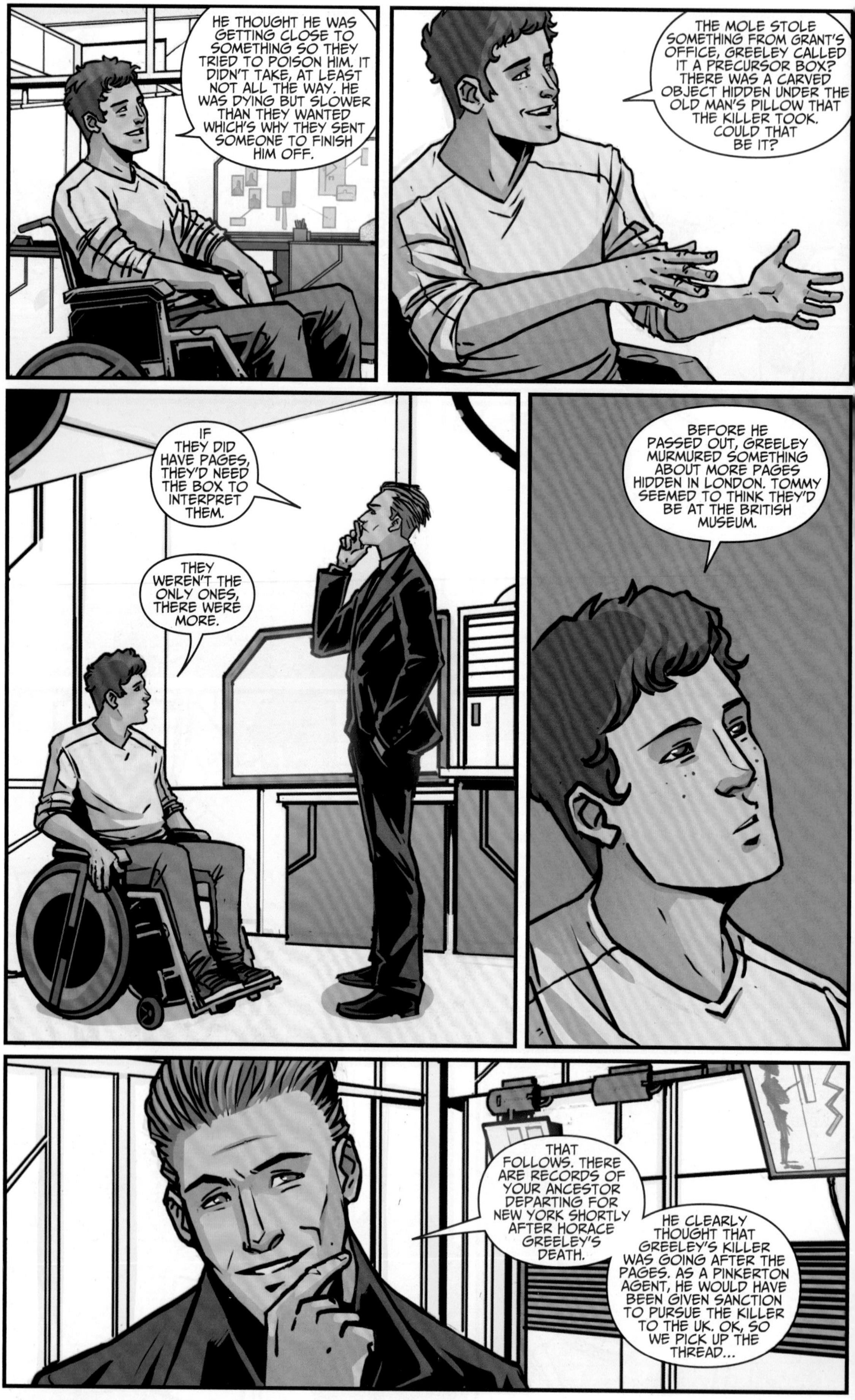
HE THOUGHT HE WAS GETTING CLOSE TO SOMETHING SO THEY TRIED TO POISON HIM. IT DIDN'T TAKE, AT LEAST NOT ALL THE WAY. HE WAS DYING BUT SLOWER THAN THEY WANTED WHICH'S WHY THEY SENT SOMEONE TO FINISH HIM OFF.
THE MOLE STOLE SOMETHING FROM GRANT'S OFFICE, GREELEY CALLED IT A PRECURSOR BOX? THERE WAS A CARVED OBJECT HIDDEN UNDER THE OLD MAN'S PILLOW THAT THE KILLER TOOK. COULD THAT BE IT?
IF THEY DID HAVE PAGES, THEY'D NEED THE BOX TO INTERPRET THEM.
THEY WEREN'T THE ONLY ONES, THERE WERE MORE.
BEFORE HE PASSED OUT, GREELEY MURMURED SOMETHING ABOUT MORE PAGES HIDDEN IN LONDON. TOMMY SEEMED TO THINK THEY'D BE AT THE BRITISH MUSEUM.
THAT FOLLOWS. THERE ARE RECORDS OF YOUR ANCESTOR DEPARTING FOR NEW YORK SHORTLY AFTER HORACE GREELEY'S DEATH.
HE CLEARLY THOUGHT THAT GREELEY'S KILLER WAS GOING AFTER THE PAGES. AS A PINKERTON AGENT, HE WOULD HAVE BEEN GIVEN SANCTION TO PURSUE THE KILLER TO THE UK. OK, SO WE PICK UP THE THREAD...

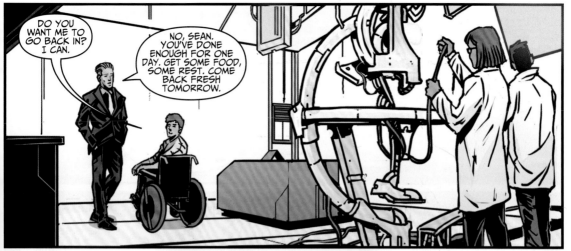

DO YOU WANT ME TO GO BACK IN? I CAN.

NO, SEAN. YOU'VE DONE ENOUGH FOR ONE DAY. GET SOME FOOD, SOME REST. COME BACK FRESH TOMORROW.

THAT'S THE ONE THING ABOUT THE PAST, IT'LL ALWAYS BE THERE.

SURE.

GO HAVE SOME FUN, YOU'RE ONLY YOUNG ONCE.

DEPENDS WHO'S LIFE YOU'RE LIVING!

LAB-06

'I DEFINITELY THINK WE'RE ONTO SOMETHING.'

THE BOY'S MEMORIES MAY WELL BE THE KEY TO WHAT WE'RE LOOKING FOR, ON HOW TO USE THE PRONGS OF EDEN.

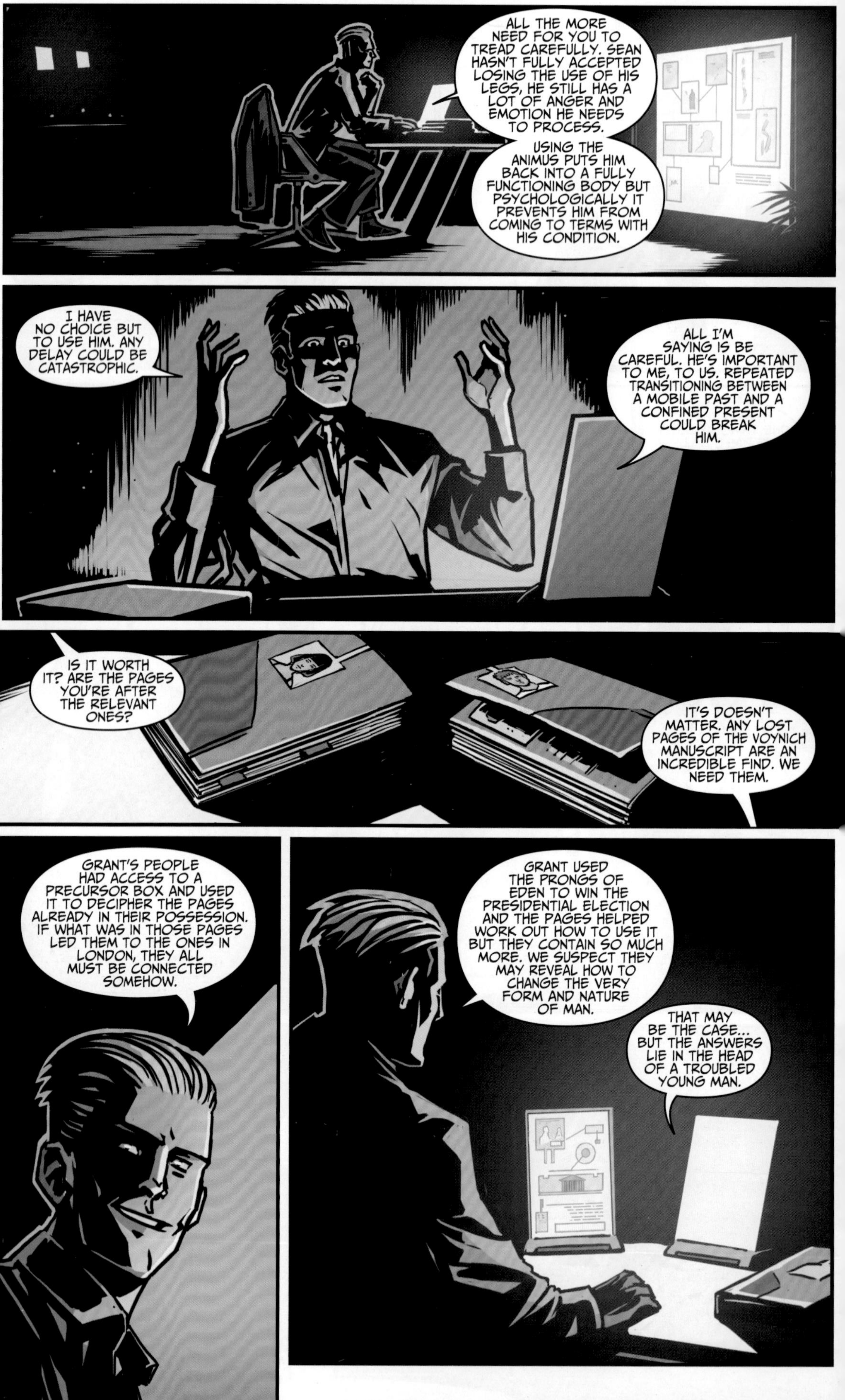
ALL THE MORE NEED FOR YOU TO TREAD CAREFULLY. SEAN HASN'T FULLY ACCEPTED LOSING THE USE OF HIS LEGS, HE STILL HAS A LOT OF ANGER AND EMOTION HE NEEDS TO PROCESS.
USING THE ANIMUS PUTS HIM BACK INTO A FULLY FUNCTIONING BODY BUT PSYCHOLOGICALLY IT PREVENTS HIM FROM COMING TO TERMS WITH HIS CONDITION.
I HAVE NO CHOICE BUT TO USE HIM. ANY DELAY COULD BE CATASTROPHIC.
ALL I'M SAYING IS BE CAREFUL. HE'S IMPORTANT TO ME, TO US. REPEATED TRANSITIONING BETWEEN A MOBILE PAST AND A CONFINED PRESENT COULD BREAK HIM.
IS IT WORTH IT? ARE THE PAGES YOU'RE AFTER THE RELEVANT ONES?
IT'S DOESN'T MATTER. ANY LOST PAGES OF THE VOYNICH MANUSCRIPT ARE AN INCREDIBLE FIND. WE NEED THEM.
GRANT'S PEOPLE HAD ACCESS TO A PRECURSOR BOX AND USED IT TO DECIPHER THE PAGES ALREADY IN THEIR POSSESSION. IF WHAT WAS IN THOSE PAGES LED THEM TO THE ONES IN LONDON, THEY ALL MUST BE CONNECTED SOMEHOW.
GRANT USED THE PRONGS OF EDEN TO WIN THE PRESIDENTIAL ELECTION AND THE PAGES HELPED WORK OUT HOW TO USE IT BUT THEY CONTAIN SO MUCH MORE. WE SUSPECT THEY MAY REVEAL HOW TO CHANGE THE VERY FORM AND NATURE OF MAN.
THAT MAY BE THE CASE... BUT THE ANSWERS LIE IN THE HEAD OF A TROUBLED YOUNG MAN.

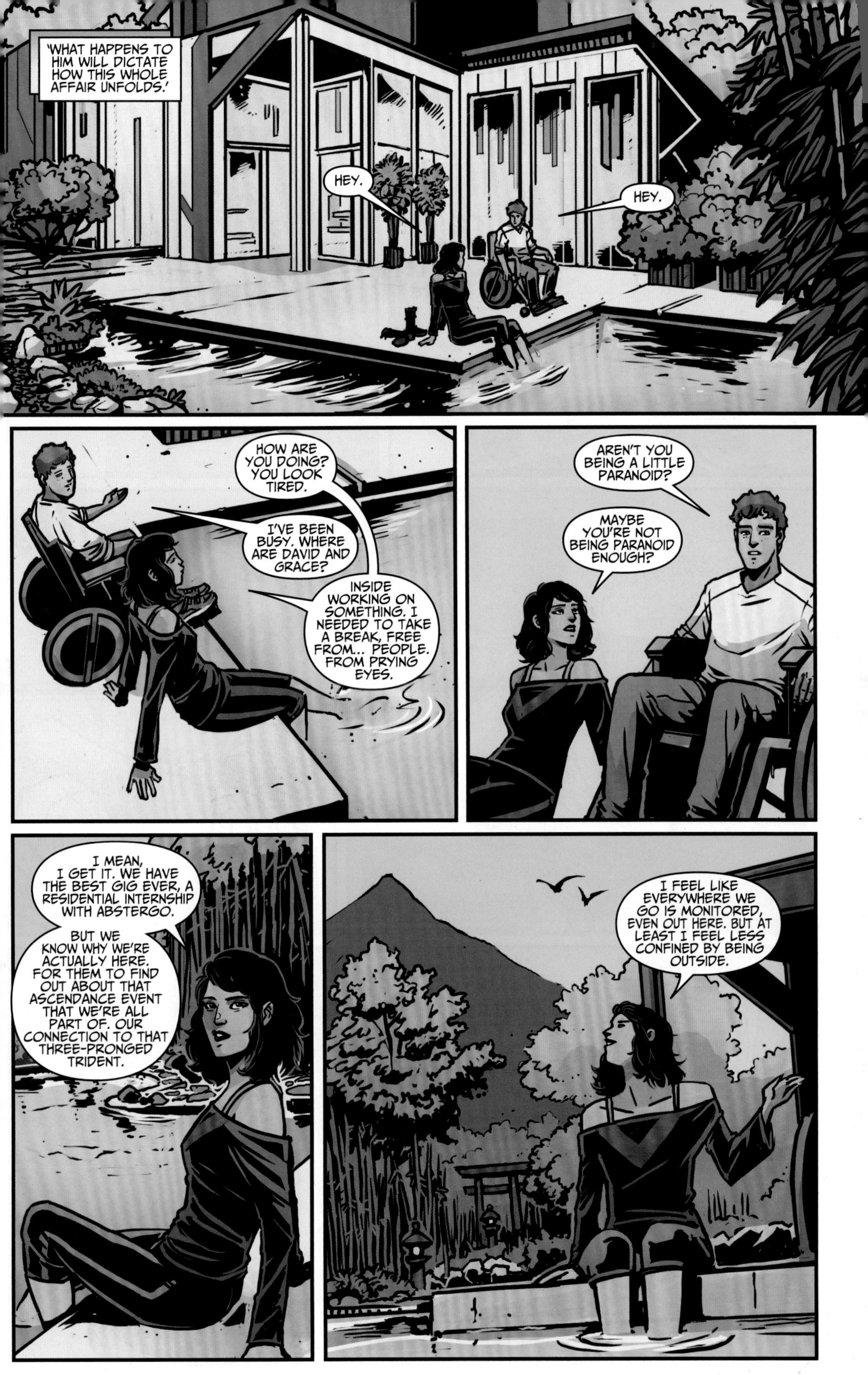
'WHAT HAPPENS TO HIM WILL DICTATE HOW THIS WHOLE AFFAIR UNFOLDS.'
HEY.
HEY.
HOW ARE YOU DOING? YOU LOOK TIRED.
I'VE BEEN BUSY. WHERE ARE DAVID AND GRACE?
INSIDE WORKING ON SOMETHING. I NEEDED TO TAKE A BREAK, FREE FROM... PEOPLE. FROM PRYING EYES.
AREN'T YOU BEING A LITTLE PARANOID?
MAYBE YOU'RE NOT BEING PARANOID ENOUGH?
I MEAN, I GET IT. WE HAVE THE BEST GIG EVER, A RESIDENTIAL INTERNSHIP WITH ABSTERGO.
BUT WE KNOW WHY WE'RE ACTUALLY HERE. FOR THEM TO FIND OUT ABOUT THAT ASCENDANCE EVENT THAT WE'RE ALL PART OF. OUR CONNECTION TO THAT THREE-PRONGED TRIDENT.
I FEEL LIKE EVERYWHERE WE GO IS MONITORED, EVEN OUT HERE. BUT AT LEAST I FEEL LESS CONFINED BY BEING OUTSIDE.

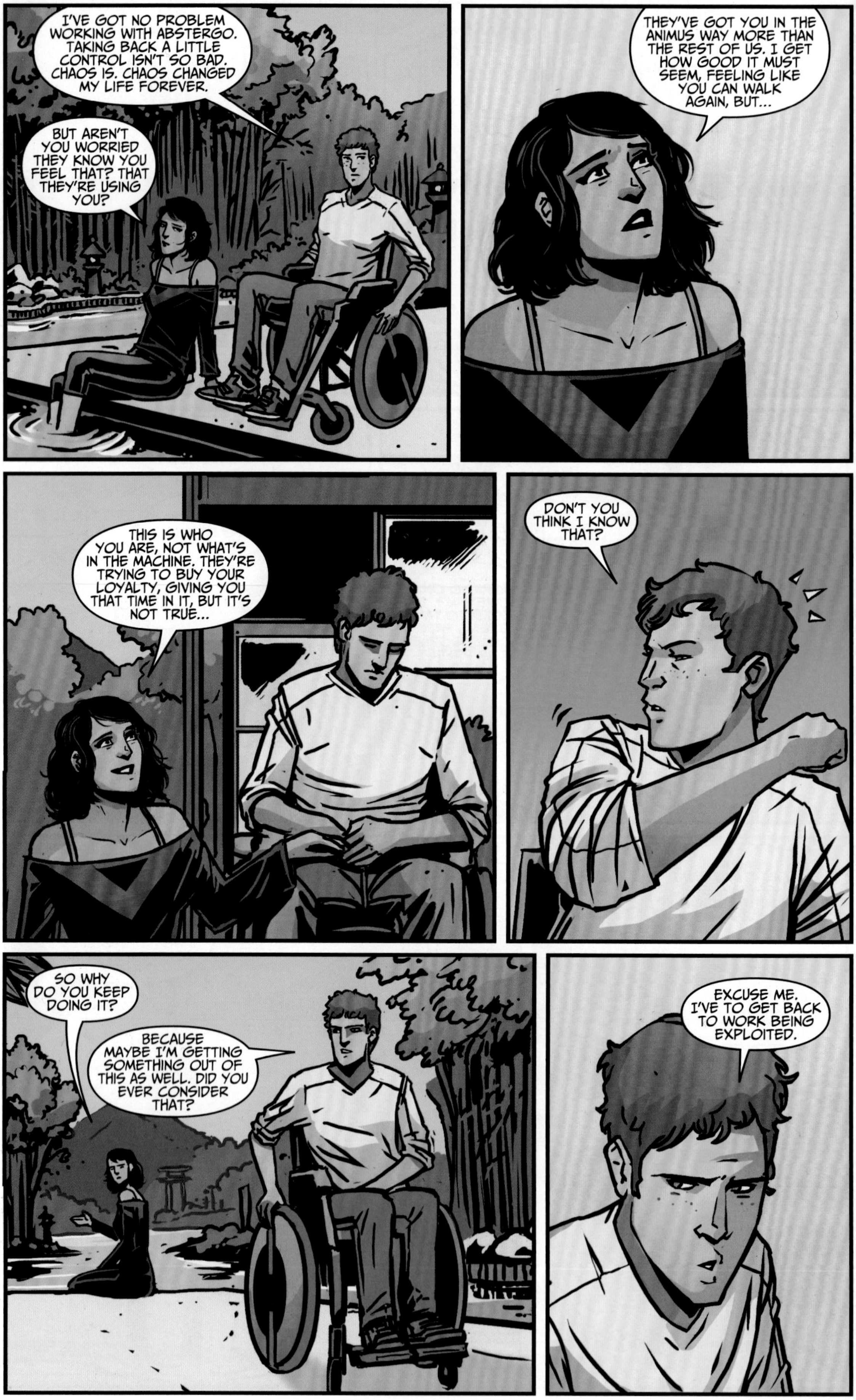
I'VE GOT NO PROBLEM WORKING WITH ABSTERGO. TAKING BACK A LITTLE CONTROL ISN'T SO BAD. CHAOS IS. CHAOS CHANGED MY LIFE FOREVER.
BUT AREN'T YOU WORRIED THEY KNOW YOU FEEL THAT? THAT THEY'RE USING YOU?
THEY'VE GOT YOU IN THE ANIMUS WAY MORE THAN THE REST OF US. I GET HOW GOOD IT MUST SEEM, FEELING LIKE YOU CAN WALK AGAIN, BUT...
THIS IS WHO YOU ARE, NOT WHAT'S IN THE MACHINE. THEY'RE TRYING TO BUY YOUR LOYALTY, GIVING YOU THAT TIME IN IT, BUT IT'S NOT TRUE...
DON'T YOU THINK I KNOW THAT?
SO WHY DO YOU KEEP DOING IT?
BECAUSE MAYBE I'M GETTING SOMETHING OUT OF THIS AS WELL. DID YOU EVER CONSIDER THAT?
EXCUSE ME. I'VE TO GET BACK TO WORK BEING EXPLOITED.

London, England, 1872.

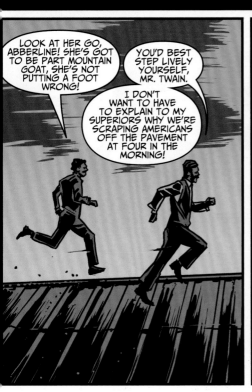

LOOK AT HER GO, ABBERLINE! SHE'S GOT TO BE PART MOUNTAIN GOAT, SHE'S NOT PUTTING A FOOT WRONG!

YOU'D BEST STEP LIVELY YOURSELF, MR. TWAIN.

I DON'T WANT TO HAVE TO EXPLAIN TO MY SUPERIORS WHY WE'RE SCRAPING AMERICANS OFF THE PAVEMENT AT FOUR IN THE MORNING!

DULY NOTED, INSPECTOR. LOOKS LIKE WE'VE GOT HER, SHE'S RUNNING OUT OF ROOF!

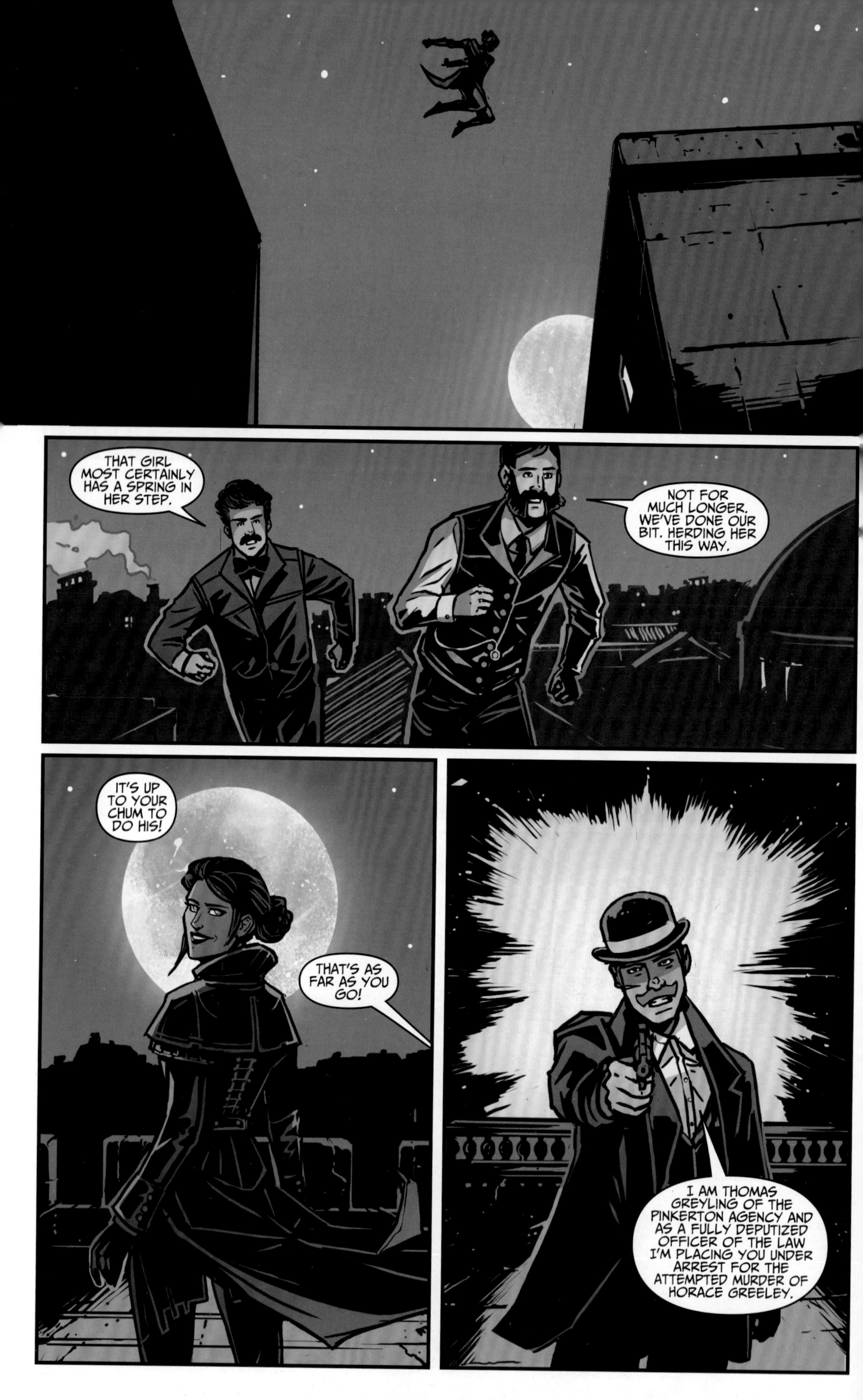
THAT GIRL MOST CERTAINLY HAS A SPRING IN HER STEP.
NOT FOR MUCH LONGER. WE'VE DONE OUR BIT. HERDING HER THIS WAY.
IT'S UP TO YOUR CHUM TO DO HIS!
THAT'S AS FAR AS YOU GO!
I AM THOMAS GREYLING OF THE PINKERTON AGENCY AND AS A FULLY DEPUTIZED OFFICER OF THE LAW I'M PLACING YOU UNDER ARREST FOR THE ATTEMPTED MURDER OF HORACE GREELEY.

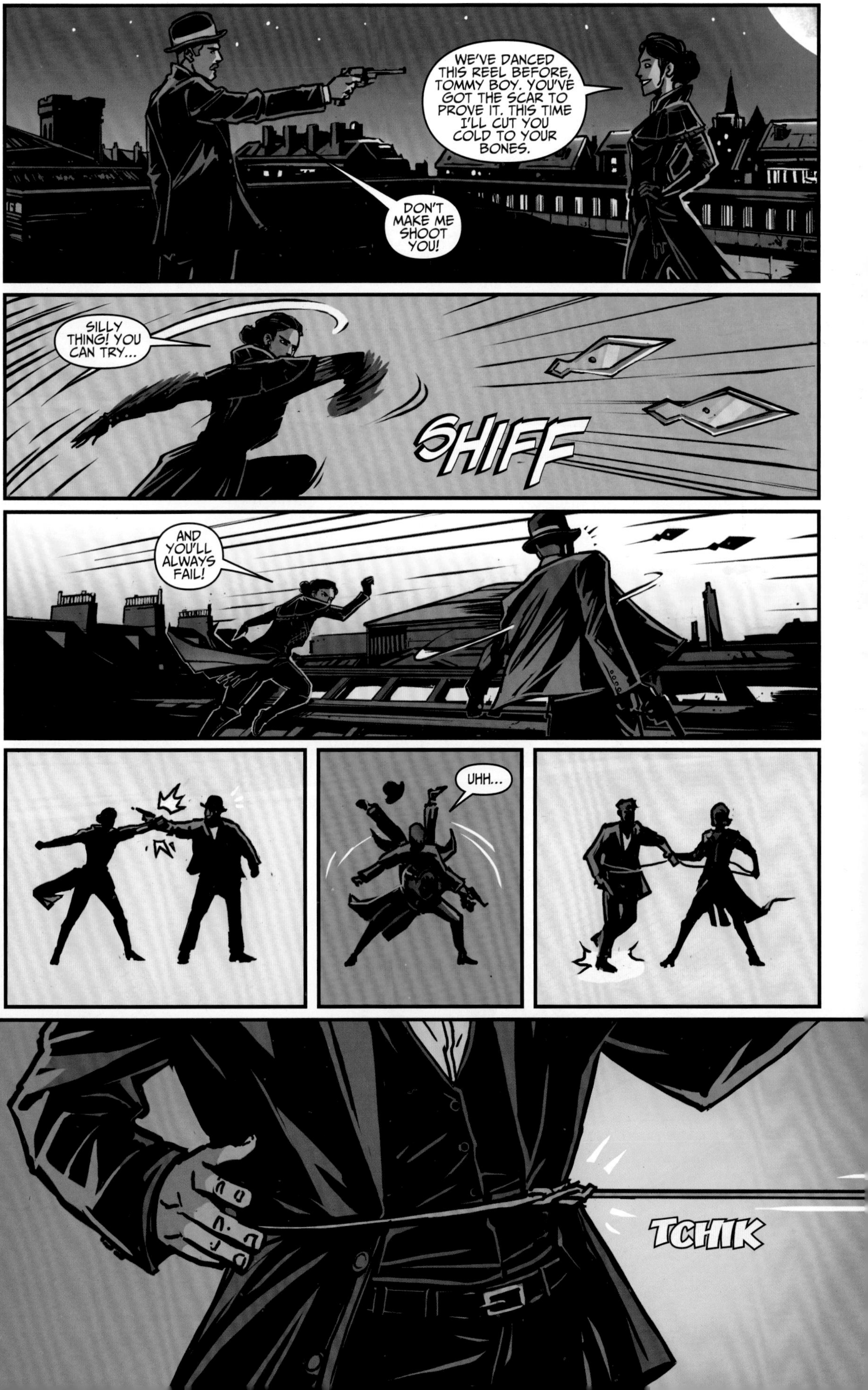
WE'VE DANCED THIS REEL BEFORE, TOMMY BOY. YOU'VE GOT THE SCAR TO PROVE IT. THIS TIME I'LL CUT YOU COLD TO YOUR BONES.
DON'T MAKE ME SHOOT YOU!
SILLY THING! YOU CAN TRY...
SHIFF
AND YOU'LL ALWAYS FAIL!
UHH...
TCHIK

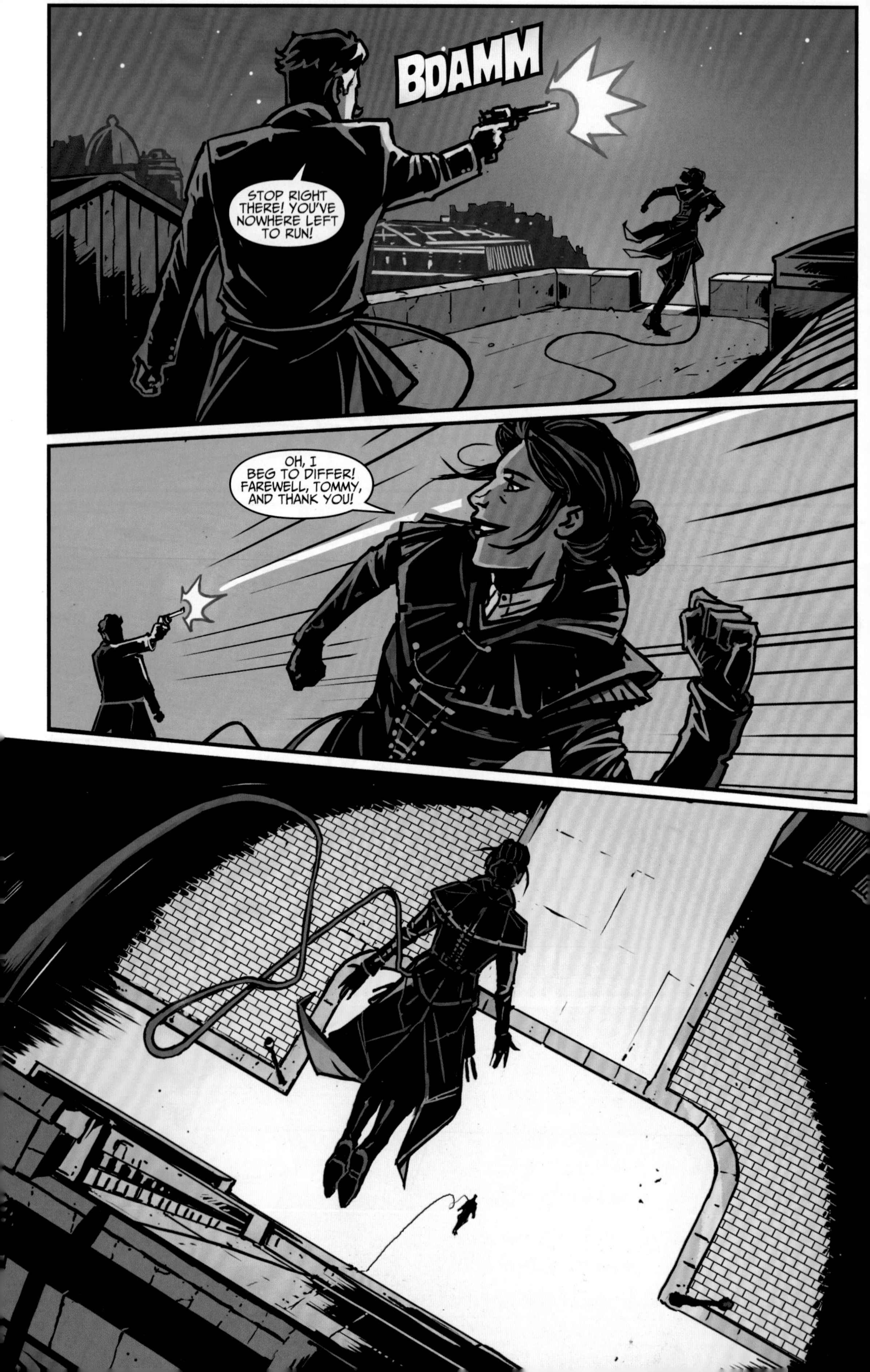
BDAMM
STOP RIGHT THERE! YOU'VE NOWHERE LEFT TO RUN!
OH, I BEG TO DIFFER! FAREWELL, TOMMY, AND THANK YOU!

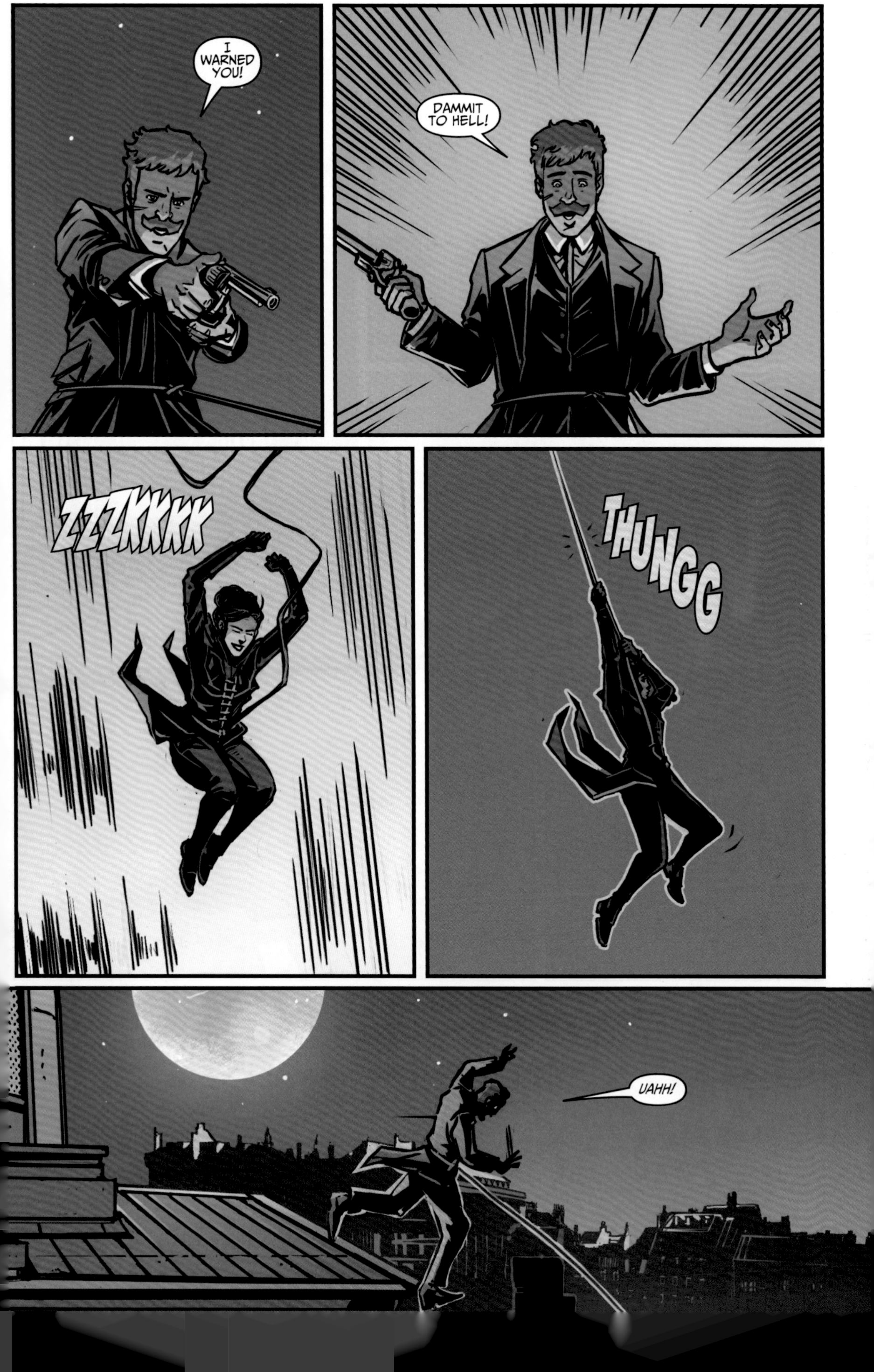
I WARNED YOU!
DAMMIT TO HELL!
ZZZKKKK
THUNGG
UAHH!

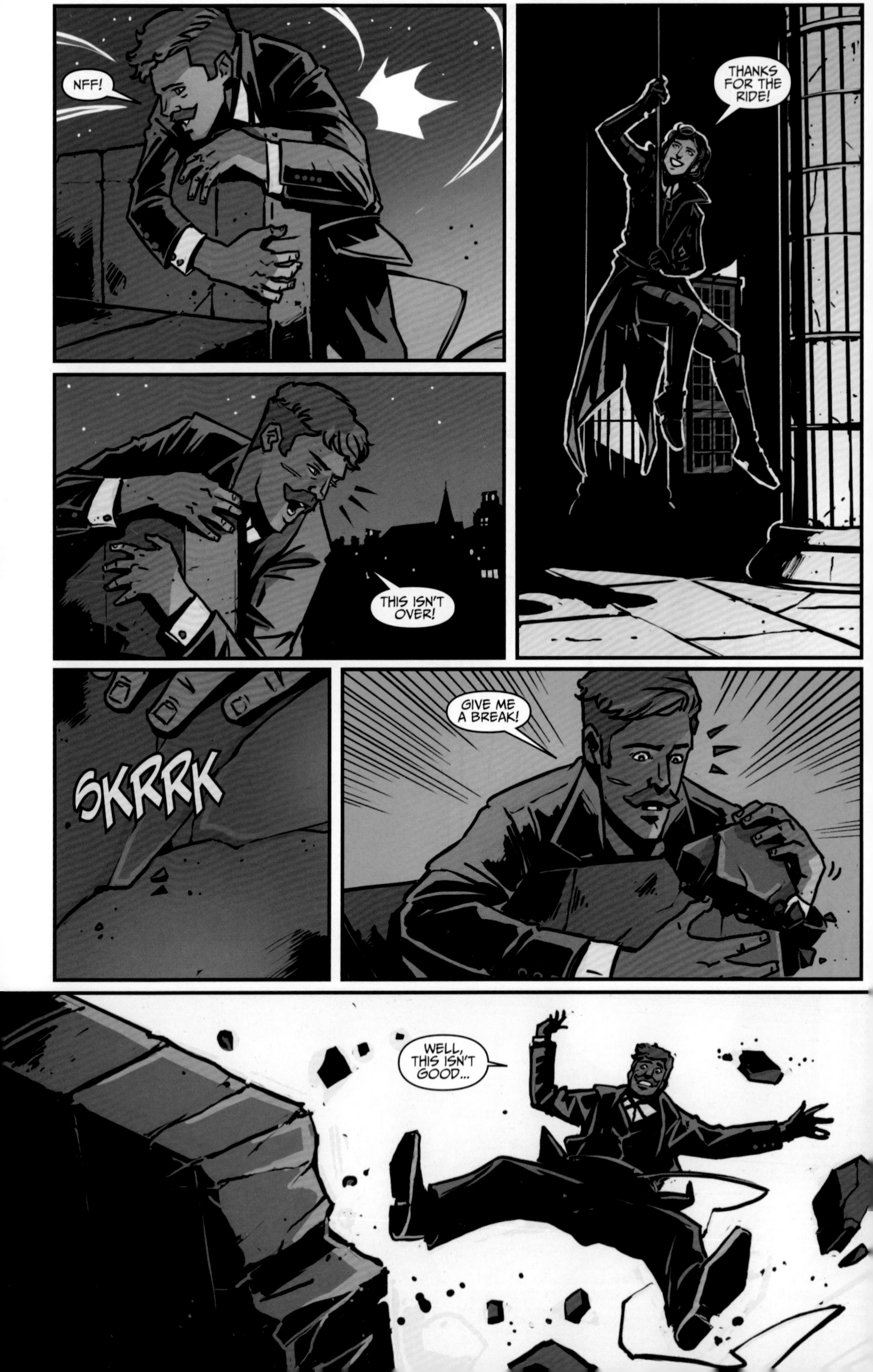
NFF!
THANKS FOR THE RIDE!
THIS ISN'T OVER!
SKRRK
GIVE ME A BREAK!
WELL, THIS ISN'T GOOD...

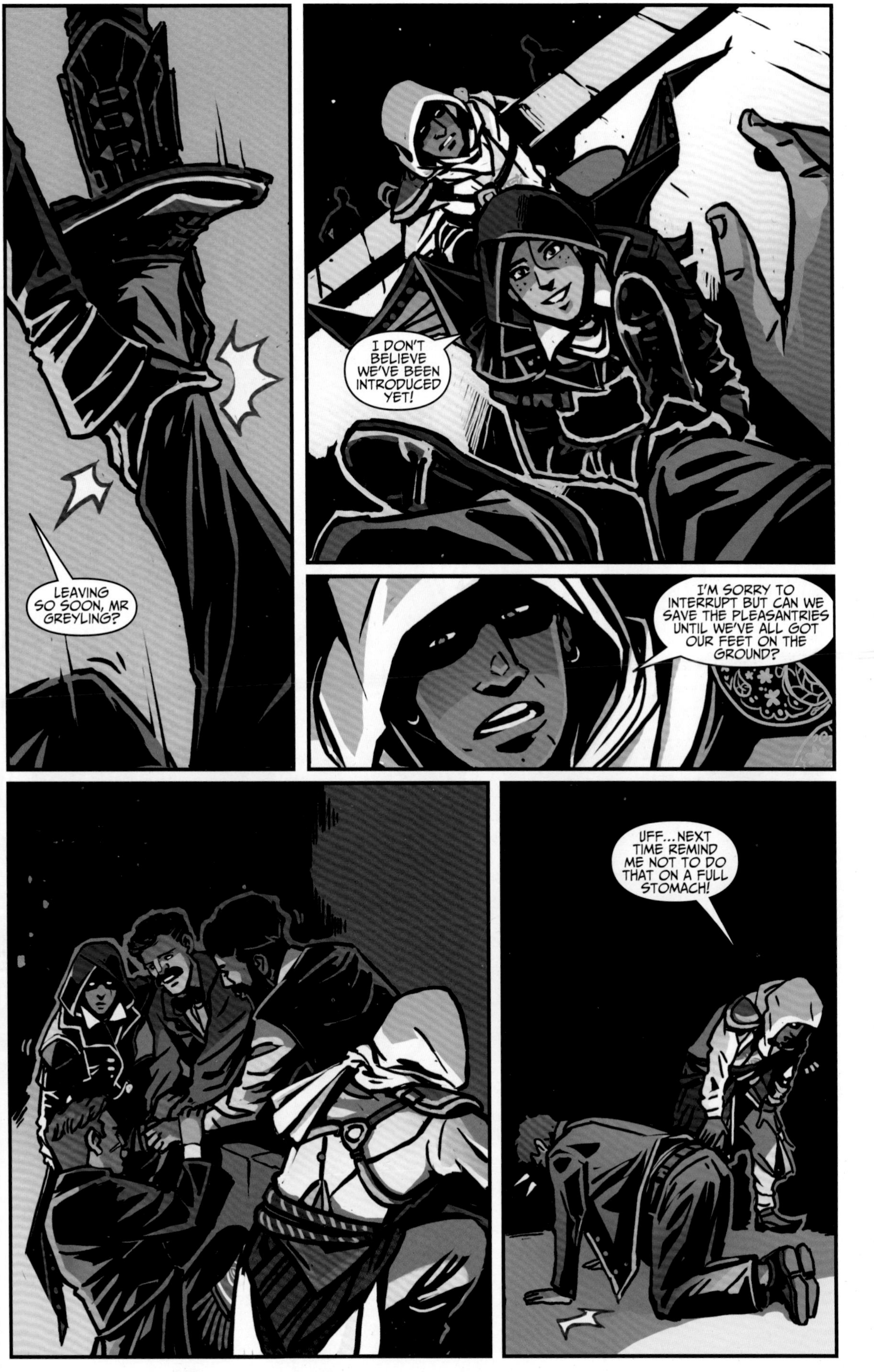
LEAVING SO SOON, MR GREYLING?
I DON'T BELIEVE WE'VE BEEN INTRODUCED YET!
I'M SORRY TO INTERRUPT BUT CAN WE SAVE THE PLEASANTRIES UNTIL WE'VE ALL GOT OUR FEET ON THE GROUND?
UFF...NEXT TIME REMIND ME NOT TO DO THAT ON A FULL STOMACH!

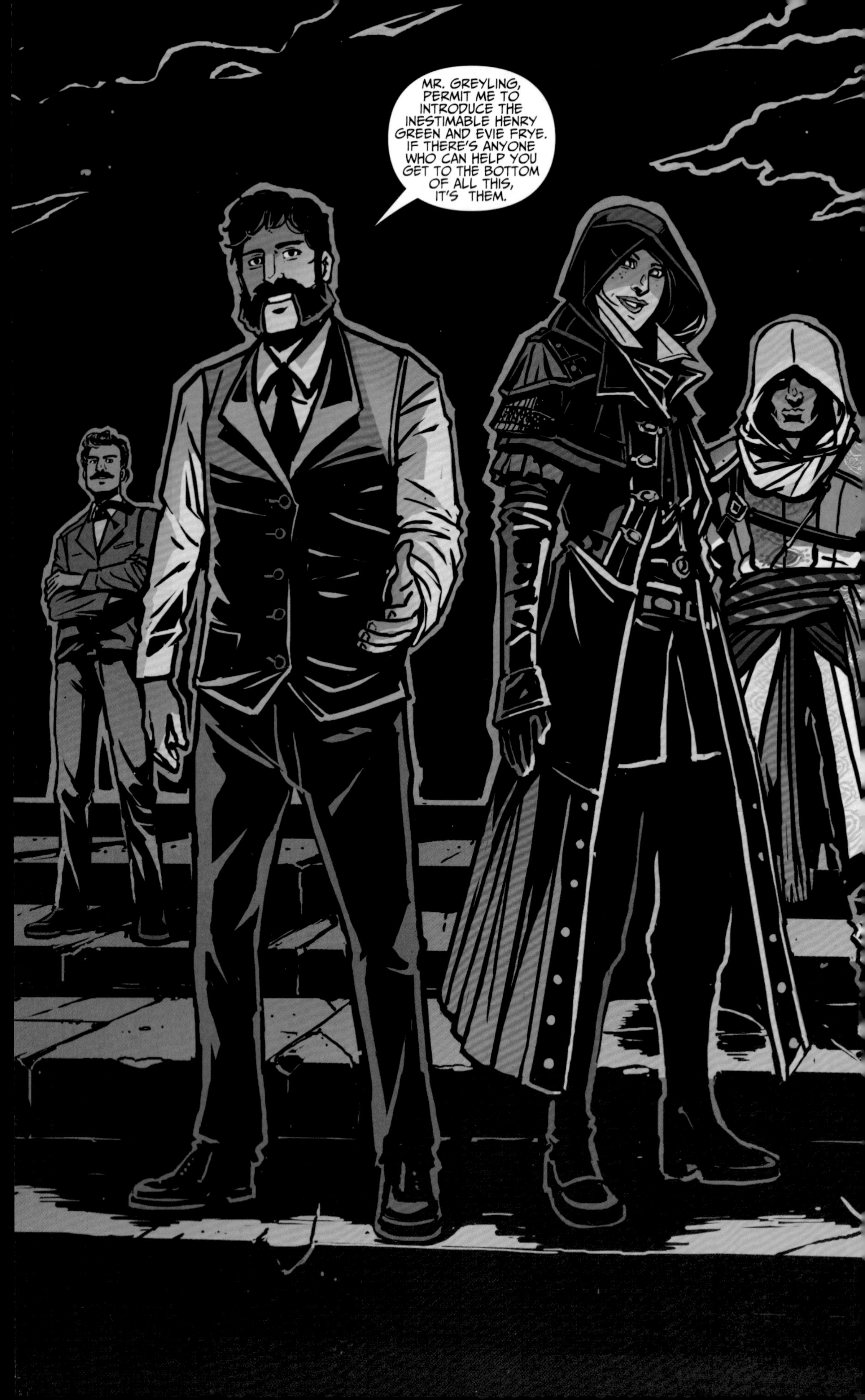
MR. GREYLING, PERMIT ME TO INTRODUCE THE INESTIMABLE HENRY GREEN AND EVIE FRYE. IF THERE'S ANYONE WHO CAN HELP YOU GET TO THE BOTTOM OF ALL THIS, IT'S THEM.

CHAPTER
2

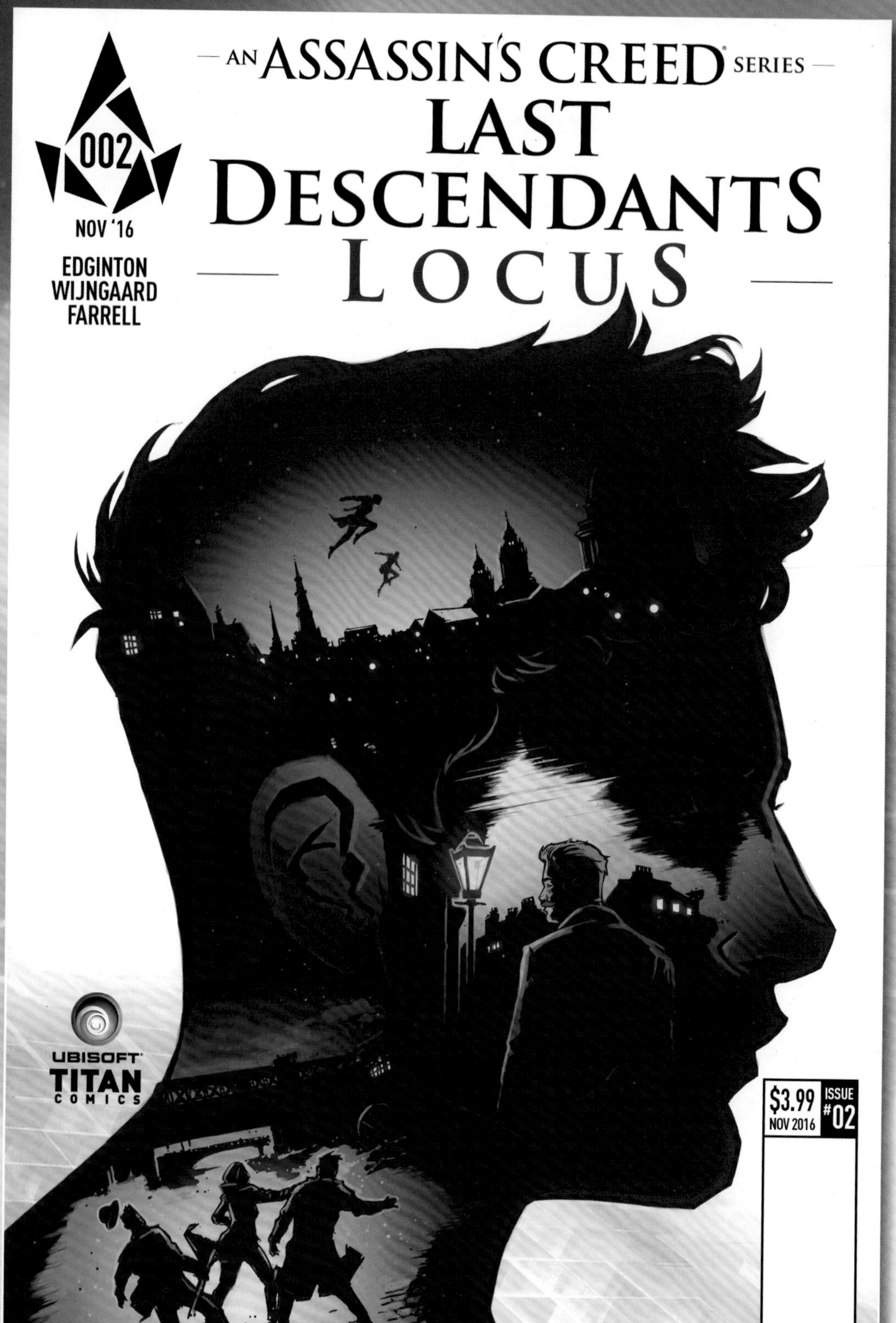

002
NOV '16
EDGINTON
WIJNGAARD
FARRELL
AN ASSASSIN'S CREED SERIES
LAST DESCENDANTS
LOCUS
UBISOFT
TITAN COMICS
$3.99
NOV 2016
ISSUE #02
CASPAR WIJNGAARD

COVER A: CASPAR WIJNGAARD

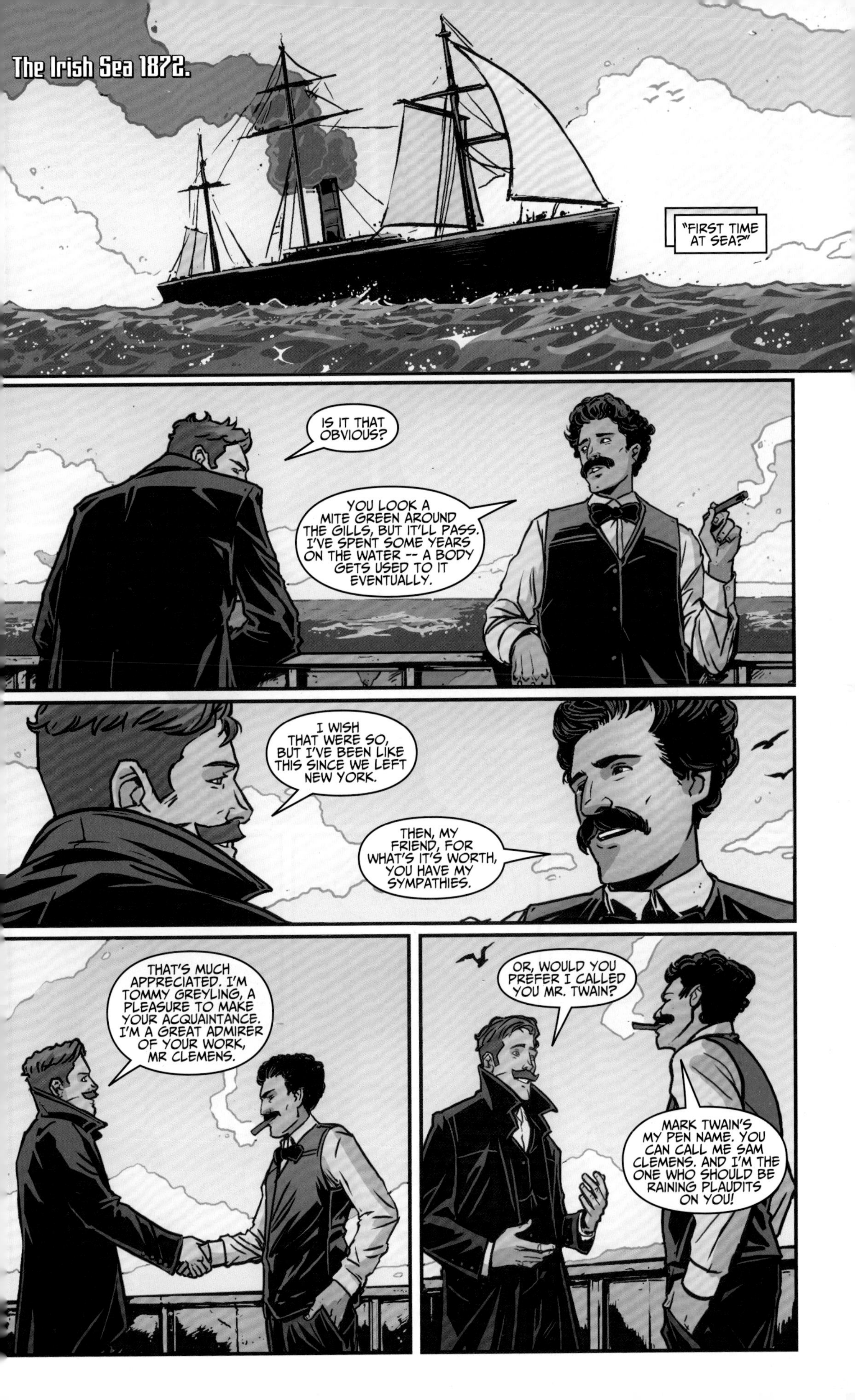

The Irish Sea 1872.
"FIRST TIME AT SEA?"
IS IT THAT OBVIOUS?
YOU LOOK A MITE GREEN AROUND THE GILLS, BUT IT'LL PASS. I'VE SPENT SOME YEARS ON THE WATER -- A BODY GETS USED TO IT EVENTUALLY.
I WISH THAT WERE SO, BUT I'VE BEEN LIKE THIS SINCE WE LEFT NEW YORK.
THEN, MY FRIEND, FOR WHAT'S IT'S WORTH, YOU HAVE MY SYMPATHIES.
THAT'S MUCH APPRECIATED. I'M TOMMY GREYLING, A PLEASURE TO MAKE YOUR ACQUAINTANCE. I'M A GREAT ADMIRER OF YOUR WORK, MR CLEMENS.
OR, WOULD YOU PREFER I CALLED YOU MR. TWAIN?
MARK TWAIN'S MY PEN NAME. YOU CAN CALL ME SAM CLEMENS. AND I'M THE ONE WHO SHOULD BE RAINING PLAUDITS ON YOU!

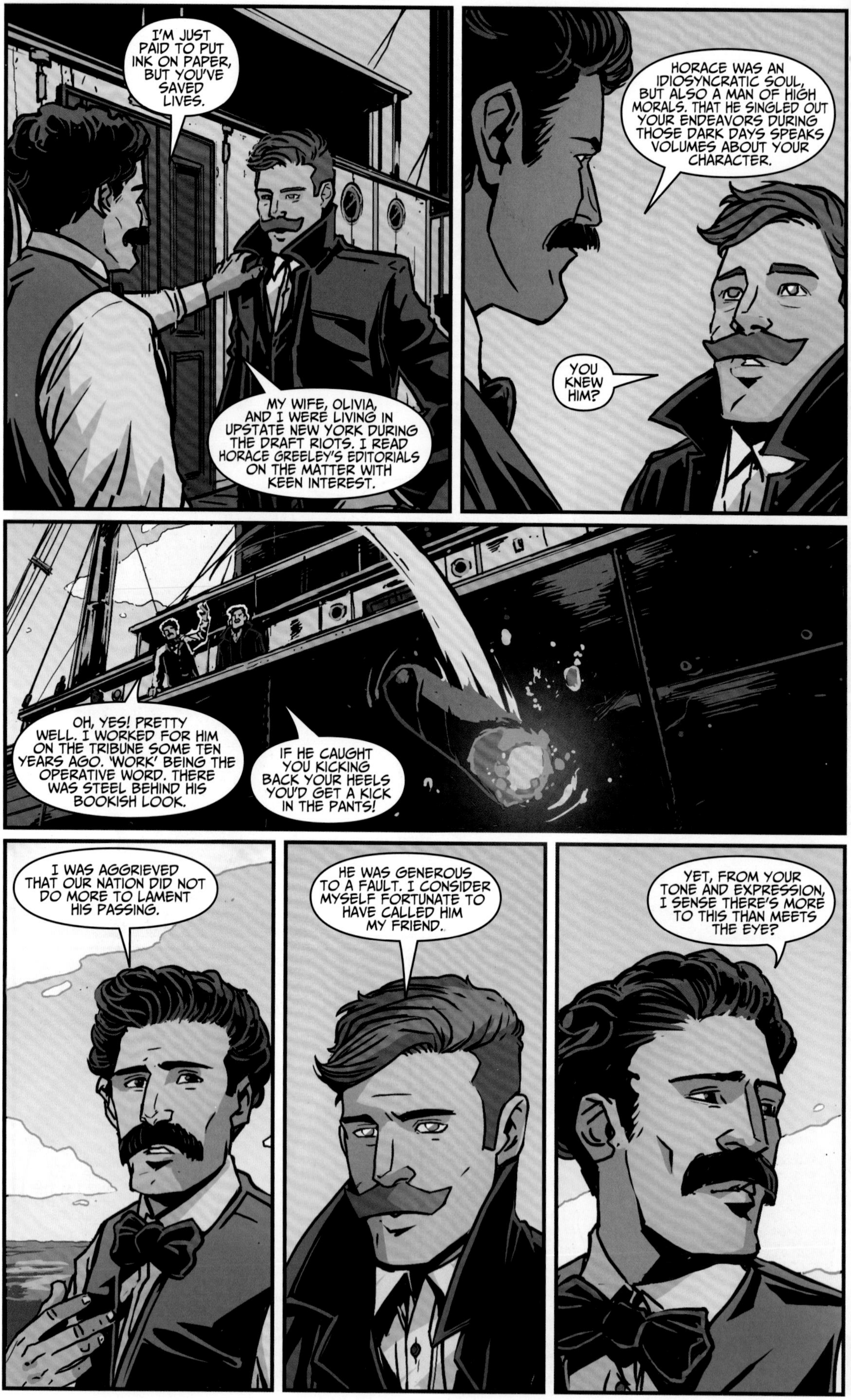
I'M JUST PAID TO PUT INK ON PAPER, BUT YOU'VE SAVED LIVES.
MY WIFE, OLIVIA, AND I WERE LIVING IN UPSTATE NEW YORK DURING THE DRAFT RIOTS. I READ HORACE GREELEY'S EDITORIALS ON THE MATTER WITH KEEN INTEREST.
HORACE WAS AN IDIOSYNCRATIC SOUL, BUT ALSO A MAN OF HIGH MORALS. THAT HE SINGLED OUT YOUR ENDEAVORS DURING THOSE DARK DAYS SPEAKS VOLUMES ABOUT YOUR CHARACTER.
YOU KNEW HIM?
OH, YES! PRETTY WELL. I WORKED FOR HIM ON THE TRIBUNE SOME TEN YEARS AGO. 'WORK' BEING THE OPERATIVE WORD. THERE WAS STEEL BEHIND HIS BOOKISH LOOK.
IF HE CAUGHT YOU KICKING BACK YOUR HEELS YOU'D GET A KICK IN THE PANTS!
I WAS AGGRIEVED THAT OUR NATION DID NOT DO MORE TO LAMENT HIS PASSING.
HE WAS GENEROUS TO A FAULT. I CONSIDER MYSELF FORTUNATE TO HAVE CALLED HIM MY FRIEND.
YET, FROM YOUR TONE AND EXPRESSION, I SENSE THERE'S MORE TO THIS THAN MEETS THE EYE?

FORGIVE ME, IT'S A BAD HABIT, CHASING STORIES LIKE A DOG AFTER A RABBIT. I DON'T KNOW WHEN TO KEEP MY NOSE OUT.

IT'S NO BOTHER. IN FACT I COULD PERHAPS DO WITH A FRESH PERSPECTIVE ON THIS. YOU SEE...

HORACE GREELEY DIDN'T DIE FROM NERVOUS COLLAPSE, BUT FROM THE EVENTUAL AFFECTS OF AN ABORTED ATTEMPT TO POISON HIM. TO PREVENT HIS RUNNING FOR THE REPUBLICAN NOMINATION.

THEY TRIED AGAIN RECENTLY, BUT FORTUNATELY I WAS THERE -- THOUGH I DID NOT COME OUT UNSCATHED.

I'M A PINKERTON AGENT CHARGED WITH INVESTIGATING HIS MURDER. THERE'S A GOOD CHANCE THE KILLER'S FLED TO GREAT BRITAIN, WHICH'S WHY I'M HERE.

I'VE TELEGRAPHED INSPECTOR ABBERLINE OF SCOTLAND YARD. HE'S EXPECTING ME.

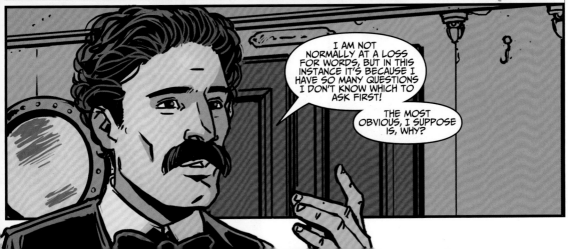

I AM NOT NORMALLY AT A LOSS FOR WORDS, BUT IN THIS INSTANCE IT'S BECAUSE I HAVE SO MANY QUESTIONS I DON'T KNOW WHICH TO ASK FIRST!

THE MOST OBVIOUS, I SUPPOSE IS, WHY?

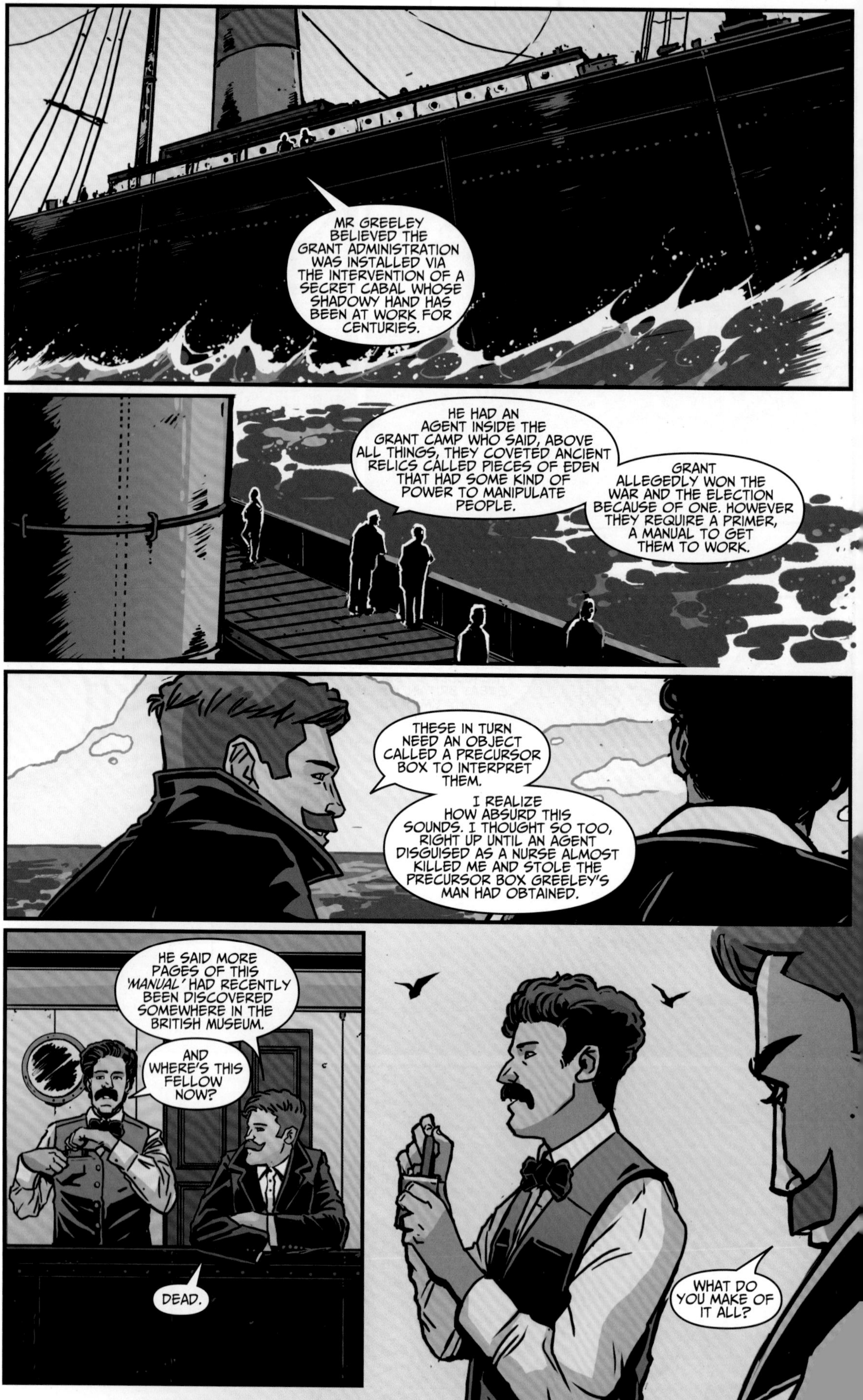
MR GREELEY BELIEVED THE GRANT ADMINISTRATION WAS INSTALLED VIA THE INTERVENTION OF A SECRET CABAL WHOSE SHADOWY HAND HAS BEEN AT WORK FOR CENTURIES.
HE HAD AN AGENT INSIDE THE GRANT CAMP WHO SAID, ABOVE ALL THINGS, THEY COVETED ANCIENT RELICS CALLED PIECES OF EDEN THAT HAD SOME KIND OF POWER TO MANIPULATE PEOPLE.
GRANT ALLEGEDLY WON THE WAR AND THE ELECTION BECAUSE OF ONE. HOWEVER THEY REQUIRE A PRIMER, A MANUAL TO GET THEM TO WORK.
THESE IN TURN NEED AN OBJECT CALLED A PRECURSOR BOX TO INTERPRET THEM.
I REALIZE HOW ABSURD THIS SOUNDS. I THOUGHT SO TOO, RIGHT UP UNTIL AN AGENT DISGUISED AS A NURSE ALMOST KILLED ME AND STOLE THE PRECURSOR BOX GREELEY'S MAN HAD OBTAINED.
HE SAID MORE PAGES OF THIS *'MANUAL'* HAD RECENTLY BEEN DISCOVERED SOMEWHERE IN THE BRITISH MUSEUM.
AND WHERE'S THIS FELLOW NOW?
DEAD.
WHAT DO YOU MAKE OF IT ALL?

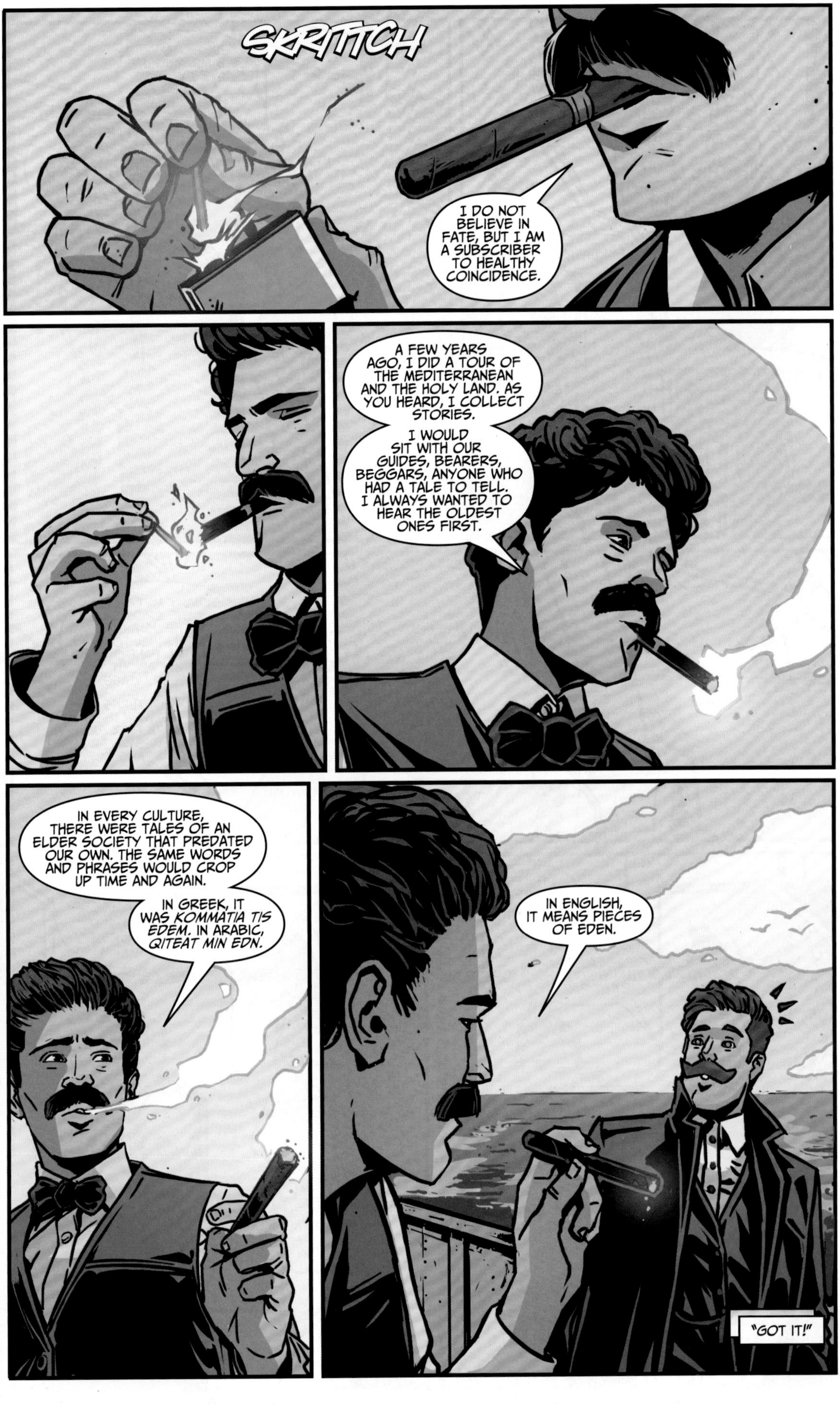
SKRITTCH
I DO NOT BELIEVE IN FATE, BUT I AM A SUBSCRIBER TO HEALTHY COINCIDENCE.
A FEW YEARS AGO, I DID A TOUR OF THE MEDITERRANEAN AND THE HOLY LAND. AS YOU HEARD, I COLLECT STORIES.
I WOULD SIT WITH OUR GUIDES, BEARERS, BEGGARS, ANYONE WHO HAD A TALE TO TELL. I ALWAYS WANTED TO HEAR THE OLDEST ONES FIRST.
IN EVERY CULTURE, THERE WERE TALES OF AN ELDER SOCIETY THAT PREDATED OUR OWN. THE SAME WORDS AND PHRASES WOULD CROP UP TIME AND AGAIN.
IN GREEK, IT WAS *KOMMATIA TIS EDEM*. IN ARABIC, *QITEAT MIN EDN*.
IN ENGLISH, IT MEANS PIECES OF EDEN.
"GOT IT!"

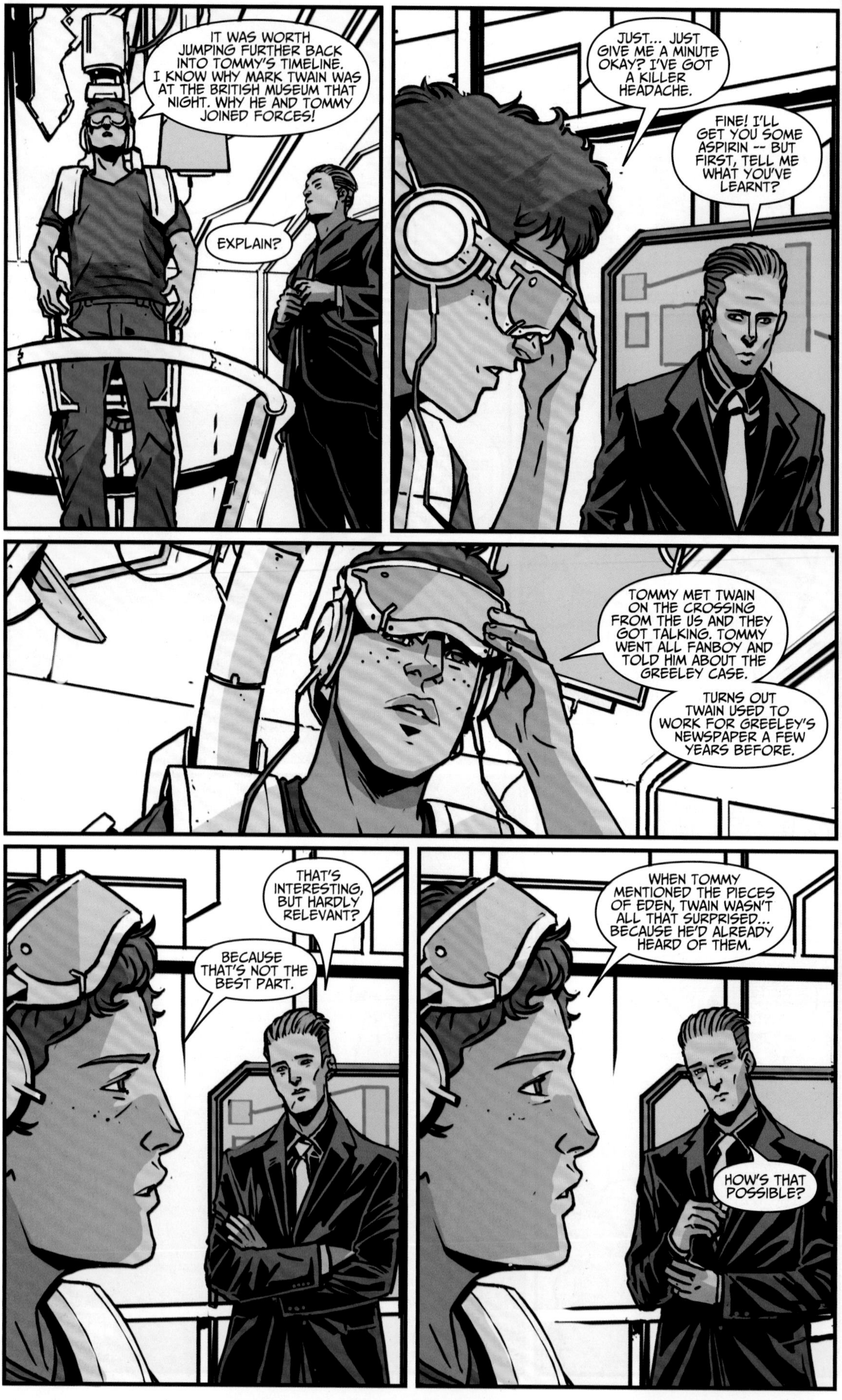
IT WAS WORTH JUMPING FURTHER BACK INTO TOMMY'S TIMELINE. I KNOW WHY MARK TWAIN WAS AT THE BRITISH MUSEUM THAT NIGHT. WHY HE AND TOMMY JOINED FORCES!
EXPLAIN?
JUST... JUST GIVE ME A MINUTE OKAY? I'VE GOT A KILLER HEADACHE.
FINE! I'LL GET YOU SOME ASPIRIN -- BUT FIRST, TELL ME WHAT YOU'VE LEARNT?
TOMMY MET TWAIN ON THE CROSSING FROM THE US AND THEY GOT TALKING. TOMMY WENT ALL FANBOY AND TOLD HIM ABOUT THE GREELEY CASE.
TURNS OUT TWAIN USED TO WORK FOR GREELEY'S NEWSPAPER A FEW YEARS BEFORE.
THAT'S INTERESTING, BUT HARDLY RELEVANT?
BECAUSE THAT'S NOT THE BEST PART.
WHEN TOMMY MENTIONED THE PIECES OF EDEN, TWAIN WASN'T ALL THAT SURPRISED... BECAUSE HE'D ALREADY HEARD OF THEM.
HOW'S THAT POSSIBLE?

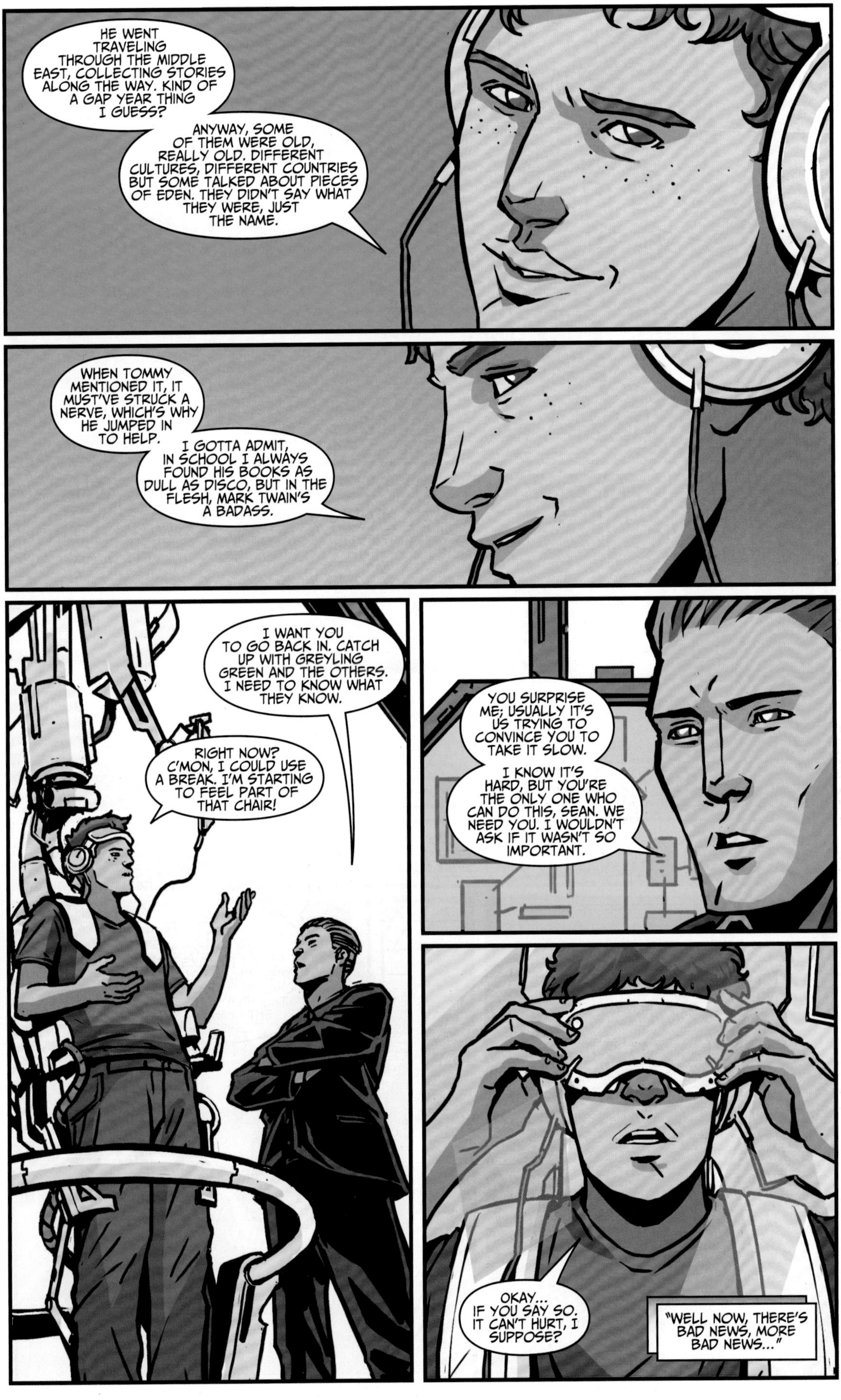
HE WENT TRAVELING THROUGH THE MIDDLE EAST, COLLECTING STORIES ALONG THE WAY. KIND OF A GAP YEAR THING I GUESS?
ANYWAY, SOME OF THEM WERE OLD, REALLY OLD. DIFFERENT CULTURES, DIFFERENT COUNTRIES BUT SOME TALKED ABOUT PIECES OF EDEN. THEY DIDN'T SAY WHAT THEY WERE, JUST THE NAME.
WHEN TOMMY MENTIONED IT, IT MUST'VE STRUCK A NERVE, WHICH'S WHY HE JUMPED IN TO HELP.
I GOTTA ADMIT, IN SCHOOL I ALWAYS FOUND HIS BOOKS AS DULL AS DISCO, BUT IN THE FLESH, MARK TWAIN'S A BADASS.
I WANT YOU TO GO BACK IN. CATCH UP WITH GREYLING GREEN AND THE OTHERS. I NEED TO KNOW WHAT THEY KNOW.
RIGHT NOW? C'MON, I COULD USE A BREAK. I'M STARTING TO FEEL PART OF THAT CHAIR!
YOU SURPRISE ME; USUALLY IT'S US TRYING TO CONVINCE YOU TO TAKE IT SLOW.
I KNOW IT'S HARD, BUT YOU'RE THE ONLY ONE WHO CAN DO THIS, SEAN. WE NEED YOU. I WOULDN'T ASK IF IT WASN'T SO IMPORTANT.
OKAY... IF YOU SAY SO. IT CAN'T HURT, I SUPPOSE?
"WELL NOW, THERE'S BAD NEWS, MORE BAD NEWS..."

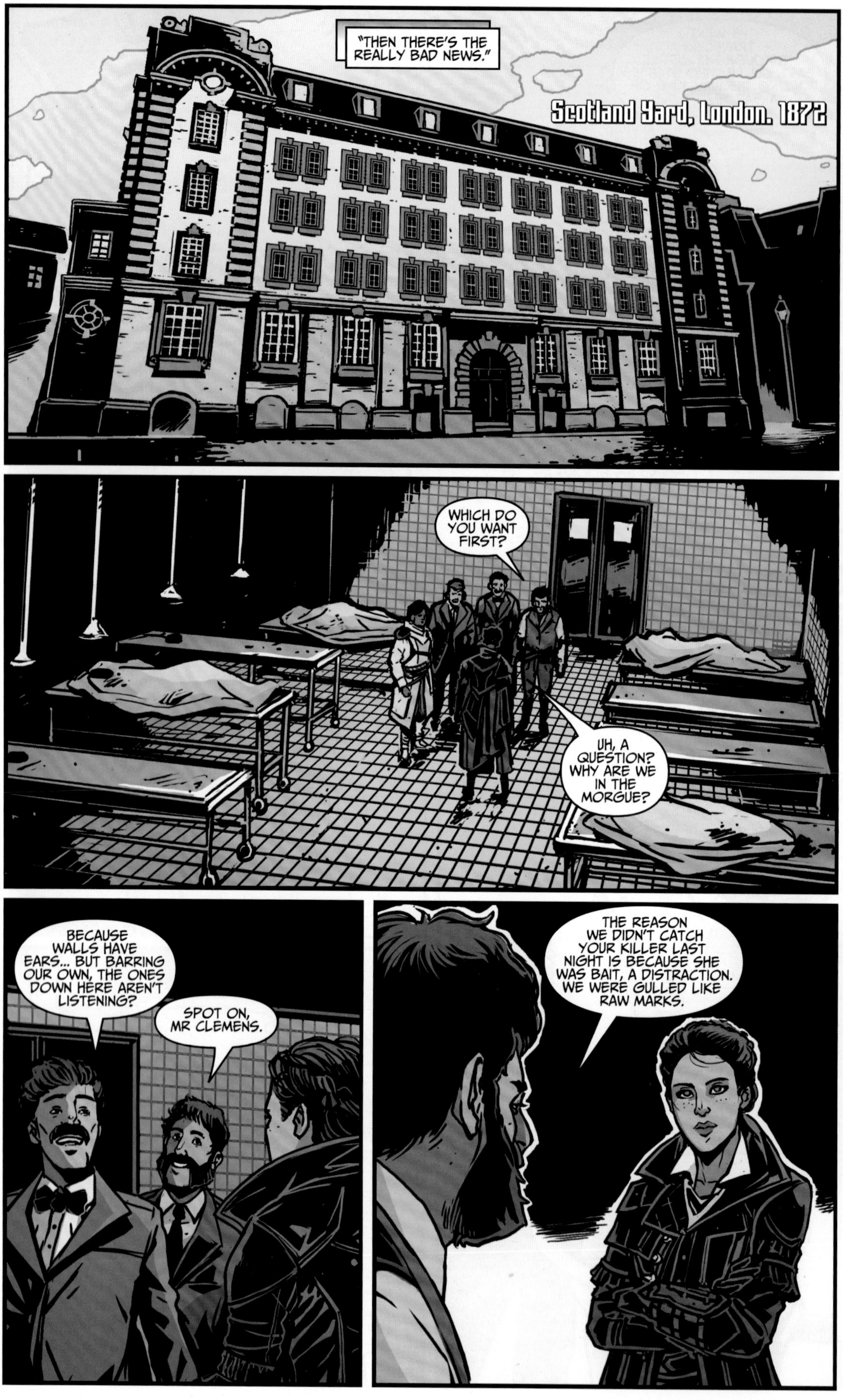
"THEN THERE'S THE REALLY BAD NEWS."
Scotland Yard, London. 1872
WHICH DO YOU WANT FIRST?
UH, A QUESTION? WHY ARE WE IN THE MORGUE?
BECAUSE WALLS HAVE EARS... BUT BARRING OUR OWN, THE ONES DOWN HERE AREN'T LISTENING?
SPOT ON, MR CLEMENS.
THE REASON WE DIDN'T CATCH YOUR KILLER LAST NIGHT IS BECAUSE SHE WAS BAIT, A DISTRACTION. WE WERE GULLED LIKE RAW MARKS.

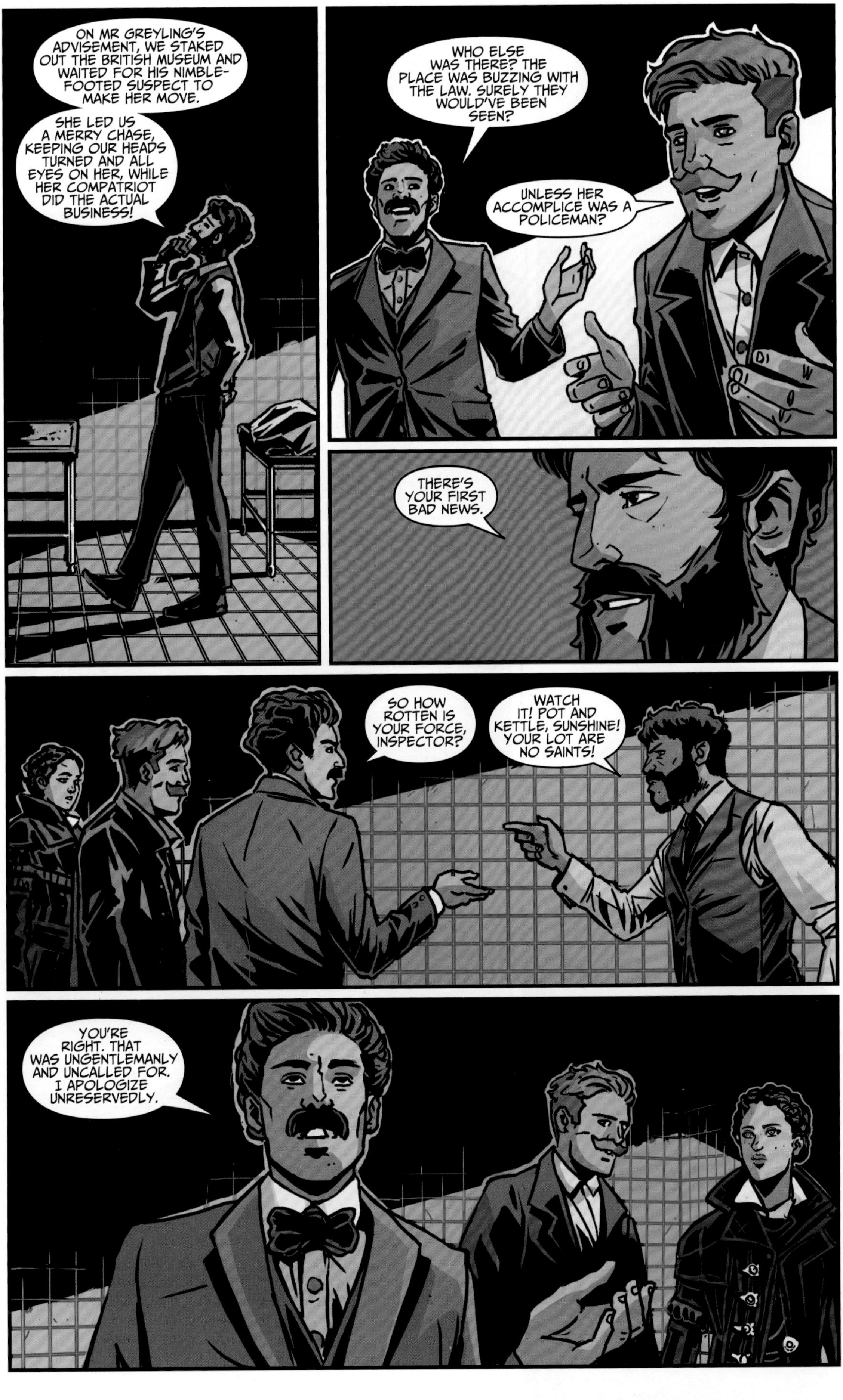
ON MR GREYLING'S ADVISEMENT, WE STAKED OUT THE BRITISH MUSEUM AND WAITED FOR HIS NIMBLE-FOOTED SUSPECT TO MAKE HER MOVE.
SHE LED US A MERRY CHASE, KEEPING OUR HEADS TURNED AND ALL EYES ON HER, WHILE HER COMPATRIOT DID THE ACTUAL BUSINESS!
WHO ELSE WAS THERE? THE PLACE WAS BUZZING WITH THE LAW. SURELY THEY WOULD'VE BEEN SEEN?
UNLESS HER ACCOMPLICE WAS A POLICEMAN?
THERE'S YOUR FIRST BAD NEWS.
SO HOW ROTTEN IS YOUR FORCE, INSPECTOR?
WATCH IT! POT AND KETTLE, SUNSHINE! YOUR LOT ARE NO SAINTS!
YOU'RE RIGHT. THAT WAS UNGENTLEMANLY AND UNCALLED FOR. I APOLOGIZE UNRESERVEDLY.

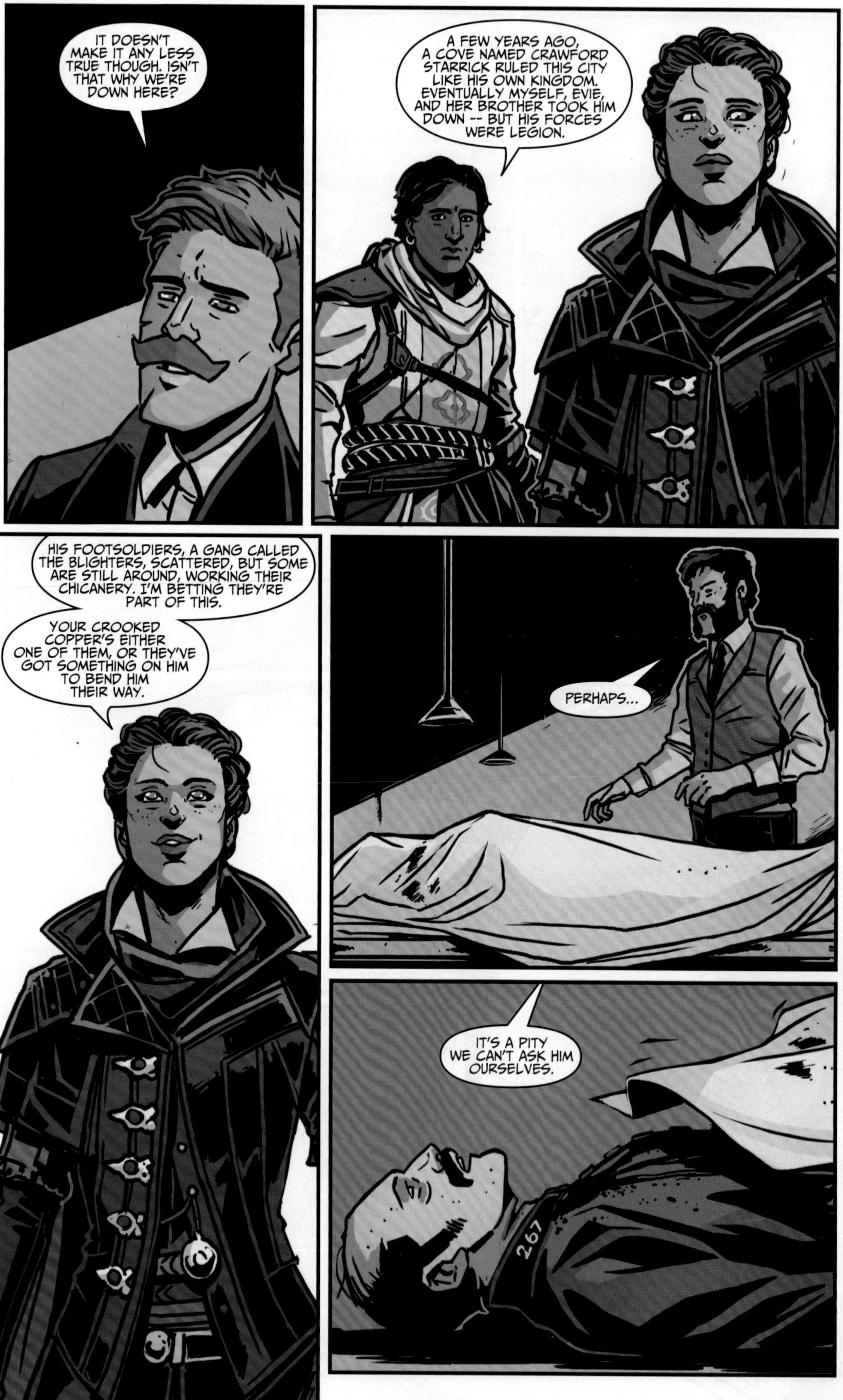
IT DOESN'T MAKE IT ANY LESS TRUE THOUGH. ISN'T THAT WHY WE'RE DOWN HERE?
A FEW YEARS AGO, A COVE NAMED CRAWFORD STARRICK RULED THIS CITY LIKE HIS OWN KINGDOM. EVENTUALLY MYSELF, EVIE, AND HER BROTHER TOOK HIM DOWN -- BUT HIS FORCES WERE LEGION.
HIS FOOTSOLDIERS, A GANG CALLED THE BLIGHTERS, SCATTERED, BUT SOME ARE STILL AROUND, WORKING THEIR CHICANERY. I'M BETTING THEY'RE PART OF THIS.
YOUR CROOKED COPPER'S EITHER ONE OF THEM, OR THEY'VE GOT SOMETHING ON HIM TO BEND HIM THEIR WAY.
PERHAPS...
IT'S A PITY WE CAN'T ASK HIM OURSELVES.
267

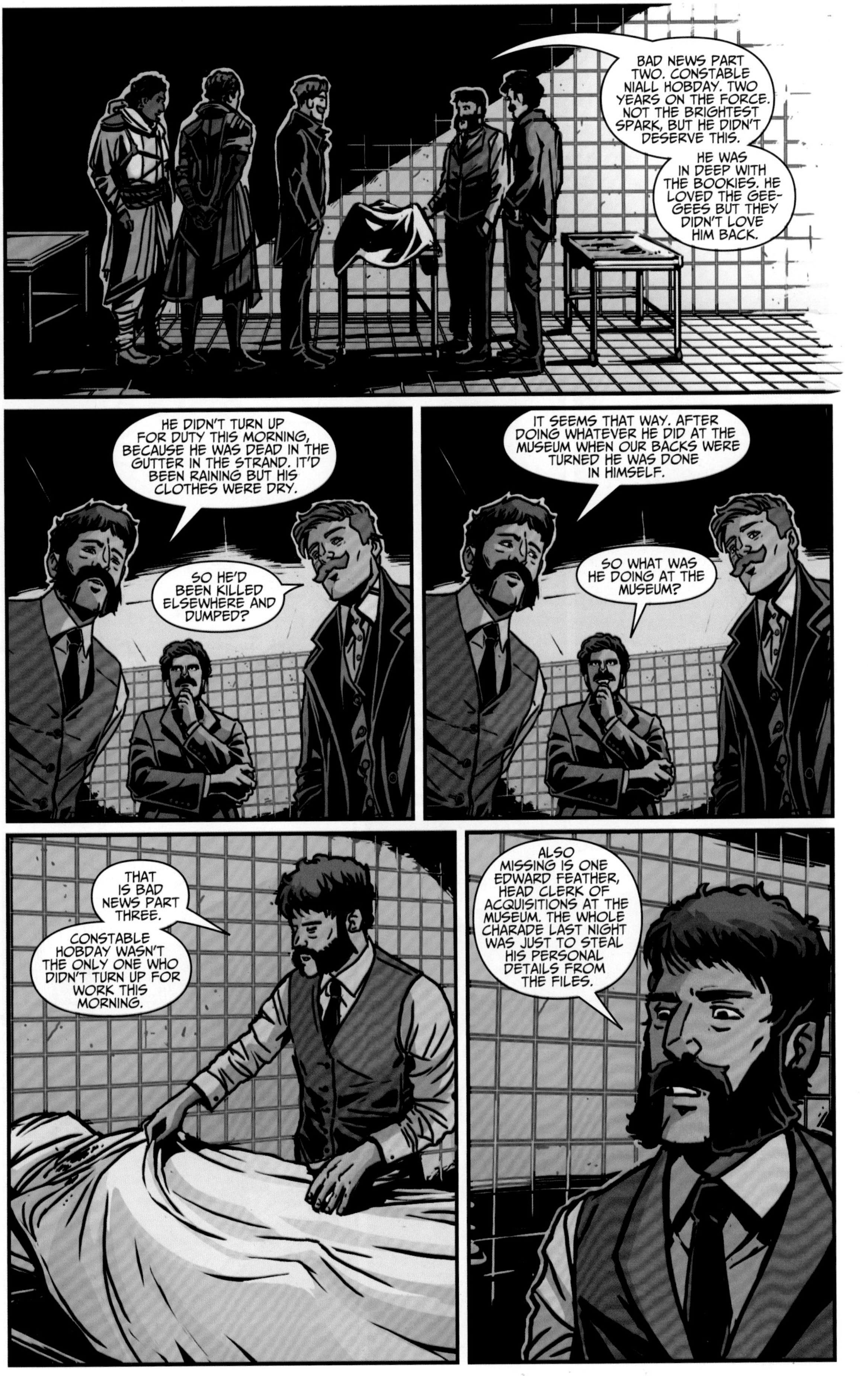
BAD NEWS PART TWO. CONSTABLE NIALL HOBDAY. TWO YEARS ON THE FORCE. NOT THE BRIGHTEST SPARK, BUT HE DIDN'T DESERVE THIS.
HE WAS IN DEEP WITH THE BOOKIES. HE LOVED THE GEE-GEES BUT THEY DIDN'T LOVE HIM BACK.
HE DIDN'T TURN UP FOR DUTY THIS MORNING, BECAUSE HE WAS DEAD IN THE GUTTER IN THE STRAND. IT'D BEEN RAINING BUT HIS CLOTHES WERE DRY.
SO HE'D BEEN KILLED ELSEWHERE AND DUMPED?
IT SEEMS THAT WAY. AFTER DOING WHATEVER HE DID AT THE MUSEUM WHEN OUR BACKS WERE TURNED HE WAS DONE IN HIMSELF.
SO WHAT WAS HE DOING AT THE MUSEUM?
THAT IS BAD NEWS PART THREE.
CONSTABLE HOBDAY WASN'T THE ONLY ONE WHO DIDN'T TURN UP FOR WORK THIS MORNING.
ALSO MISSING IS ONE EDWARD FEATHER, HEAD CLERK OF ACQUISITIONS AT THE MUSEUM. THE WHOLE CHARADE LAST NIGHT WAS JUST TO STEAL HIS PERSONAL DETAILS FROM THE FILES.

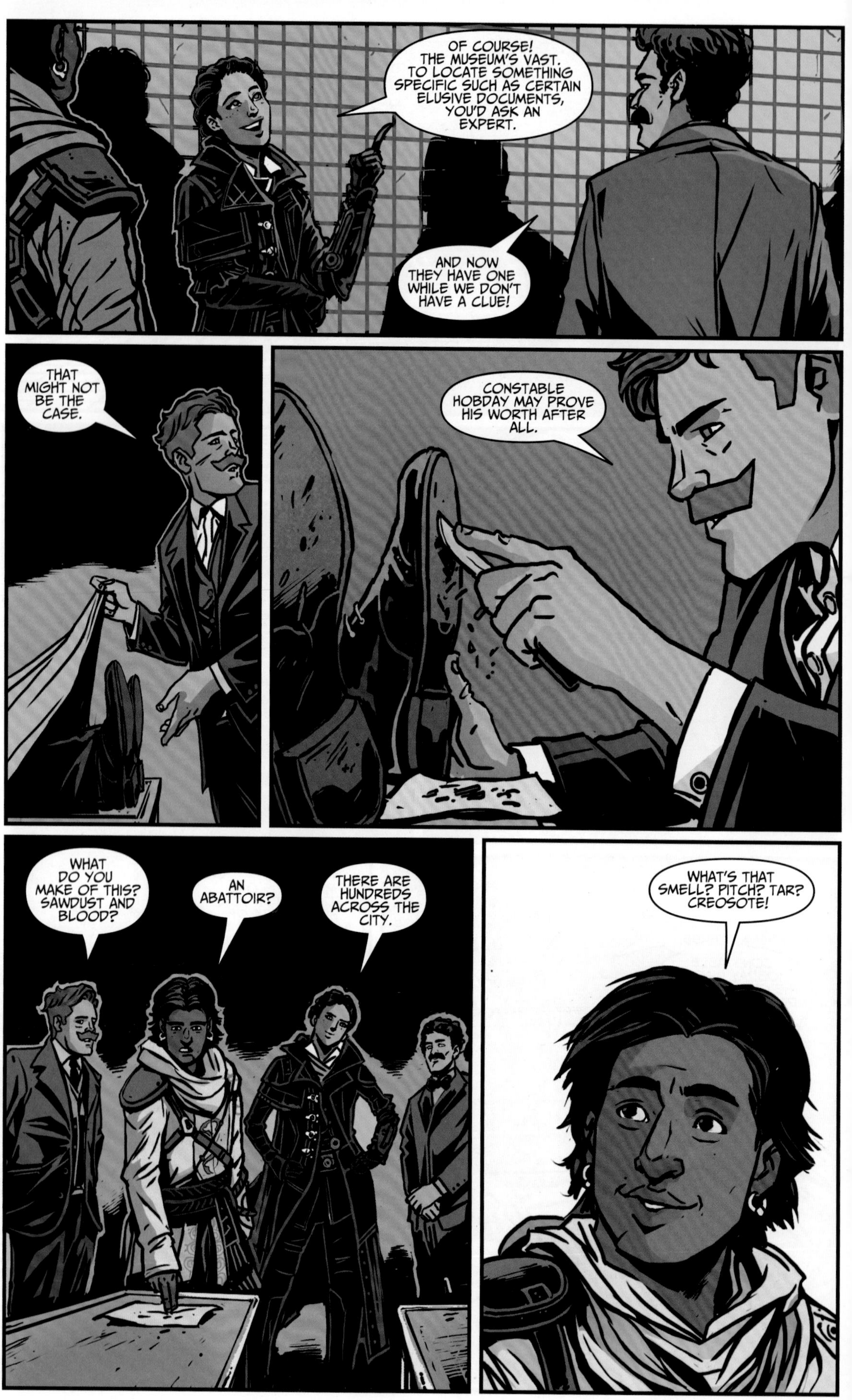
OF COURSE! THE MUSEUM'S VAST. TO LOCATE SOMETHING SPECIFIC SUCH AS CERTAIN ELUSIVE DOCUMENTS, YOU'D ASK AN EXPERT.
AND NOW THEY HAVE ONE WHILE WE DON'T HAVE A CLUE!
THAT MIGHT NOT BE THE CASE.
CONSTABLE HOBDAY MAY PROVE HIS WORTH AFTER ALL.
WHAT DO YOU MAKE OF THIS? SAWDUST AND BLOOD?
AN ABATTOIR?
THERE ARE HUNDREDS ACROSS THE CITY.
WHAT'S THAT SMELL? PITCH? TAR? CREOSOTE!

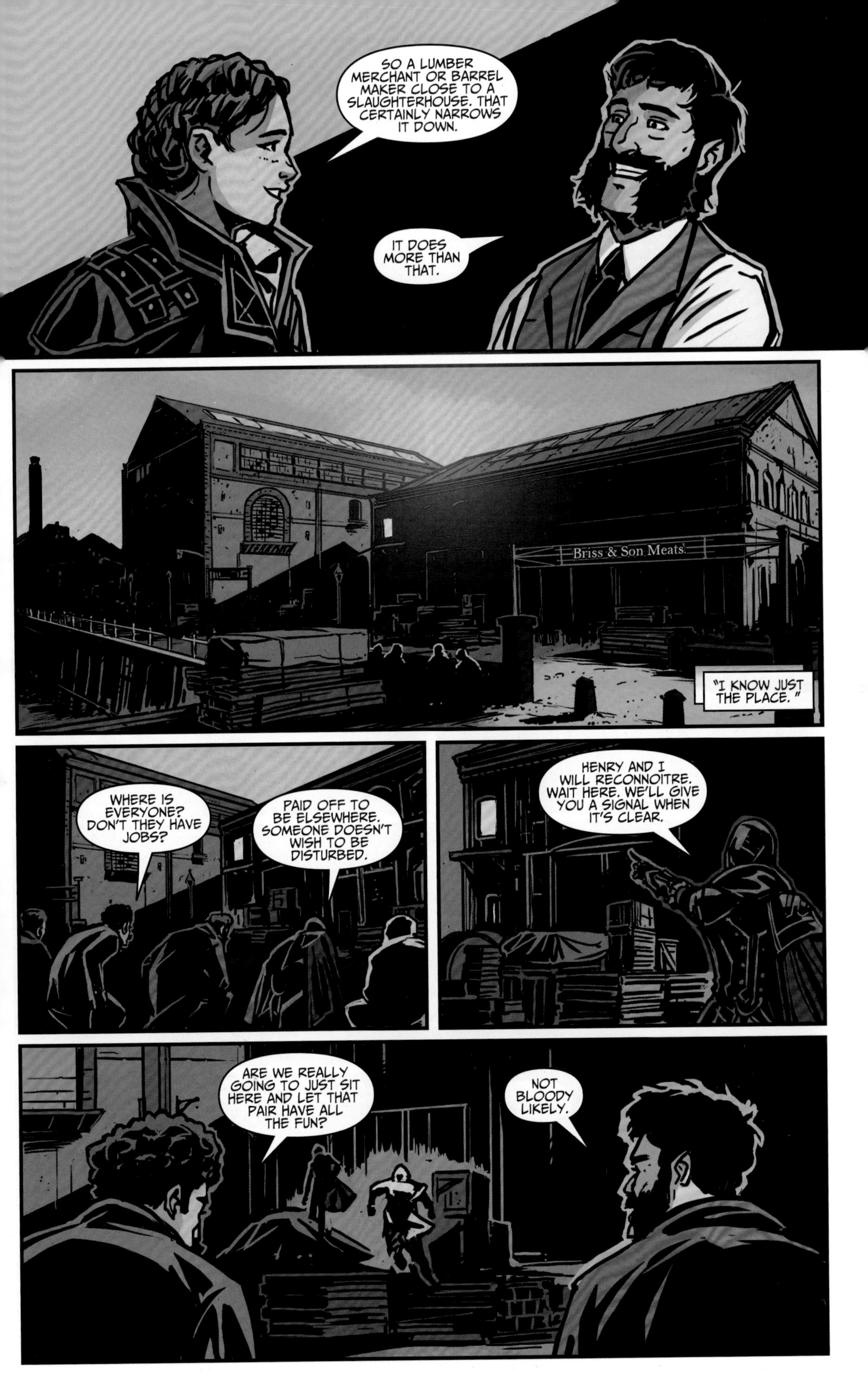
SO A LUMBER MERCHANT OR BARREL MAKER CLOSE TO A SLAUGHTERHOUSE. THAT CERTAINLY NARROWS IT DOWN.
IT DOES MORE THAN THAT.
Briss & Son Meats.
"I KNOW JUST THE PLACE."
WHERE IS EVERYONE? DON'T THEY HAVE JOBS?
PAID OFF TO BE ELSEWHERE. SOMEONE DOESN'T WISH TO BE DISTURBED.
HENRY AND I WILL RECONNOITRE. WAIT HERE. WE'LL GIVE YOU A SIGNAL WHEN IT'S CLEAR.
ARE WE REALLY GOING TO JUST SIT HERE AND LET THAT PAIR HAVE ALL THE FUN?
NOT BLOODY LIKELY.

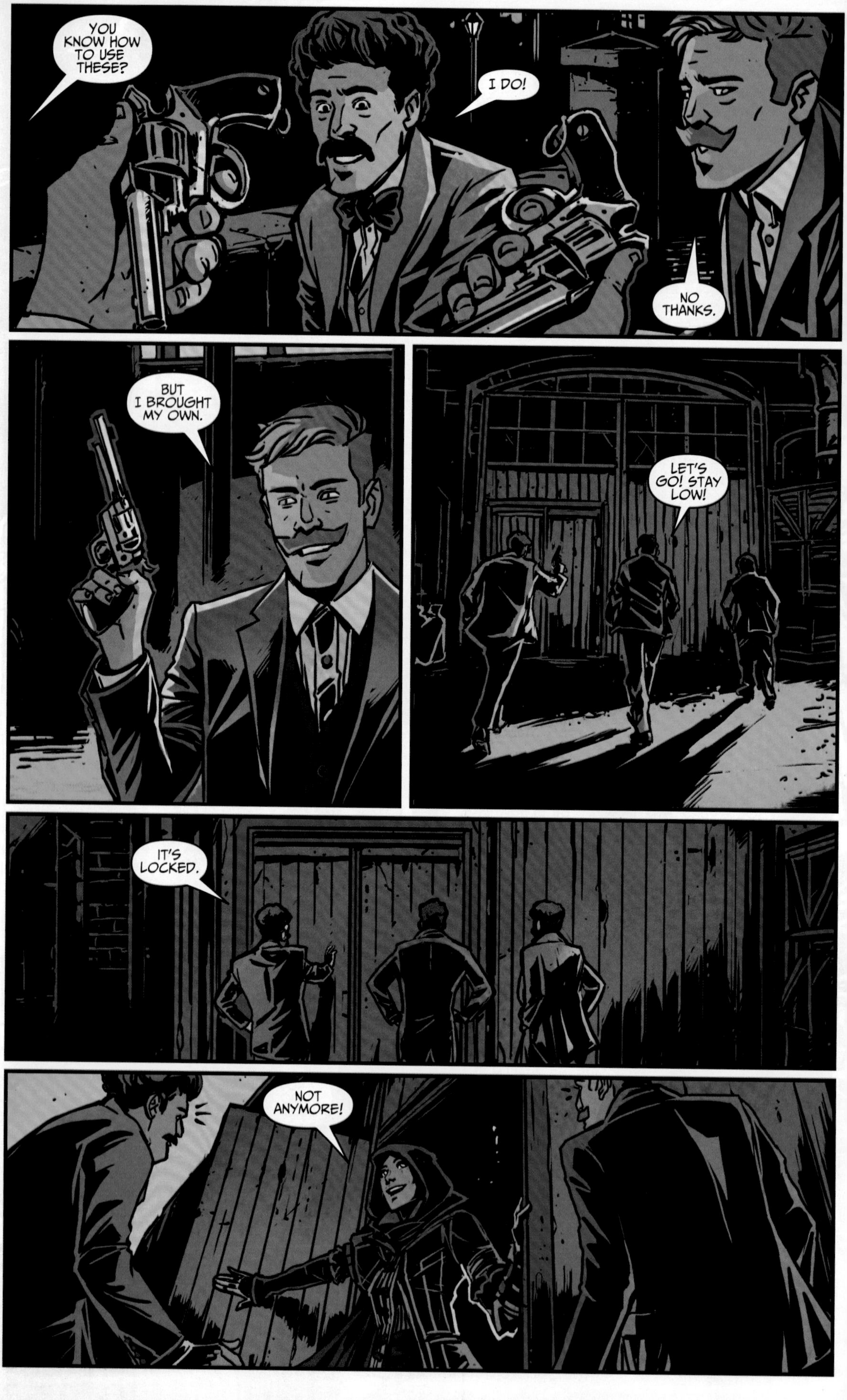
YOU KNOW HOW TO USE THESE?
I DO!
NO THANKS.
BUT I BROUGHT MY OWN.
LET'S GO! STAY LOW!
IT'S LOCKED.
NOT ANYMORE!

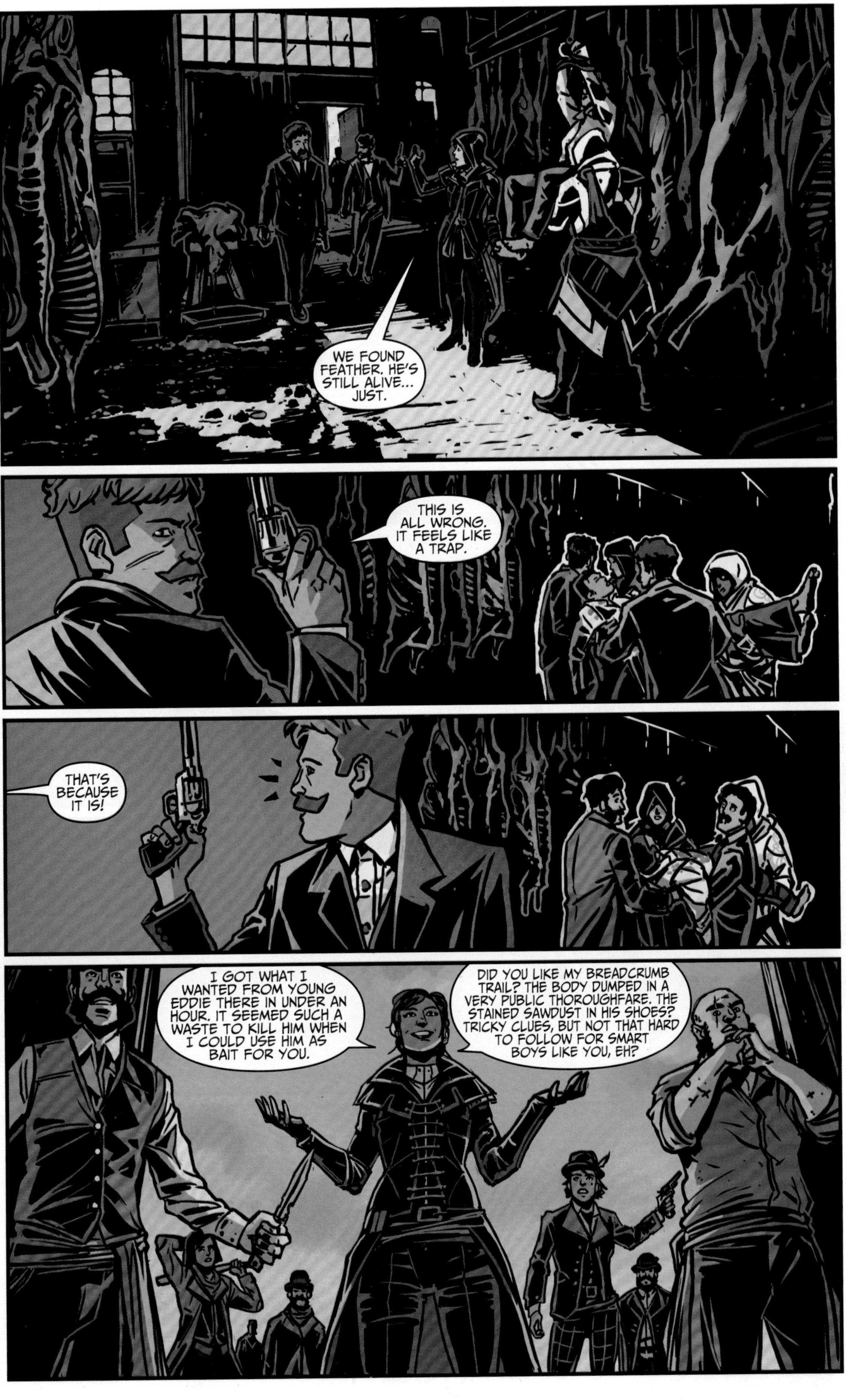
WE FOUND FEATHER. HE'S STILL ALIVE... JUST.
THIS IS ALL WRONG. IT FEELS LIKE A TRAP.
THAT'S BECAUSE IT IS!
I GOT WHAT I WANTED FROM YOUNG EDDIE THERE IN UNDER AN HOUR. IT SEEMED SUCH A WASTE TO KILL HIM WHEN I COULD USE HIM AS BAIT FOR YOU.
DID YOU LIKE MY BREADCRUMB TRAIL? THE BODY DUMPED IN A VERY PUBLIC THOROUGHFARE. THE STAINED SAWDUST IN HIS SHOES? TRICKY CLUES, BUT NOT THAT HARD TO FOLLOW FOR SMART BOYS LIKE YOU, EH?

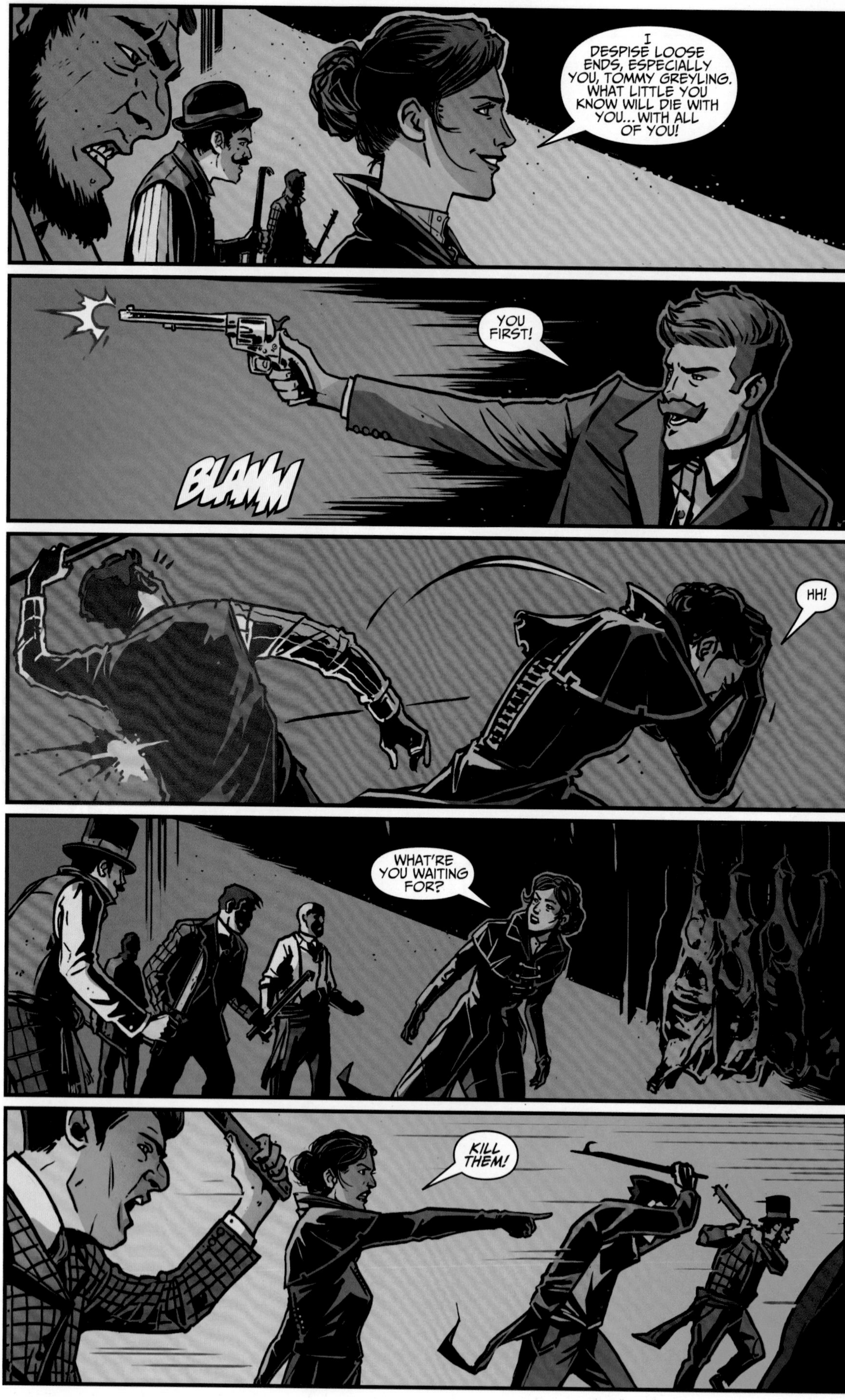
I DESPISE LOOSE ENDS, ESPECIALLY YOU, TOMMY GREYLING. WHAT LITTLE YOU KNOW WILL DIE WITH YOU...WITH ALL OF YOU!
YOU FIRST!
BLAMM
HH!
WHAT'RE YOU WAITING FOR?
KILL THEM!

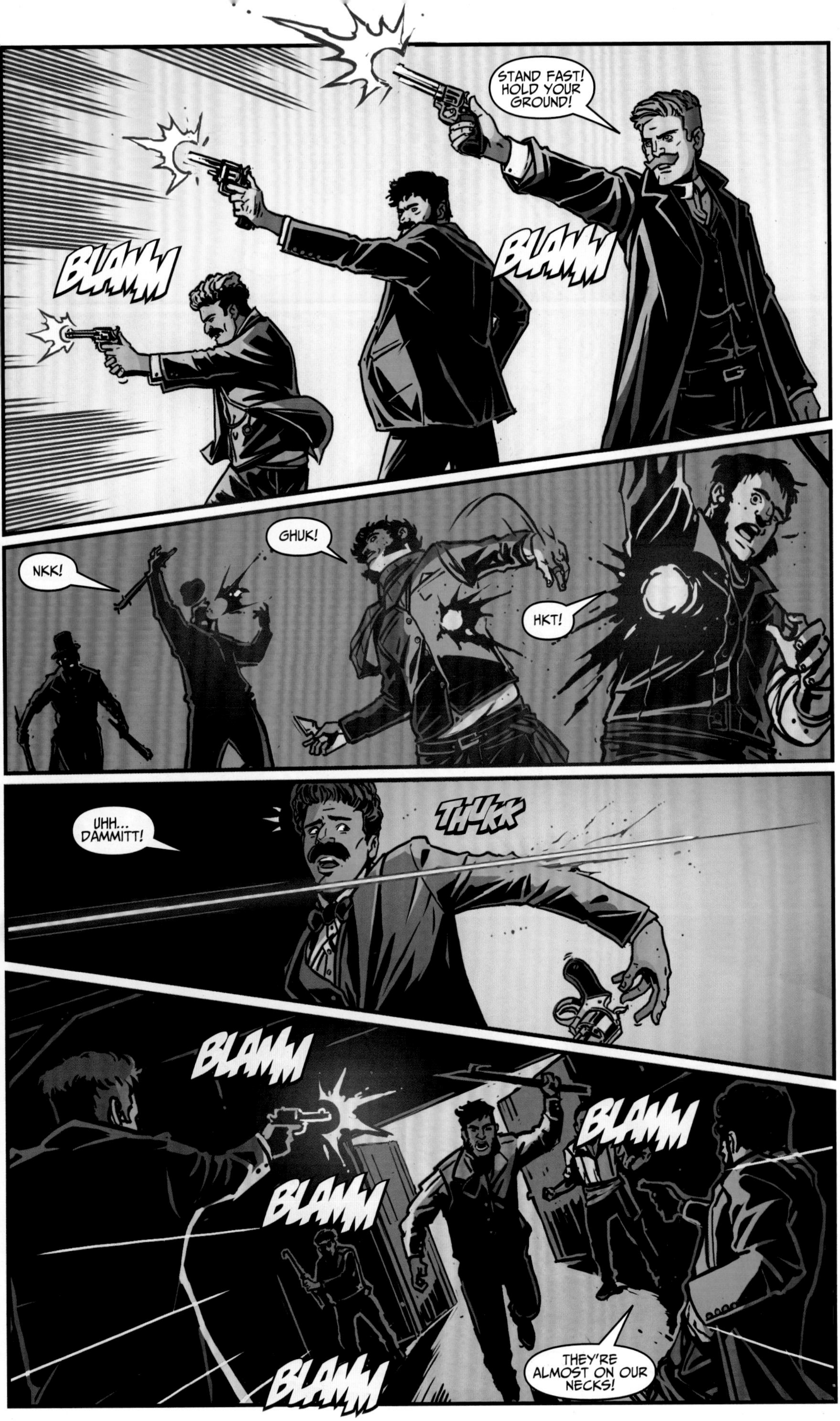
STAND FAST! HOLD YOUR GROUND!
BLAMM
BLAMM
NKK!
GHUK!
HKT!
UHH... DAMMITT!
THUKK
BLAMM
BLAMM
BLAMM
BLAMM
THEY'RE ALMOST ON OUR NECKS!

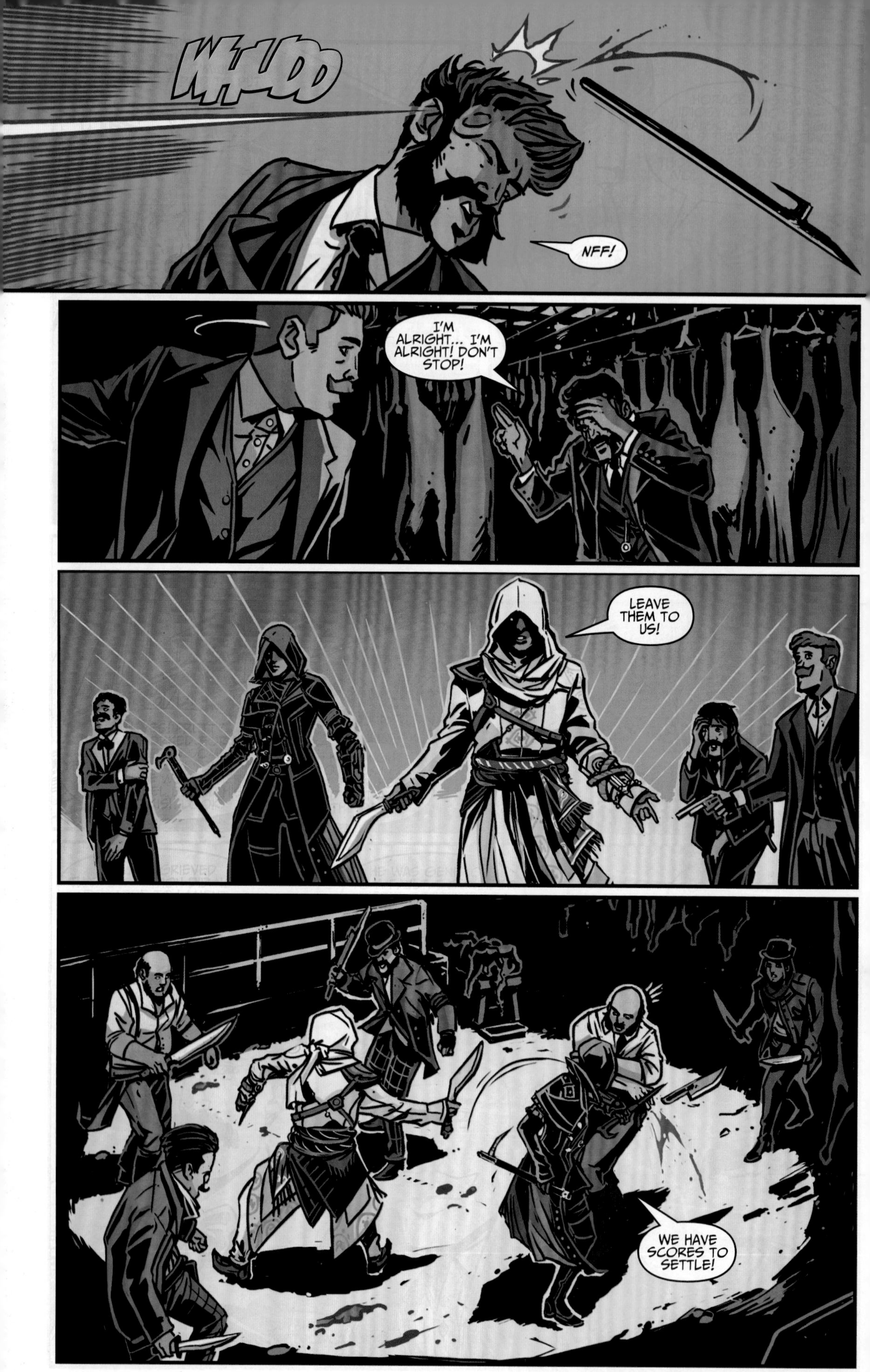
WHUDD
NFF!
I'M ALRIGHT... I'M ALRIGHT! DON'T STOP!
LEAVE THEM TO US!
WE HAVE SCORES TO SETTLE!

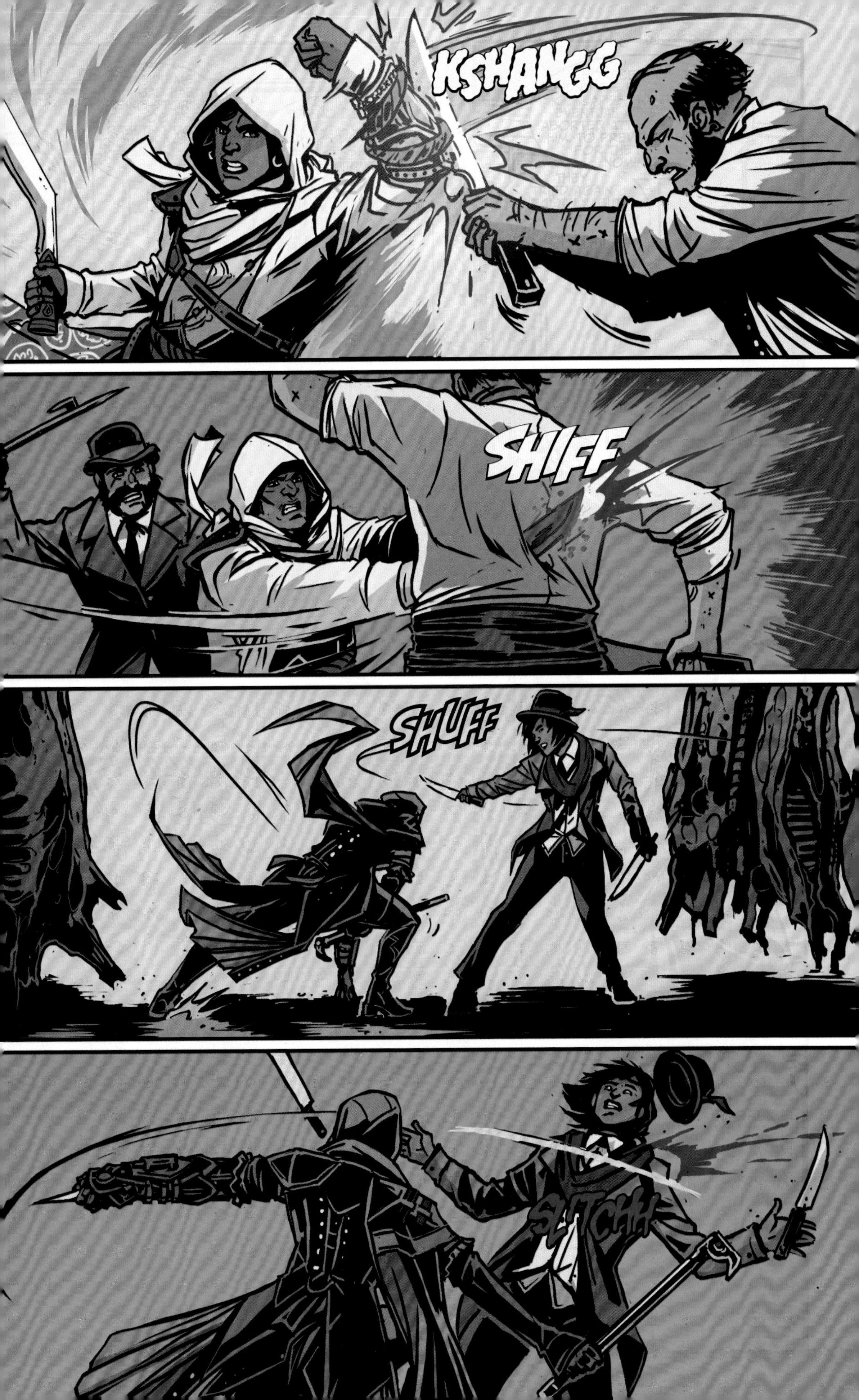
KSHANGG
SHIFF
SHUFF
SLITCHH

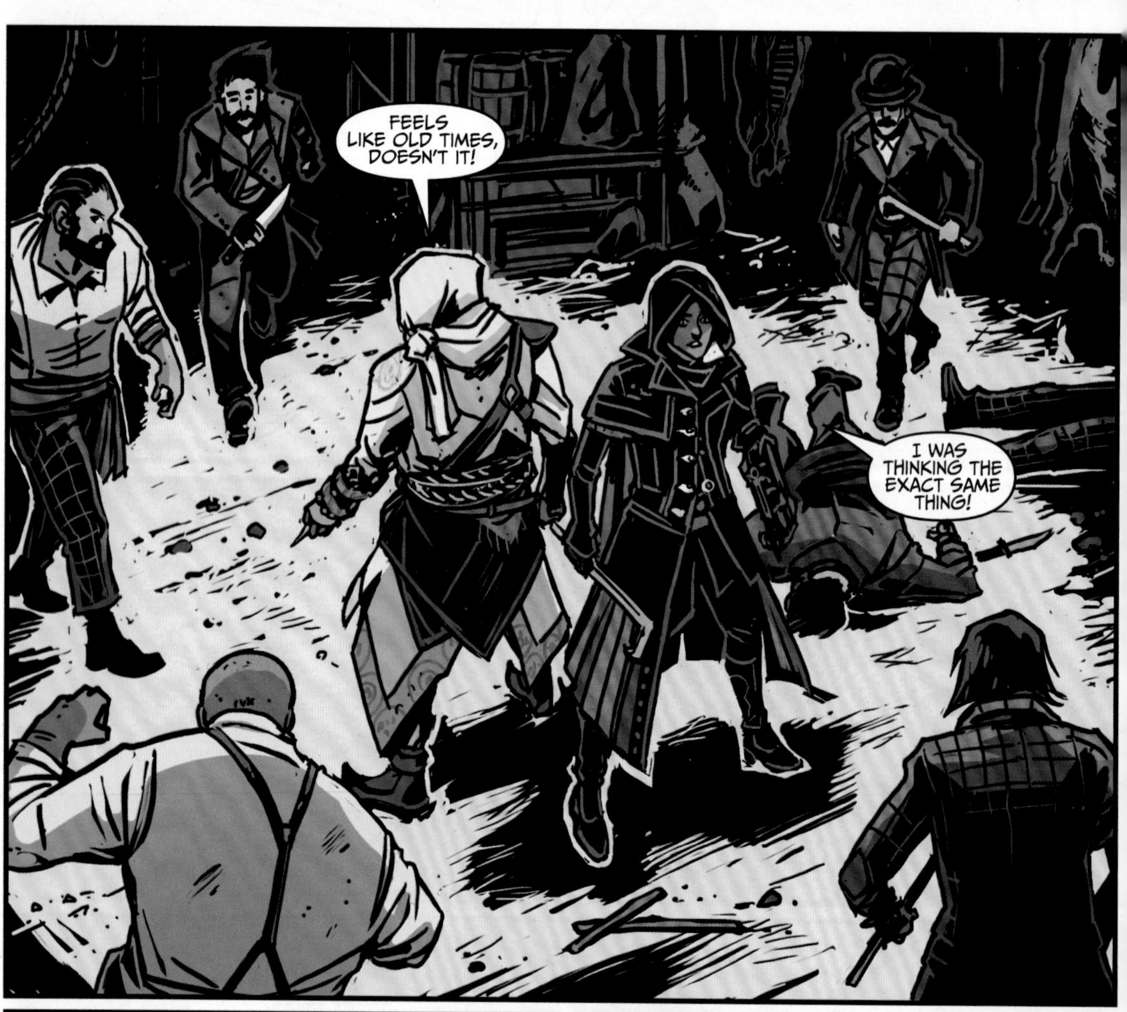
FEELS LIKE OLD TIMES, DOESN'T IT!
I WAS THINKING THE EXACT SAME THING!

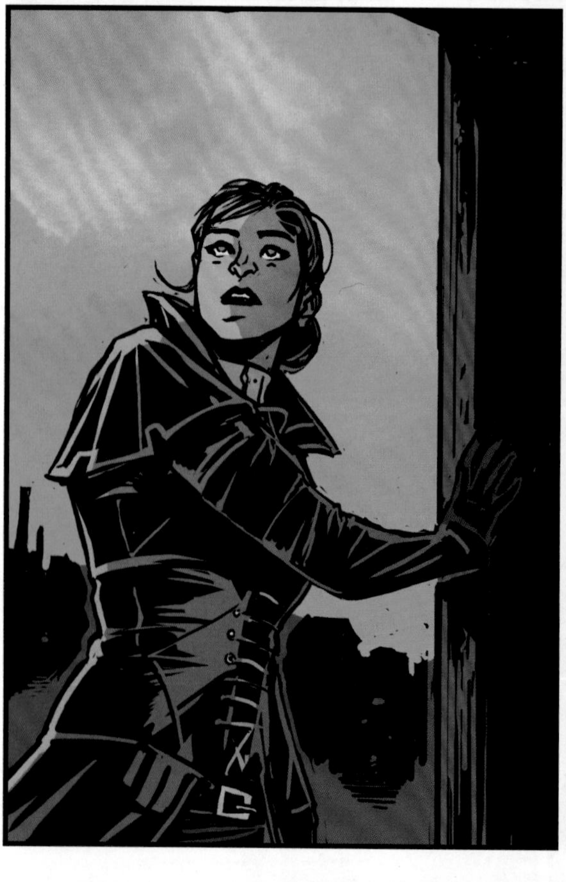

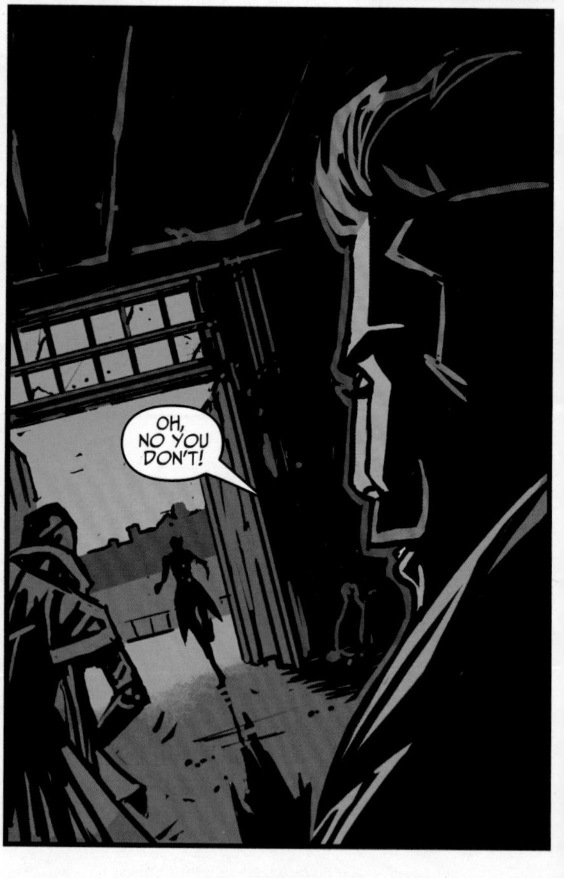
OH, NO YOU DON'T!

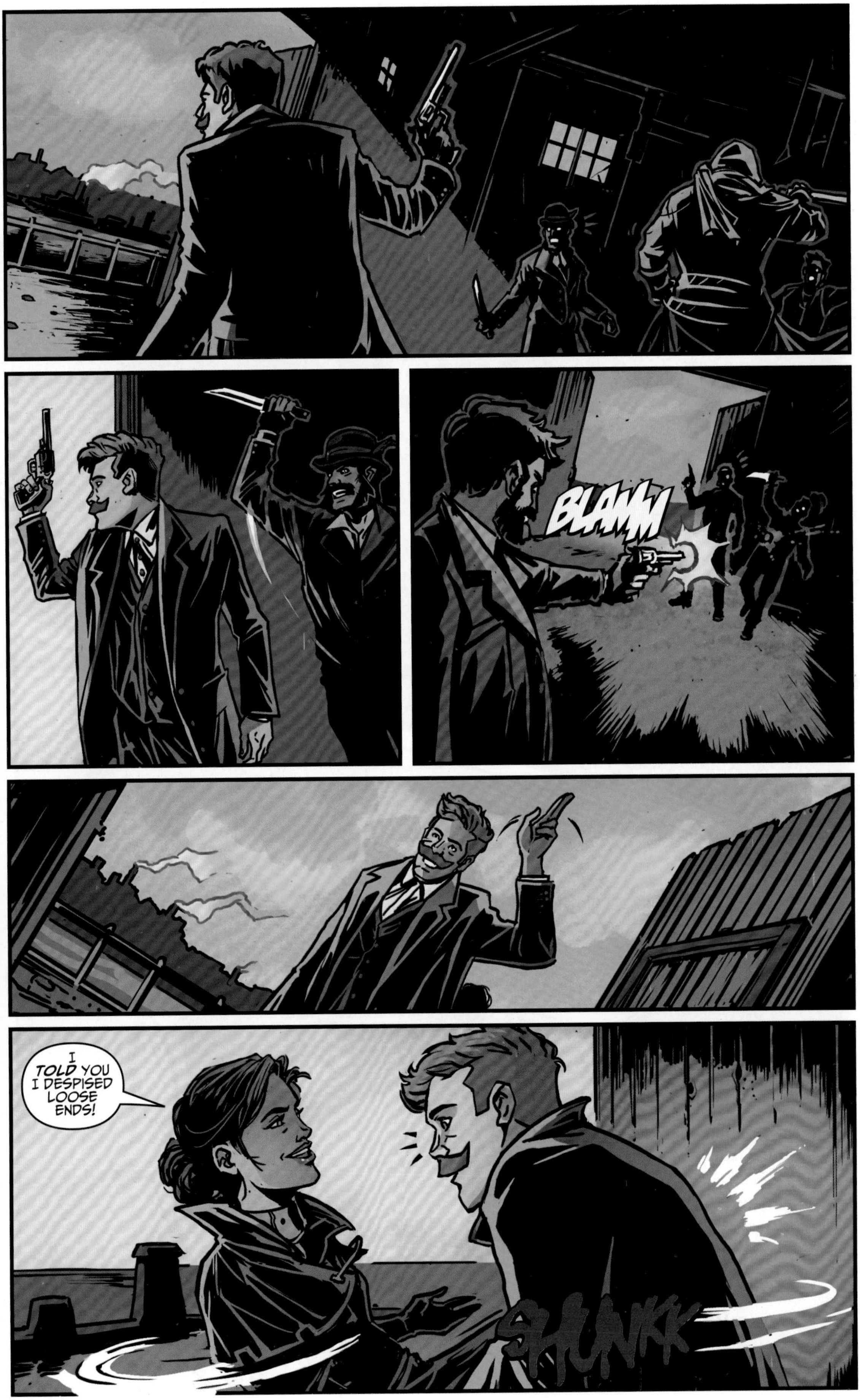
BLAMM
I TOLD YOU I DESPISED LOOSE ENDS!
SHUNKK

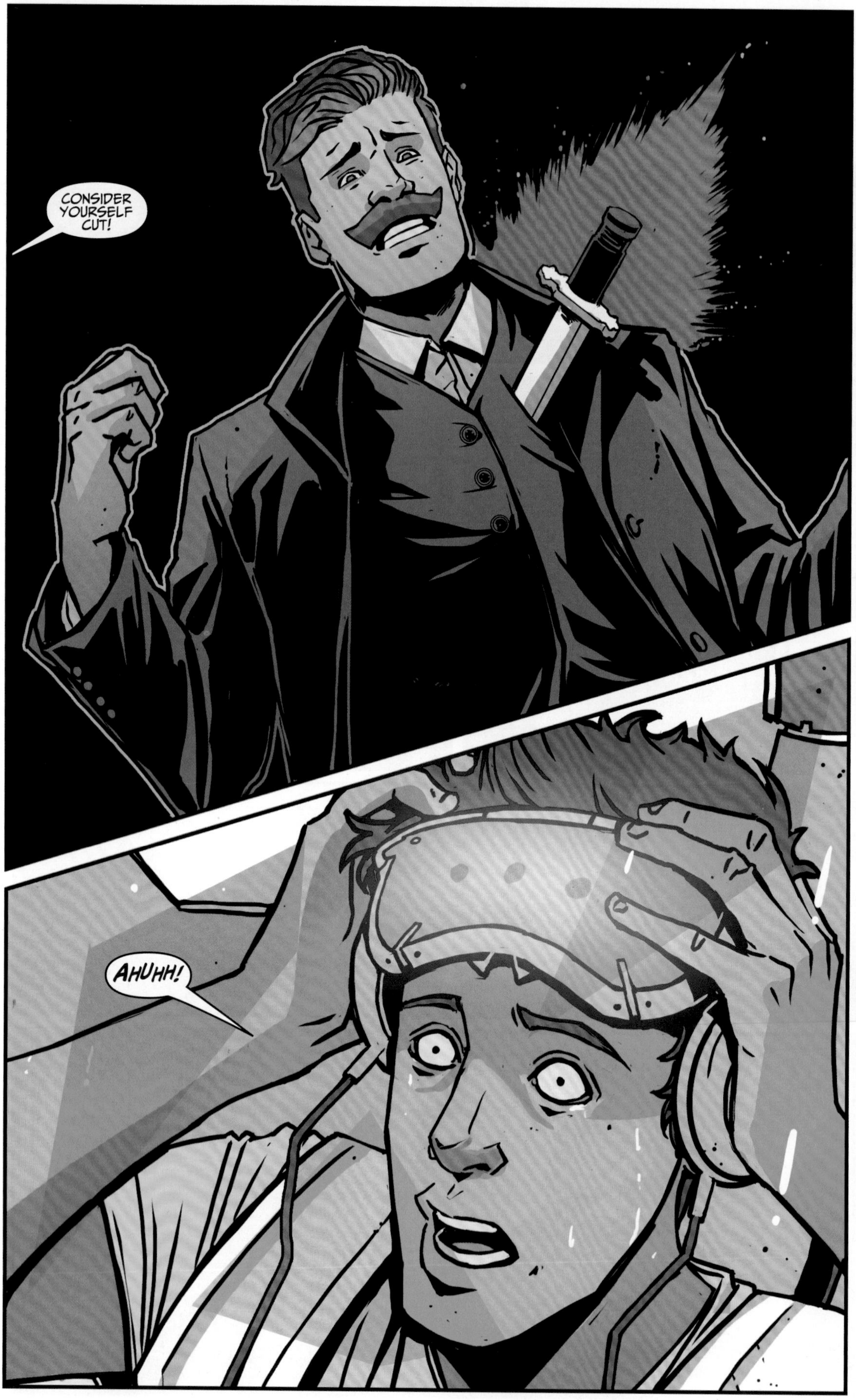
CONSIDER YOURSELF CUT!
AHUHH!

CHAPTER

3

AN ASSASSIN'S CREED SERIES
LAST DESCENDANTS
LOCUS

003

EDGINTON
WIJNGAARD
FARRELL

COVER A: CASPAR WIJNGAARD

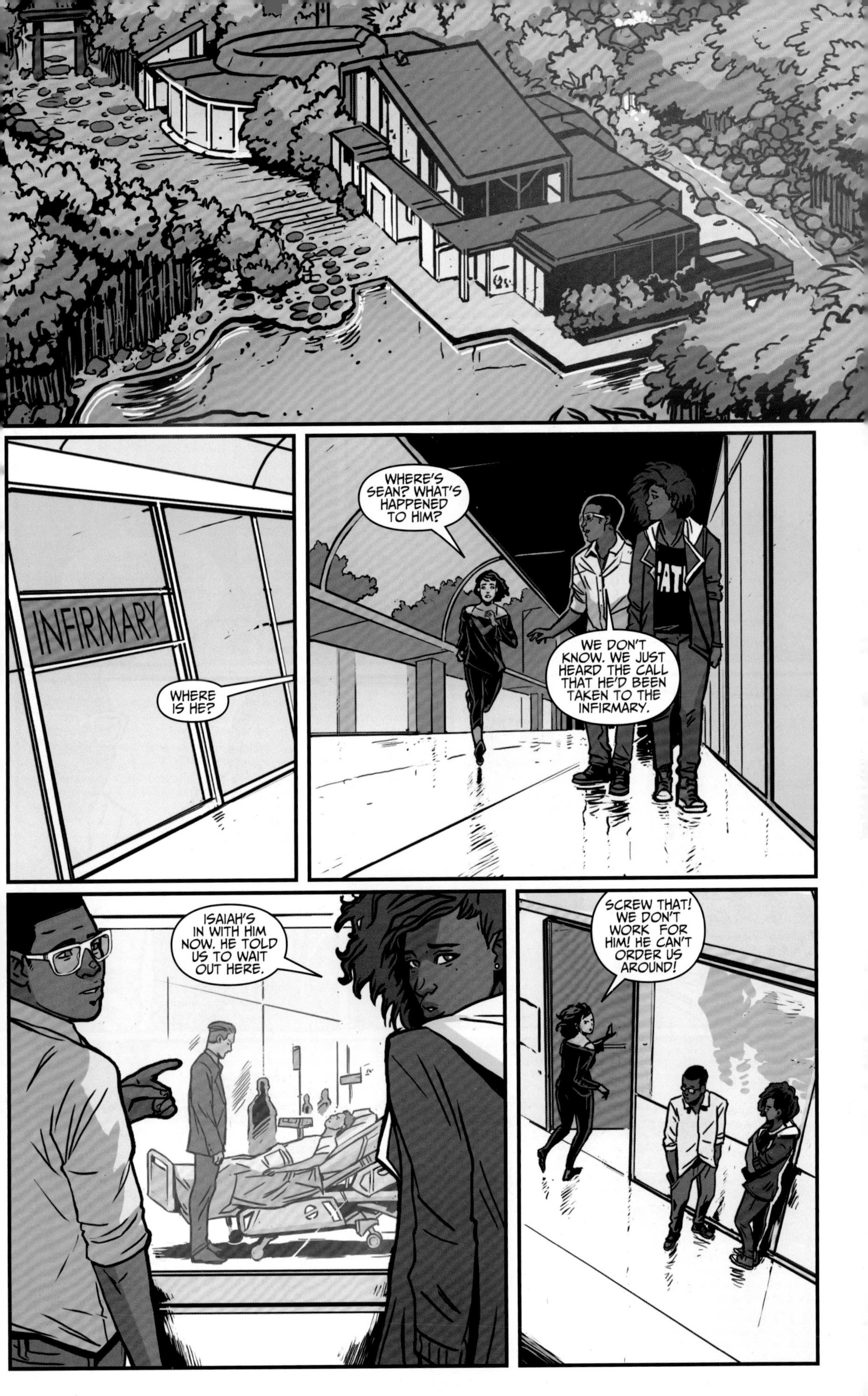
INFIRMARY
WHERE IS HE?
WHERE'S SEAN? WHAT'S HAPPENED TO HIM?
WE DON'T KNOW. WE JUST HEARD THE CALL THAT HE'D BEEN TAKEN TO THE INFIRMARY.
ISAIAH'S IN WITH HIM NOW. HE TOLD US TO WAIT OUT HERE.
SCREW THAT! WE DON'T WORK FOR HIM! HE CAN'T ORDER US AROUND!

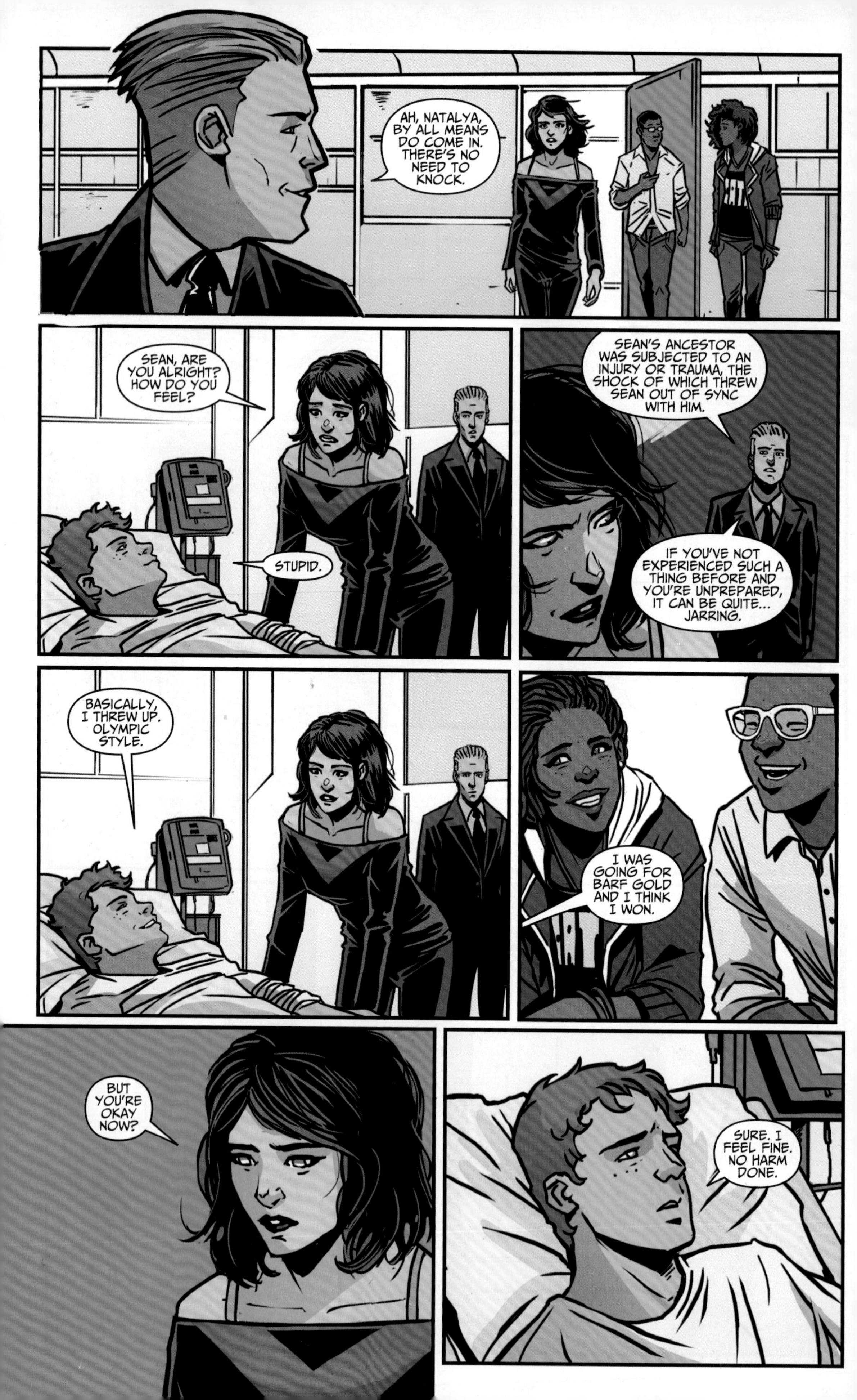
AH, NATALYA, BY ALL MEANS DO COME IN. THERE'S NO NEED TO KNOCK.
SEAN, ARE YOU ALRIGHT? HOW DO YOU FEEL?
STUPID.
SEAN'S ANCESTOR WAS SUBJECTED TO AN INJURY OR TRAUMA, THE SHOCK OF WHICH THREW SEAN OUT OF SYNC WITH HIM.
IF YOU'VE NOT EXPERIENCED SUCH A THING BEFORE AND YOU'RE UNPREPARED, IT CAN BE QUITE... JARRING.
BASICALLY, I THREW UP. OLYMPIC STYLE.
I WAS GOING FOR BARF GOLD AND I THINK I WON.
BUT YOU'RE OKAY NOW?
SURE. I FEEL FINE. NO HARM DONE.

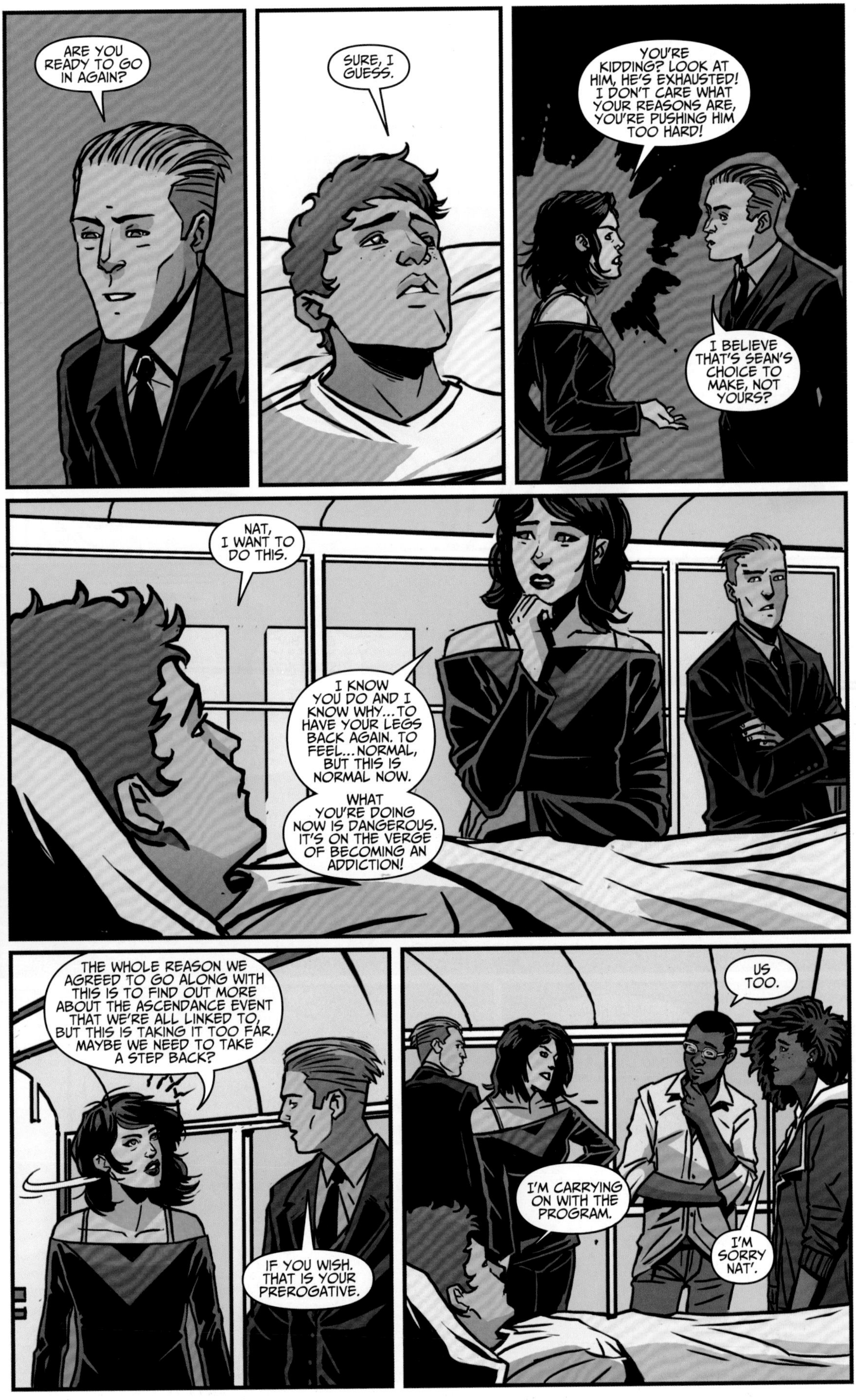

ARE YOU READY TO GO IN AGAIN?
SURE, I GUESS.
YOU'RE KIDDING? LOOK AT HIM, HE'S EXHAUSTED! I DON'T CARE WHAT YOUR REASONS ARE, YOU'RE PUSHING HIM TOO HARD!
I BELIEVE THAT'S SEAN'S CHOICE TO MAKE, NOT YOURS?
NAT, I WANT TO DO THIS.
I KNOW YOU DO AND I KNOW WHY...TO HAVE YOUR LEGS BACK AGAIN. TO FEEL...NORMAL, BUT THIS IS NORMAL NOW.
WHAT YOU'RE DOING NOW IS DANGEROUS. IT'S ON THE VERGE OF BECOMING AN ADDICTION!
THE WHOLE REASON WE AGREED TO GO ALONG WITH THIS IS TO FIND OUT MORE ABOUT THE ASCENDANCE EVENT THAT WE'RE ALL LINKED TO, BUT THIS IS TAKING IT TOO FAR. MAYBE WE NEED TO TAKE A STEP BACK?
IF YOU WISH. THAT IS YOUR PREROGATIVE.
US TOO.
I'M CARRYING ON WITH THE PROGRAM.
I'M SORRY NAT'.

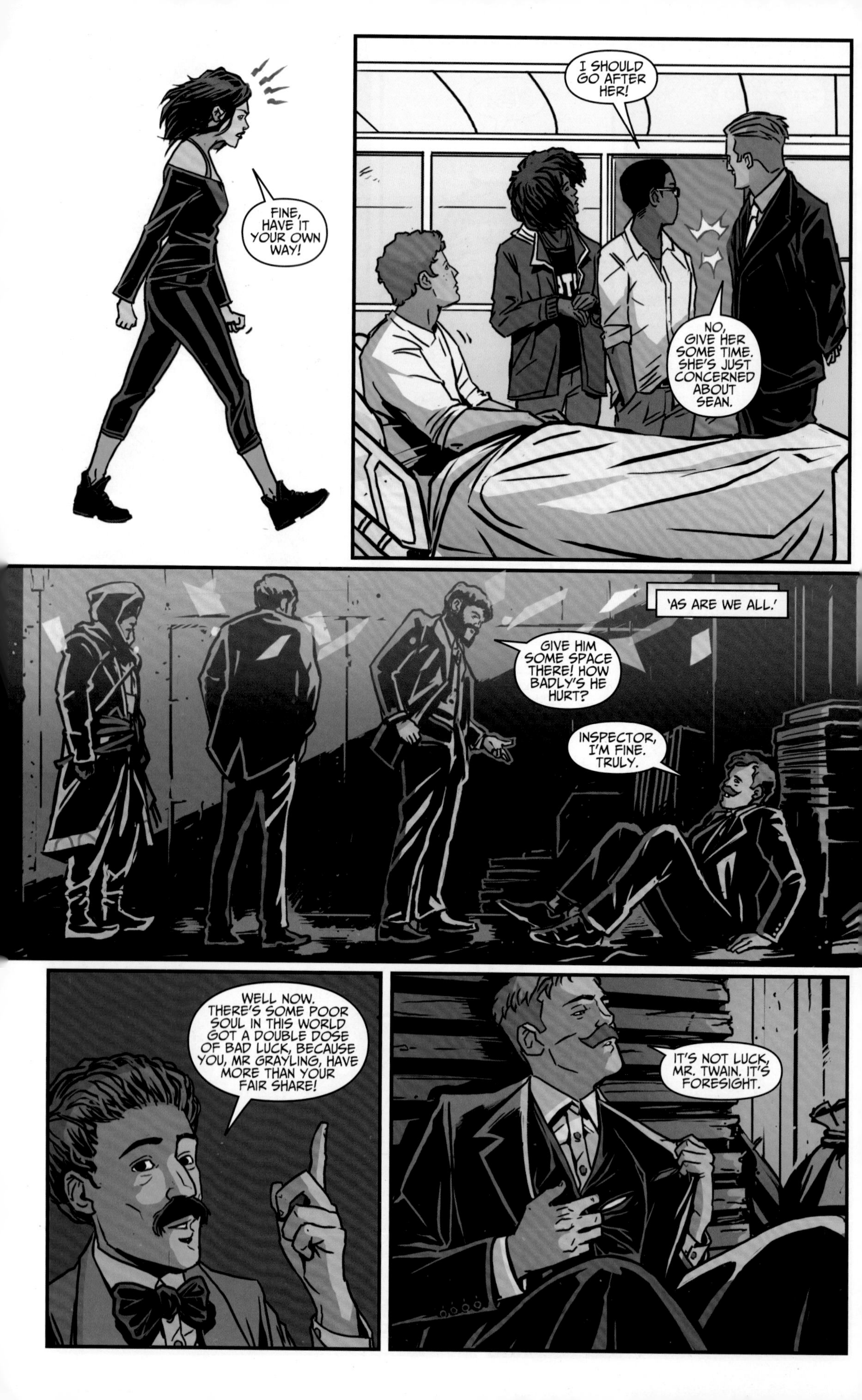

FINE, HAVE IT YOUR OWN WAY!
I SHOULD GO AFTER HER!
NO, GIVE HER SOME TIME. SHE'S JUST CONCERNED ABOUT SEAN.
'AS ARE WE ALL.'
GIVE HIM SOME SPACE THERE! HOW BADLY'S HE HURT?
INSPECTOR, I'M FINE. TRULY.
WELL NOW. THERE'S SOME POOR SOUL IN THIS WORLD GOT A DOUBLE DOSE OF BAD LUCK, BECAUSE YOU, MR GRAYLING, HAVE MORE THAN YOUR FAIR SHARE!
IT'S NOT LUCK, MR. TWAIN. IT'S FORESIGHT.

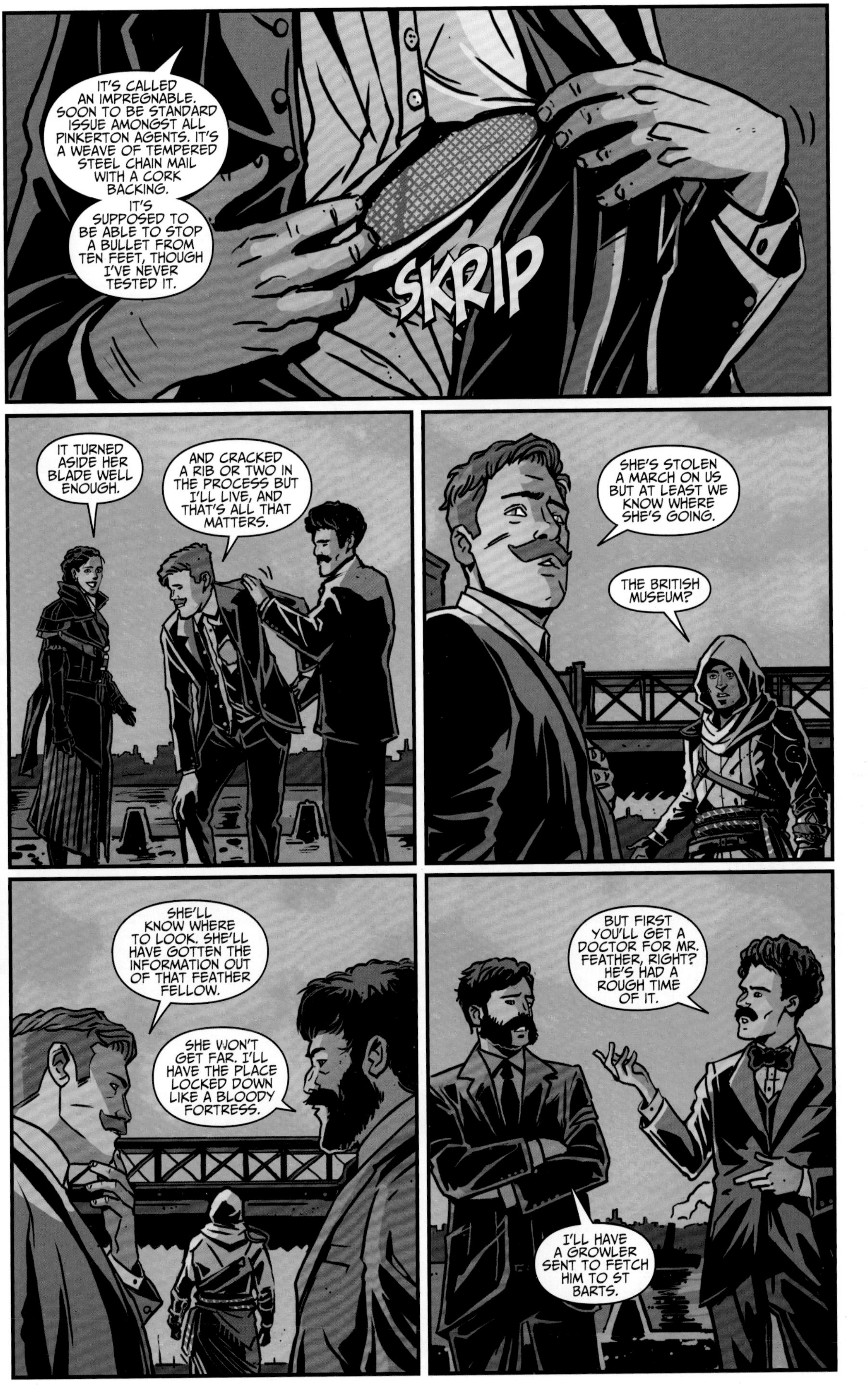
IT'S CALLED AN IMPREGNABLE. SOON TO BE STANDARD ISSUE AMONGST ALL PINKERTON AGENTS. IT'S A WEAVE OF TEMPERED STEEL CHAIN MAIL WITH A CORK BACKING.
IT'S SUPPOSED TO BE ABLE TO STOP A BULLET FROM TEN FEET, THOUGH I'VE NEVER TESTED IT.
SKRIP
IT TURNED ASIDE HER BLADE WELL ENOUGH.
AND CRACKED A RIB OR TWO IN THE PROCESS BUT I'LL LIVE, AND THAT'S ALL THAT MATTERS.
SHE'S STOLEN A MARCH ON US BUT AT LEAST WE KNOW WHERE SHE'S GOING.
THE BRITISH MUSEUM?
SHE'LL KNOW WHERE TO LOOK. SHE'LL HAVE GOTTEN THE INFORMATION OUT OF THAT FEATHER FELLOW.
SHE WON'T GET FAR. I'LL HAVE THE PLACE LOCKED DOWN LIKE A BLOODY FORTRESS.
BUT FIRST YOU'LL GET A DOCTOR FOR MR. FEATHER, RIGHT? HE'S HAD A ROUGH TIME OF IT.
I'LL HAVE A GROWLER SENT TO FETCH HIM TO ST BARTS.

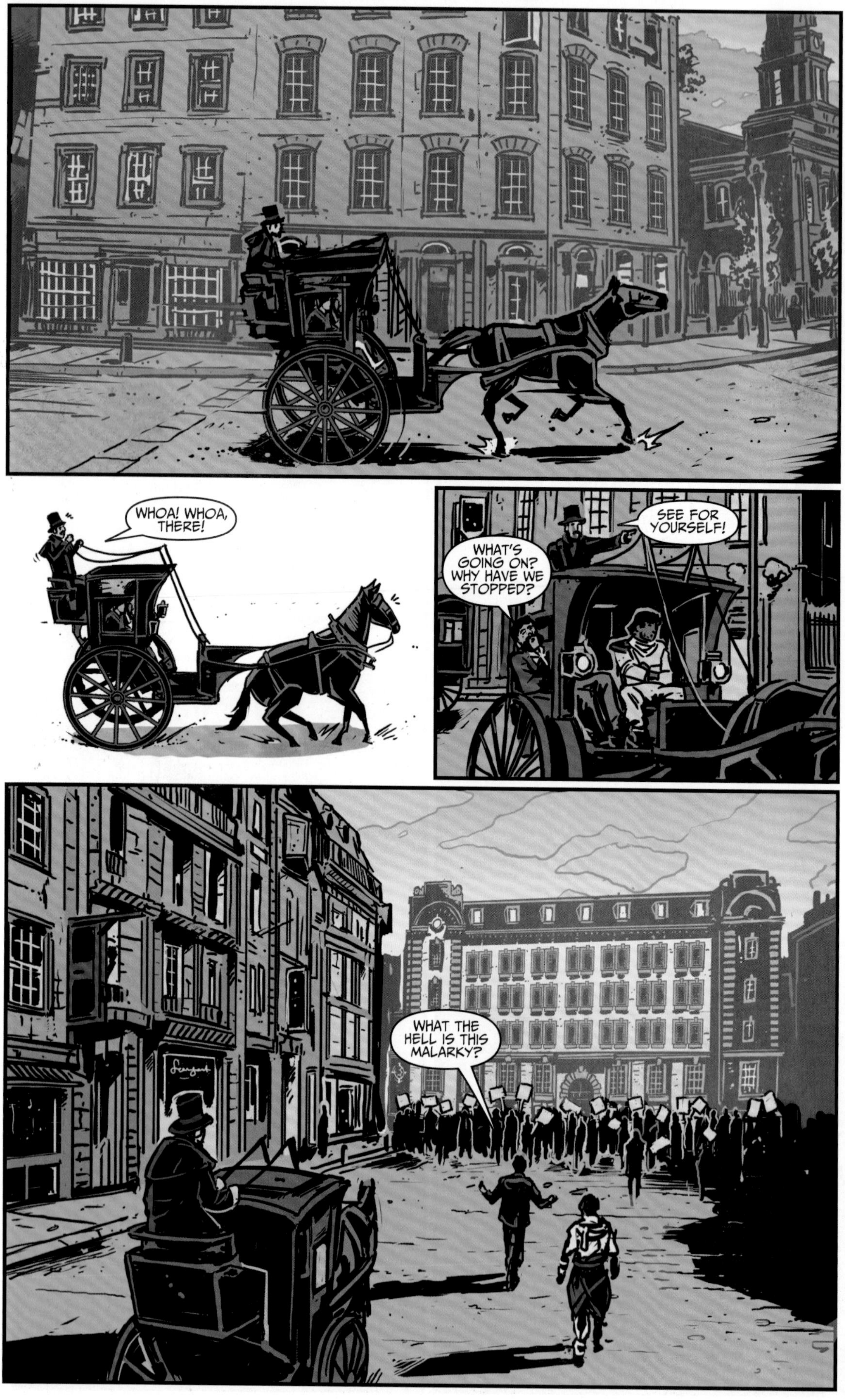
WHOA! WHOA, THERE!
WHAT'S GOING ON? WHY HAVE WE STOPPED?
SEE FOR YOURSELF!
WHAT THE HELL IS THIS MALARKY?

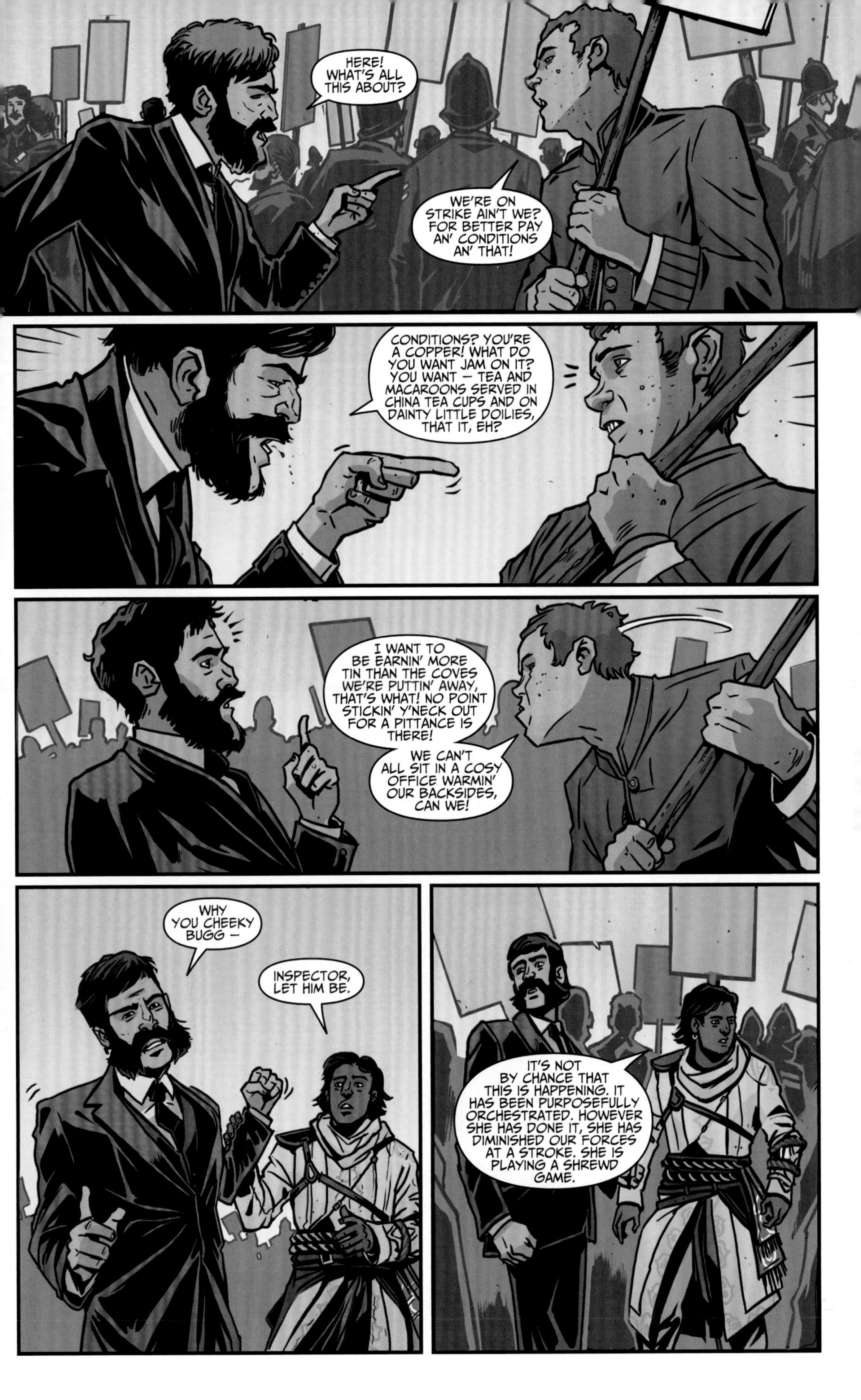
HERE! WHAT'S ALL THIS ABOUT?
WE'RE ON STRIKE AIN'T WE? FOR BETTER PAY AN' CONDITIONS AN' THAT!
CONDITIONS? YOU'RE A COPPER! WHAT DO YOU WANT JAM ON IT? YOU WANT — TEA AND MACAROONS SERVED IN CHINA TEA CUPS AND ON DAINTY LITTLE DOILIES, THAT IT, EH?
I WANT TO BE EARNIN' MORE TIN THAN THE COVES WE'RE PUTTIN' AWAY, THAT'S WHAT! NO POINT STICKIN' Y'NECK OUT FOR A PITTANCE IS THERE!
WE CAN'T ALL SIT IN A COSY OFFICE WARMIN' OUR BACKSIDES, CAN WE!
WHY YOU CHEEKY BUGG —
INSPECTOR, LET HIM BE.
IT'S NOT BY CHANCE THAT THIS IS HAPPENING. IT HAS BEEN PURPOSEFULLY ORCHESTRATED. HOWEVER SHE HAS DONE IT, SHE HAS DIMINISHED OUR FORCES AT A STROKE. SHE IS PLAYING A SHREWD GAME.

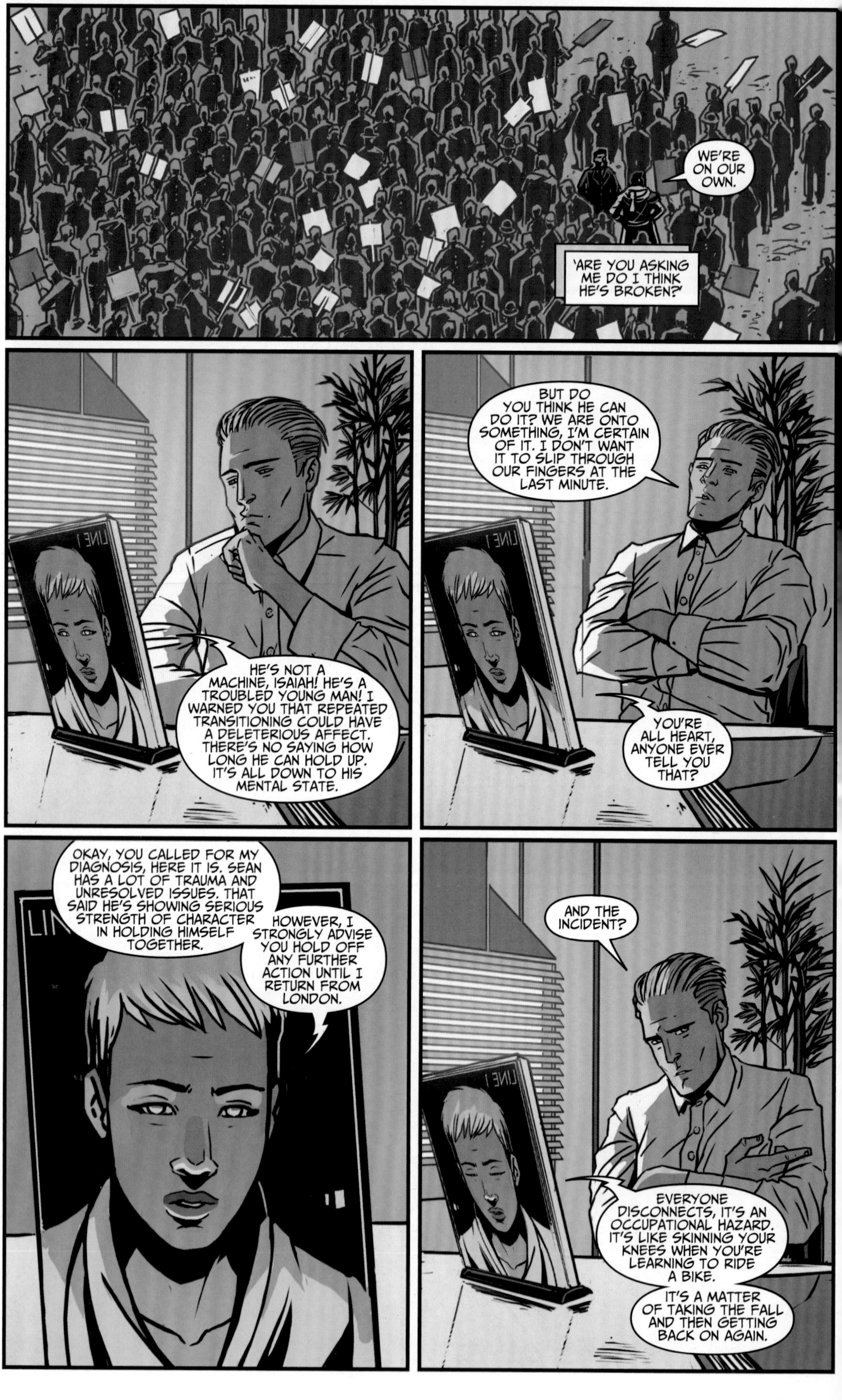
WE'RE ON OUR OWN.
'ARE YOU ASKING ME DO I THINK HE'S BROKEN?'
HE'S NOT A MACHINE, ISAIAH! HE'S A TROUBLED YOUNG MAN! I WARNED YOU THAT REPEATED TRANSITIONING COULD HAVE A DELETERIOUS AFFECT. THERE'S NO SAYING HOW LONG HE CAN HOLD UP. IT'S ALL DOWN TO HIS MENTAL STATE.
BUT DO YOU THINK HE CAN DO IT? WE ARE ONTO SOMETHING, I'M CERTAIN OF IT. I DON'T WANT IT TO SLIP THROUGH OUR FINGERS AT THE LAST MINUTE.
YOU'RE ALL HEART, ANYONE EVER TELL YOU THAT?
OKAY, YOU CALLED FOR MY DIAGNOSIS, HERE IT IS. SEAN HAS A LOT OF TRAUMA AND UNRESOLVED ISSUES. THAT SAID HE'S SHOWING SERIOUS STRENGTH OF CHARACTER IN HOLDING HIMSELF TOGETHER.
HOWEVER, I STRONGLY ADVISE YOU HOLD OFF ANY FURTHER ACTION UNTIL I RETURN FROM LONDON.
AND THE INCIDENT?
EVERYONE DISCONNECTS, IT'S AN OCCUPATIONAL HAZARD. IT'S LIKE SKINNING YOUR KNEES WHEN YOU'RE LEARNING TO RIDE A BIKE.
IT'S A MATTER OF TAKING THE FALL AND THEN GETTING BACK ON AGAIN.

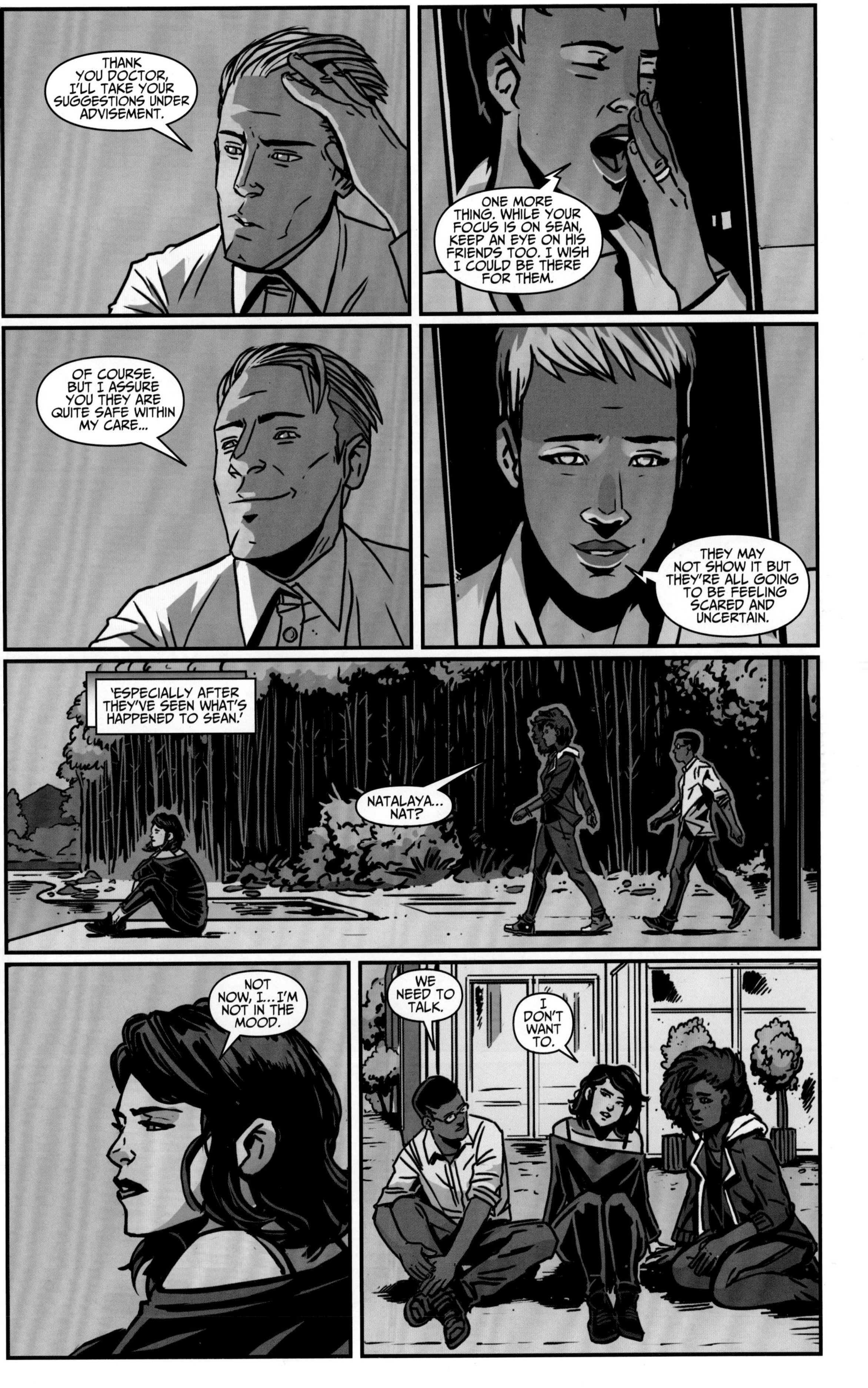
THANK YOU DOCTOR, I'LL TAKE YOUR SUGGESTIONS UNDER ADVISEMENT.
ONE MORE THING. WHILE YOUR FOCUS IS ON SEAN, KEEP AN EYE ON HIS FRIENDS TOO. I WISH I COULD BE THERE FOR THEM.
OF COURSE. BUT I ASSURE YOU THEY ARE QUITE SAFE WITHIN MY CARE...
THEY MAY NOT SHOW IT BUT THEY'RE ALL GOING TO BE FEELING SCARED AND UNCERTAIN.
'ESPECIALLY AFTER THEY'VE SEEN WHAT'S HAPPENED TO SEAN.'
NATALAYA... NAT?
NOT NOW, I... I'M NOT IN THE MOOD.
WE NEED TO TALK.
I DON'T WANT TO.

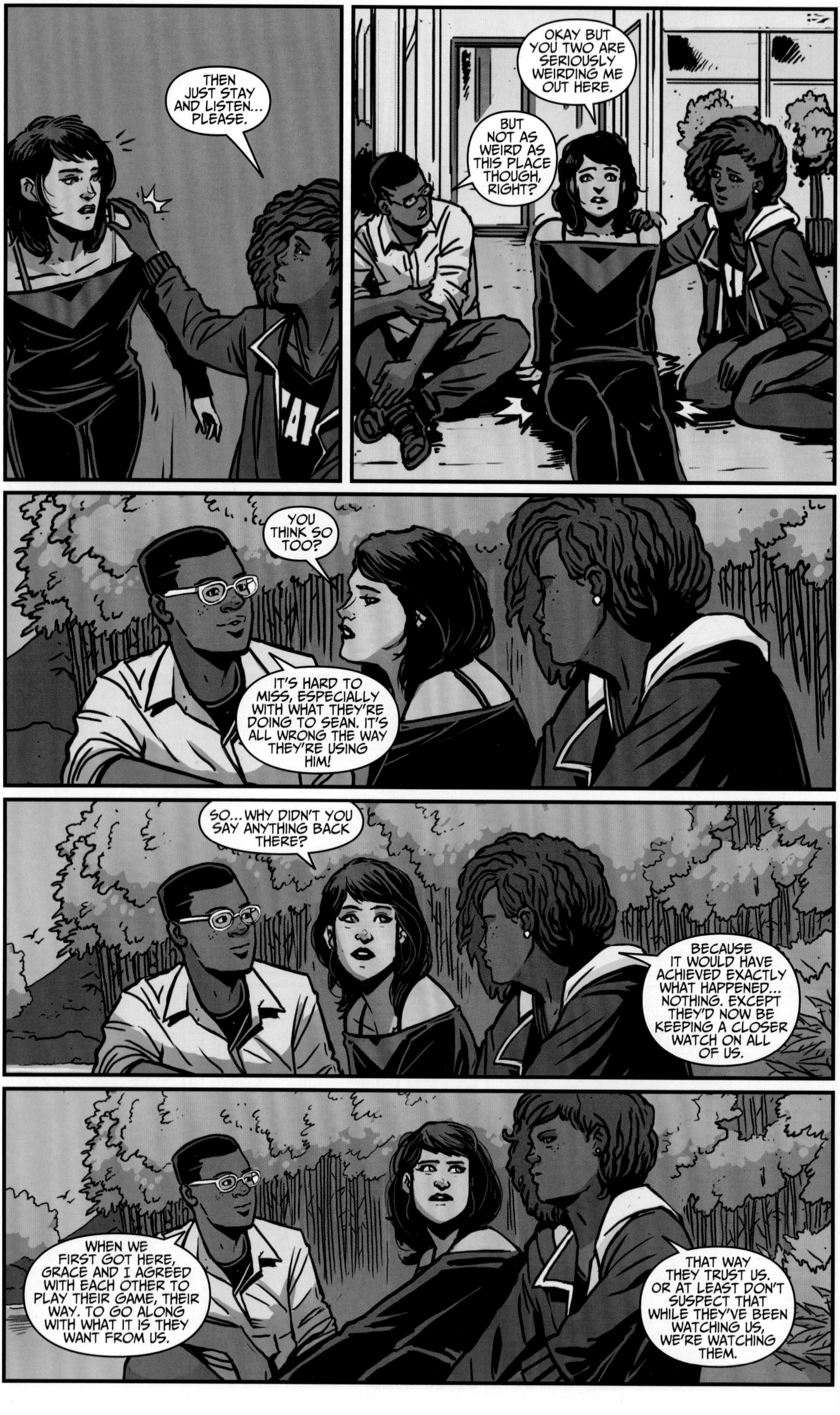
THEN JUST STAY AND LISTEN... PLEASE.
OKAY BUT YOU TWO ARE SERIOUSLY WEIRDING ME OUT HERE.
BUT NOT AS WEIRD AS THIS PLACE THOUGH, RIGHT?
YOU THINK SO TOO?
IT'S HARD TO MISS, ESPECIALLY WITH WHAT THEY'RE DOING TO SEAN. IT'S ALL WRONG THE WAY THEY'RE USING HIM!
SO... WHY DIDN'T YOU SAY ANYTHING BACK THERE?
BECAUSE IT WOULD HAVE ACHIEVED EXACTLY WHAT HAPPENED... NOTHING. EXCEPT THEY'D NOW BE KEEPING A CLOSER WATCH ON ALL OF US.
WHEN WE FIRST GOT HERE, GRACE AND I AGREED WITH EACH OTHER TO PLAY THEIR GAME, THEIR WAY. TO GO ALONG WITH WHAT IT IS THEY WANT FROM US.
THAT WAY THEY TRUST US. OR AT LEAST DON'T SUSPECT THAT WHILE THEY'VE BEEN WATCHING US, WE'RE WATCHING THEM.

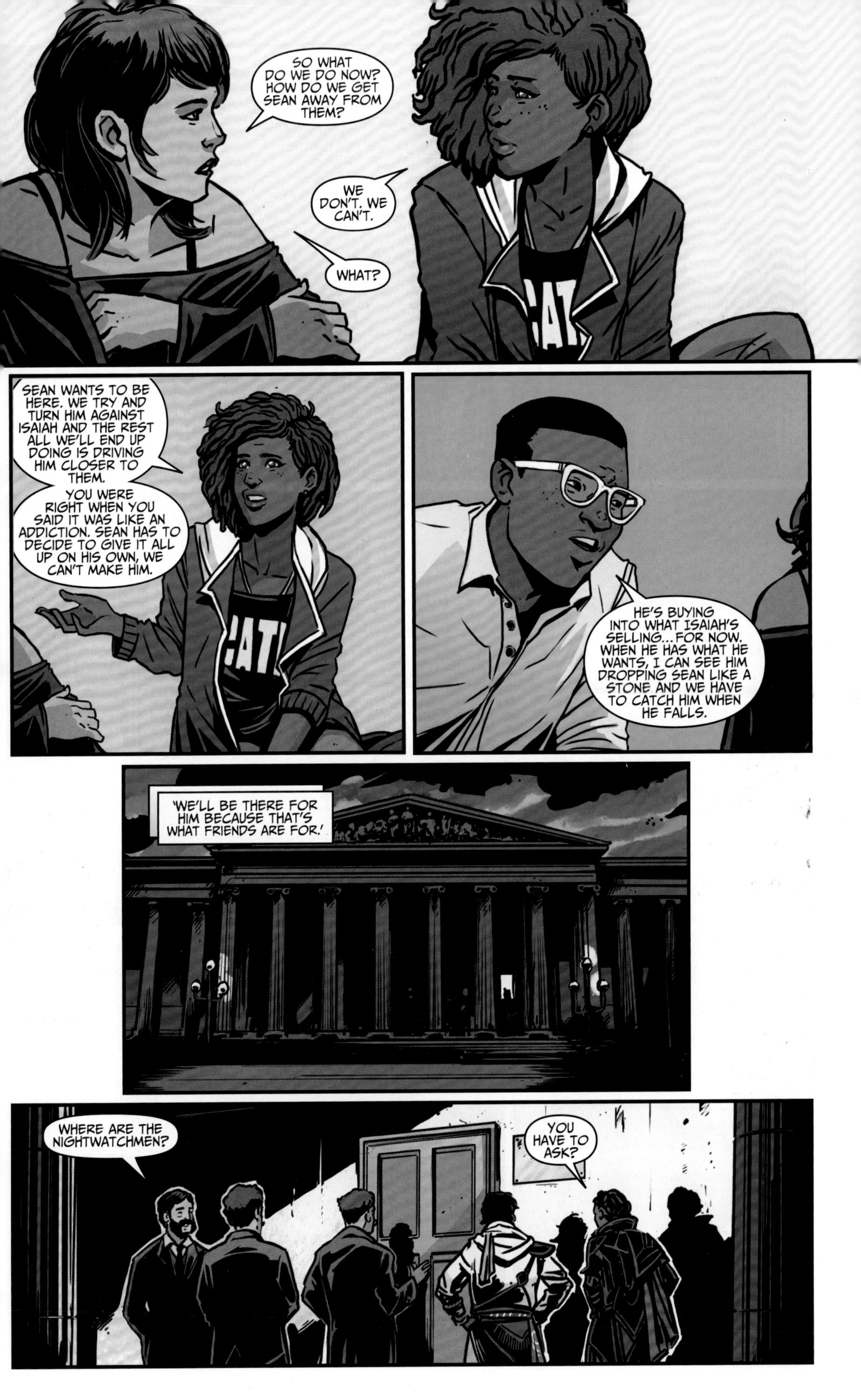
SO WHAT DO WE DO NOW? HOW DO WE GET SEAN AWAY FROM THEM?
WE DON'T. WE CAN'T.
WHAT?
SEAN WANTS TO BE HERE. WE TRY AND TURN HIM AGAINST ISAIAH AND THE REST ALL WE'LL END UP DOING IS DRIVING HIM CLOSER TO THEM.
YOU WERE RIGHT WHEN YOU SAID IT WAS LIKE AN ADDICTION. SEAN HAS TO DECIDE TO GIVE IT ALL UP ON HIS OWN, WE CAN'T MAKE HIM.
HE'S BUYING INTO WHAT ISAIAH'S SELLING... FOR NOW. WHEN HE HAS WHAT HE WANTS, I CAN SEE HIM DROPPING SEAN LIKE A STONE AND WE HAVE TO CATCH HIM WHEN HE FALLS.
'WE'LL BE THERE FOR HIM BECAUSE THAT'S WHAT FRIENDS ARE FOR.'
WHERE ARE THE NIGHTWATCHMEN?
YOU HAVE TO ASK?

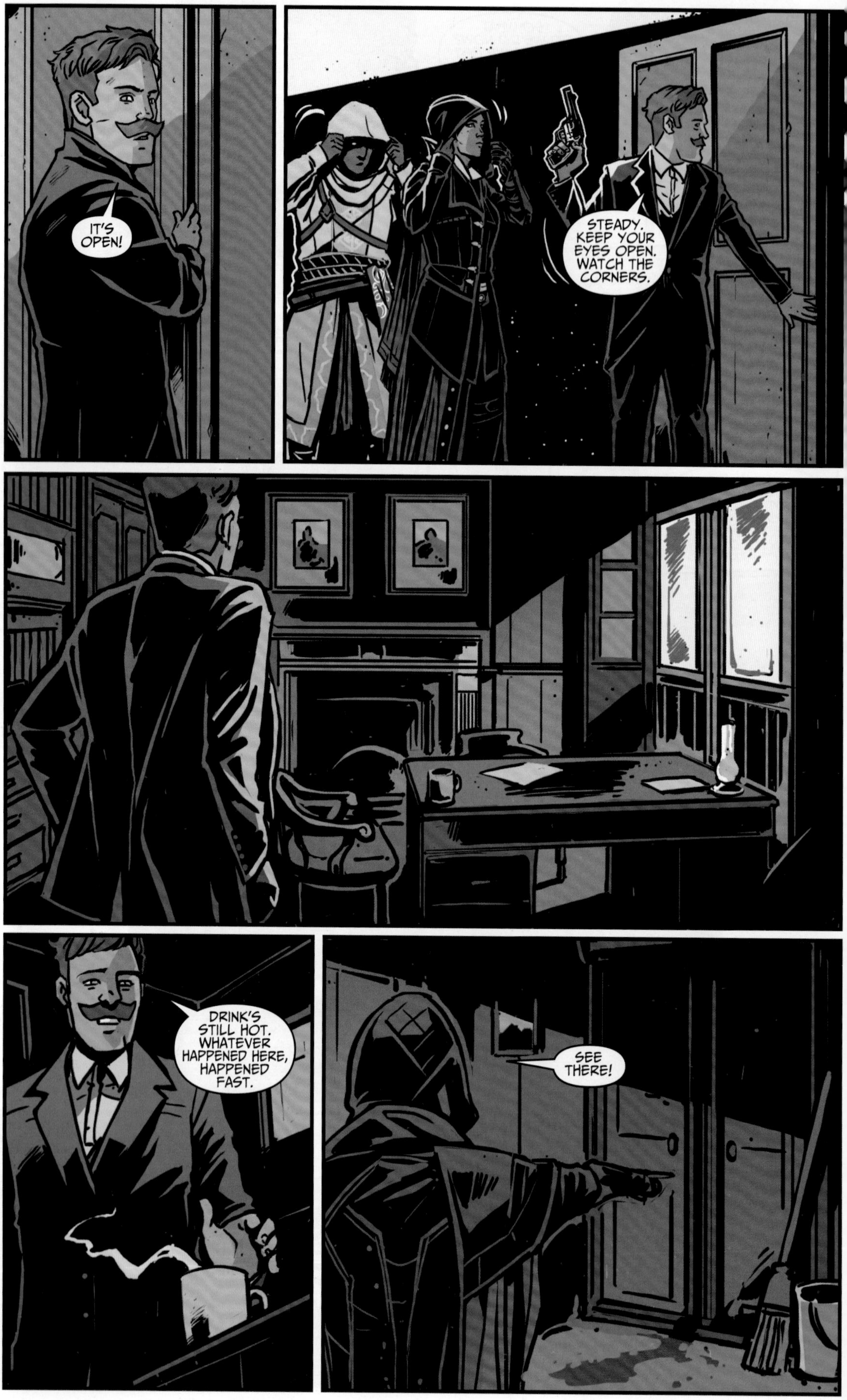
IT'S OPEN!
STEADY. KEEP YOUR EYES OPEN. WATCH THE CORNERS.
DRINK'S STILL HOT. WHATEVER HAPPENED HERE, HAPPENED FAST.
SEE THERE!

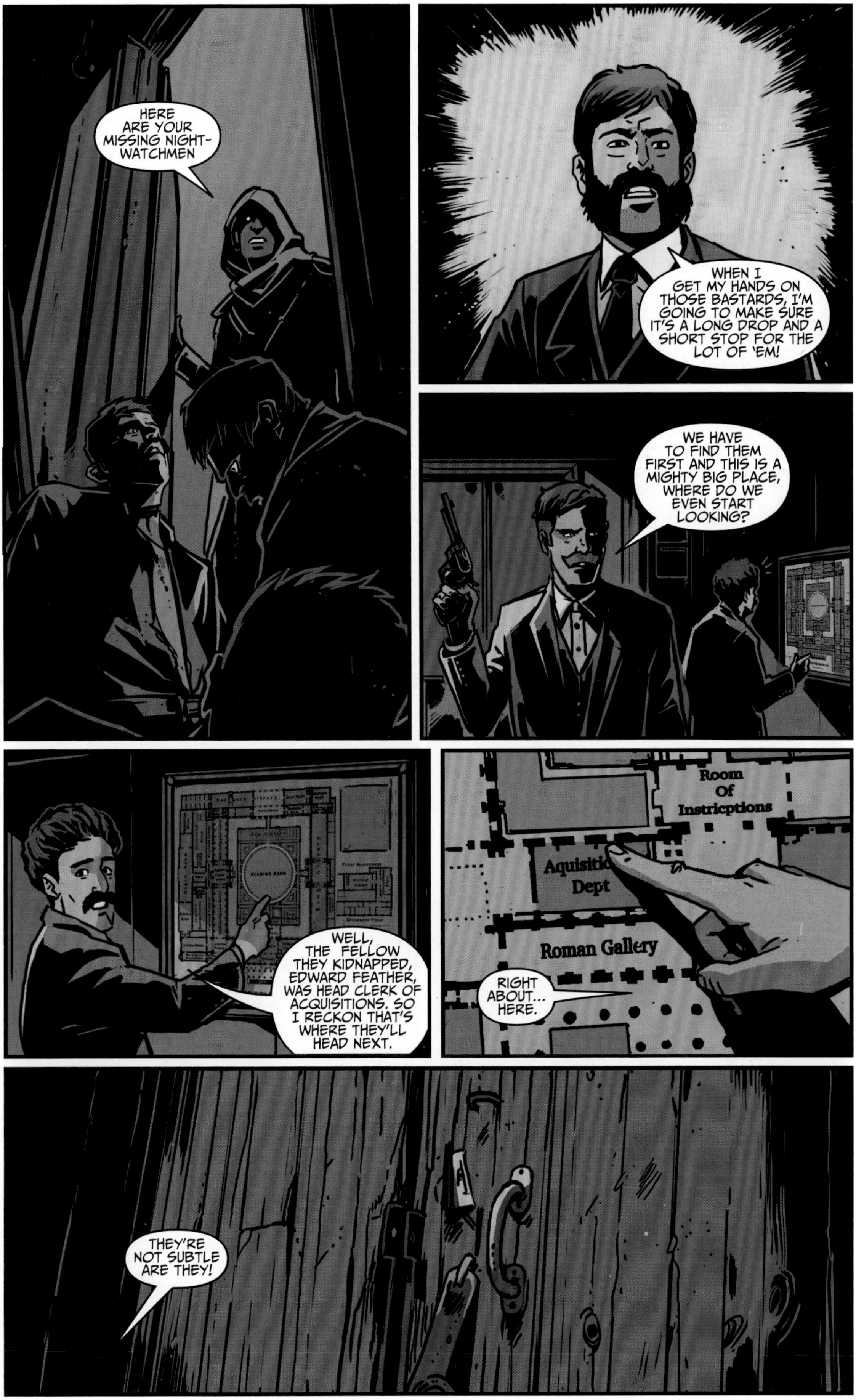
HERE ARE YOUR MISSING NIGHT-WATCHMEN
WHEN I GET MY HANDS ON THOSE BASTARDS, I'M GOING TO MAKE SURE IT'S A LONG DROP AND A SHORT STOP FOR THE LOT OF 'EM!
WE HAVE TO FIND THEM FIRST AND THIS IS A MIGHTY BIG PLACE, WHERE DO WE EVEN START LOOKING?
WELL, THE FELLOW THEY KIDNAPPED, EDWARD FEATHER, WAS HEAD CLERK OF ACQUISITIONS. SO I RECKON THAT'S WHERE THEY'LL HEAD NEXT.
Room Of Instrictions
Aquisitio Dept
Roman Gallery
RIGHT ABOUT... HERE.
THEY'RE NOT SUBTLE ARE THEY!

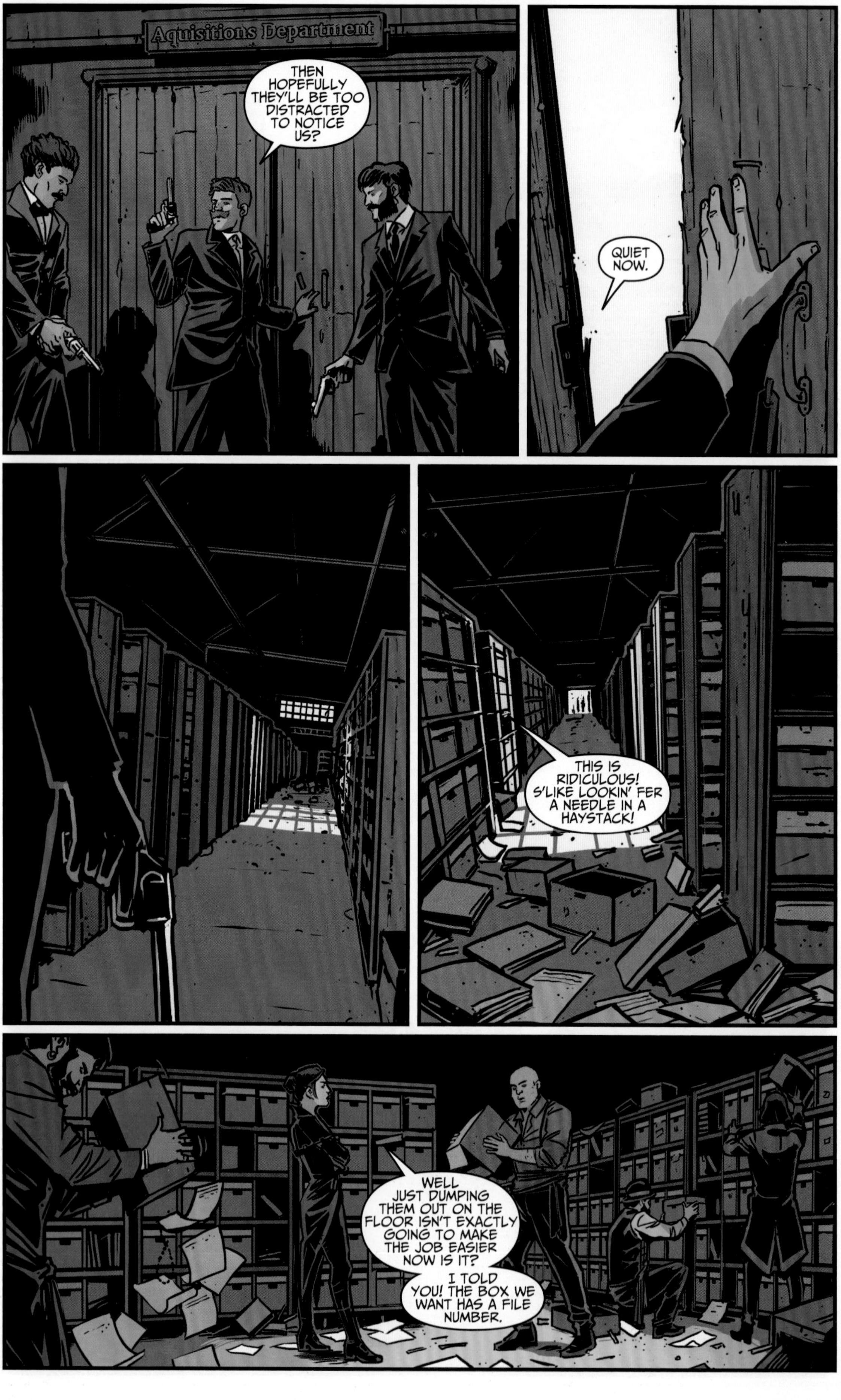
Aquisitions Department
THEN HOPEFULLY THEY'LL BE TOO DISTRACTED TO NOTICE US?
QUIET NOW.
THIS IS RIDICULOUS! S'LIKE LOOKIN' FER A NEEDLE IN A HAYSTACK!
WELL JUST DUMPING THEM OUT ON THE FLOOR ISN'T EXACTLY GOING TO MAKE THE JOB EASIER NOW IS IT?
I TOLD YOU! THE BOX WE WANT HAS A FILE NUMBER.

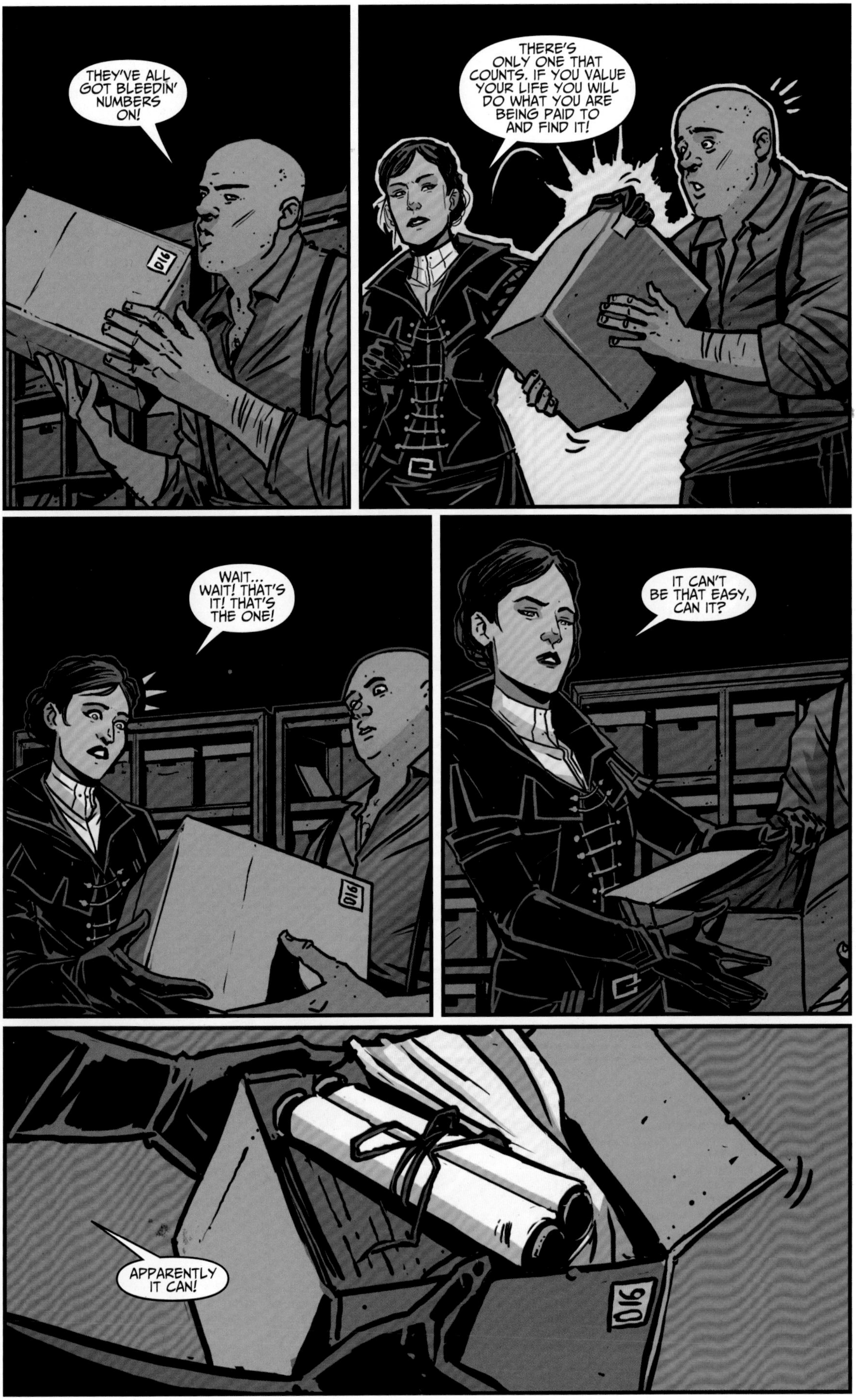
THEY'VE ALL GOT BLEEDIN' NUMBERS ON!
016
THERE'S ONLY ONE THAT COUNTS. IF YOU VALUE YOUR LIFE YOU WILL DO WHAT YOU ARE BEING PAID TO AND FIND IT!
WAIT... WAIT! THAT'S IT! THAT'S THE ONE!
016
IT CAN'T BE THAT EASY, CAN IT?
APPARENTLY IT CAN!
016

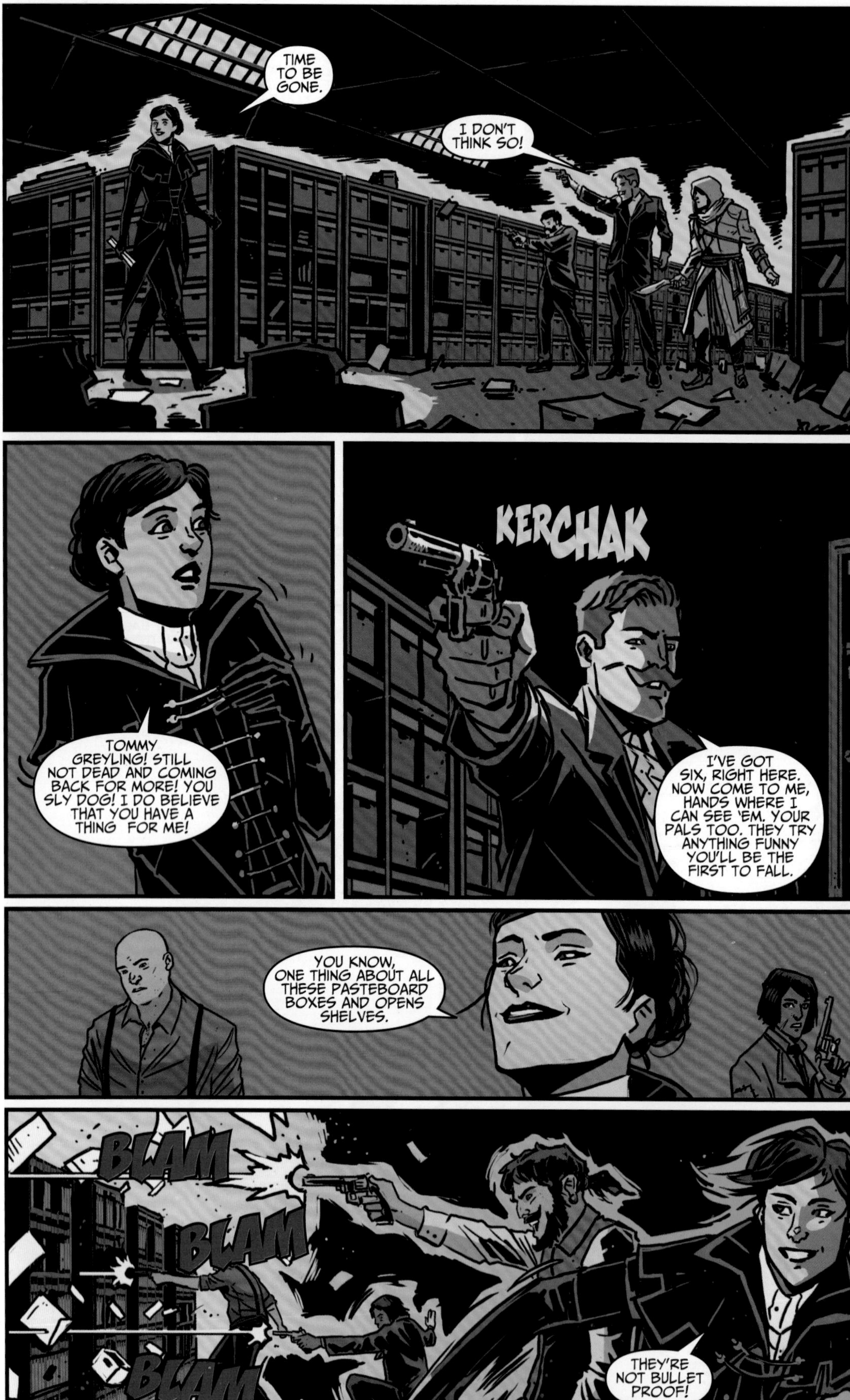
TIME TO BE GONE.
I DON'T THINK SO!
TOMMY GREYLING! STILL NOT DEAD AND COMING BACK FOR MORE! YOU SLY DOG! I DO BELIEVE THAT YOU HAVE A THING FOR ME!
KERCHAK
I'VE GOT SIX, RIGHT HERE. NOW COME TO ME, HANDS WHERE I CAN SEE 'EM. YOUR PALS TOO. THEY TRY ANYTHING FUNNY YOU'LL BE THE FIRST TO FALL.
YOU KNOW, ONE THING ABOUT ALL THESE PASTEBOARD BOXES AND OPENS SHELVES.
BLAM
BLAM
BLAM
THEY'RE NOT BULLET PROOF!

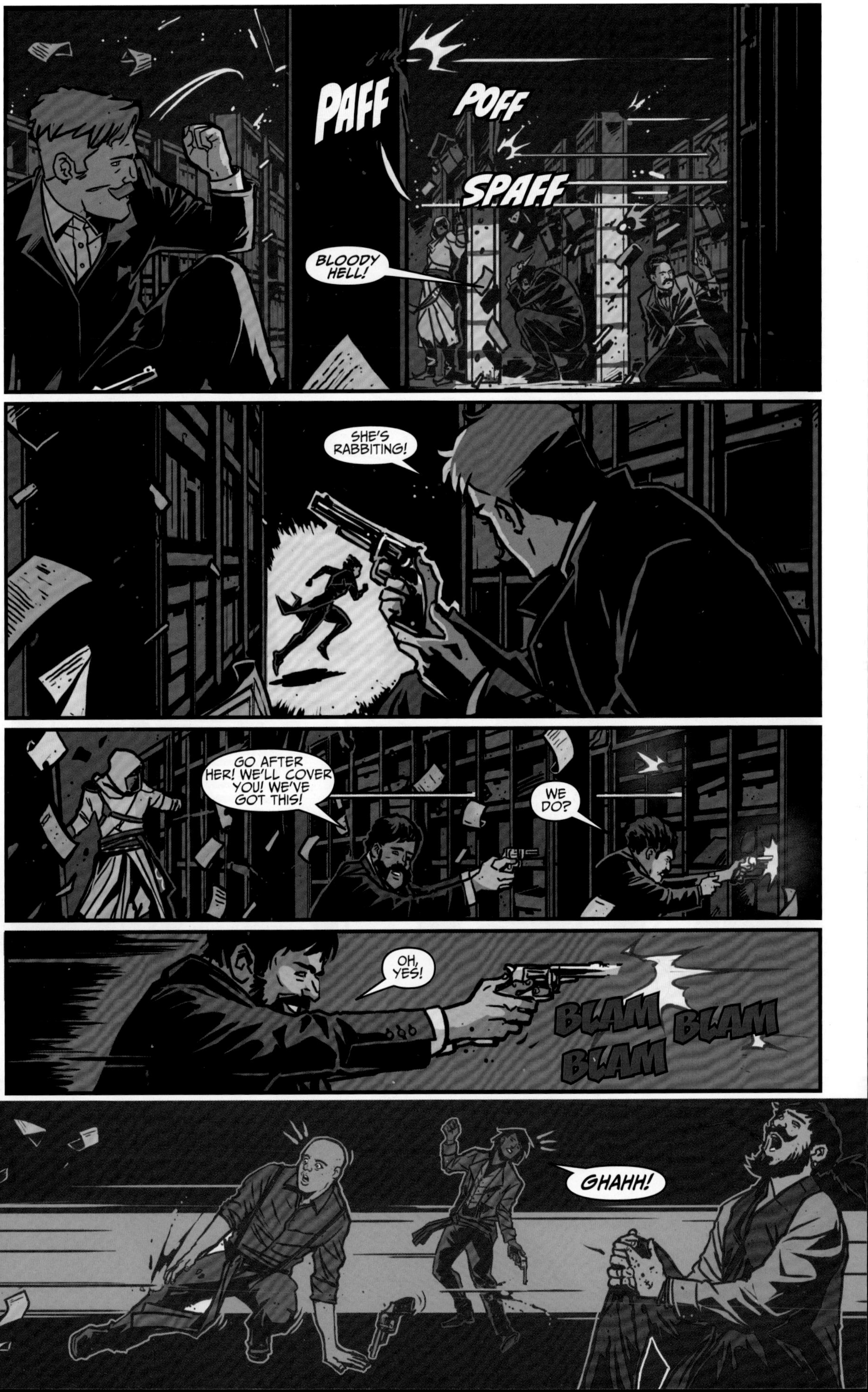
PAFF
POFF
SPAFF
BLOODY HELL!
SHE'S RABBITING!
GO AFTER HER! WE'LL COVER YOU! WE'VE GOT THIS!
WE DO?
OH, YES!
BLAM
BLAM
BLAM
GHAHH!

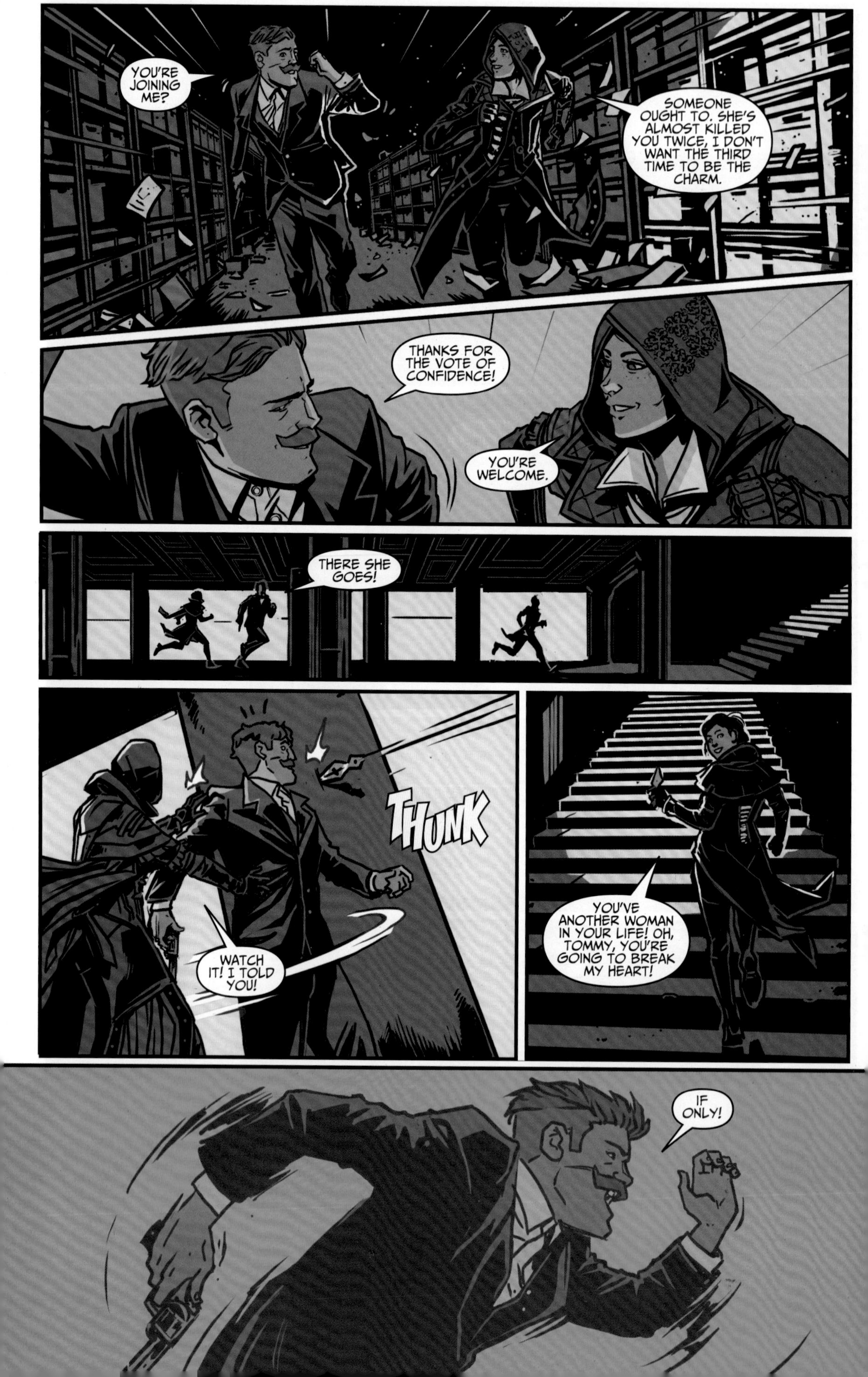
YOU'RE JOINING ME?
SOMEONE OUGHT TO. SHE'S ALMOST KILLED YOU TWICE, I DON'T WANT THE THIRD TIME TO BE THE CHARM.
THANKS FOR THE VOTE OF CONFIDENCE!
YOU'RE WELCOME.
THERE SHE GOES!
THUNK
WATCH IT! I TOLD YOU!
YOU'VE ANOTHER WOMAN IN YOUR LIFE! OH, TOMMY, YOU'RE GOING TO BREAK MY HEART!
IF ONLY!

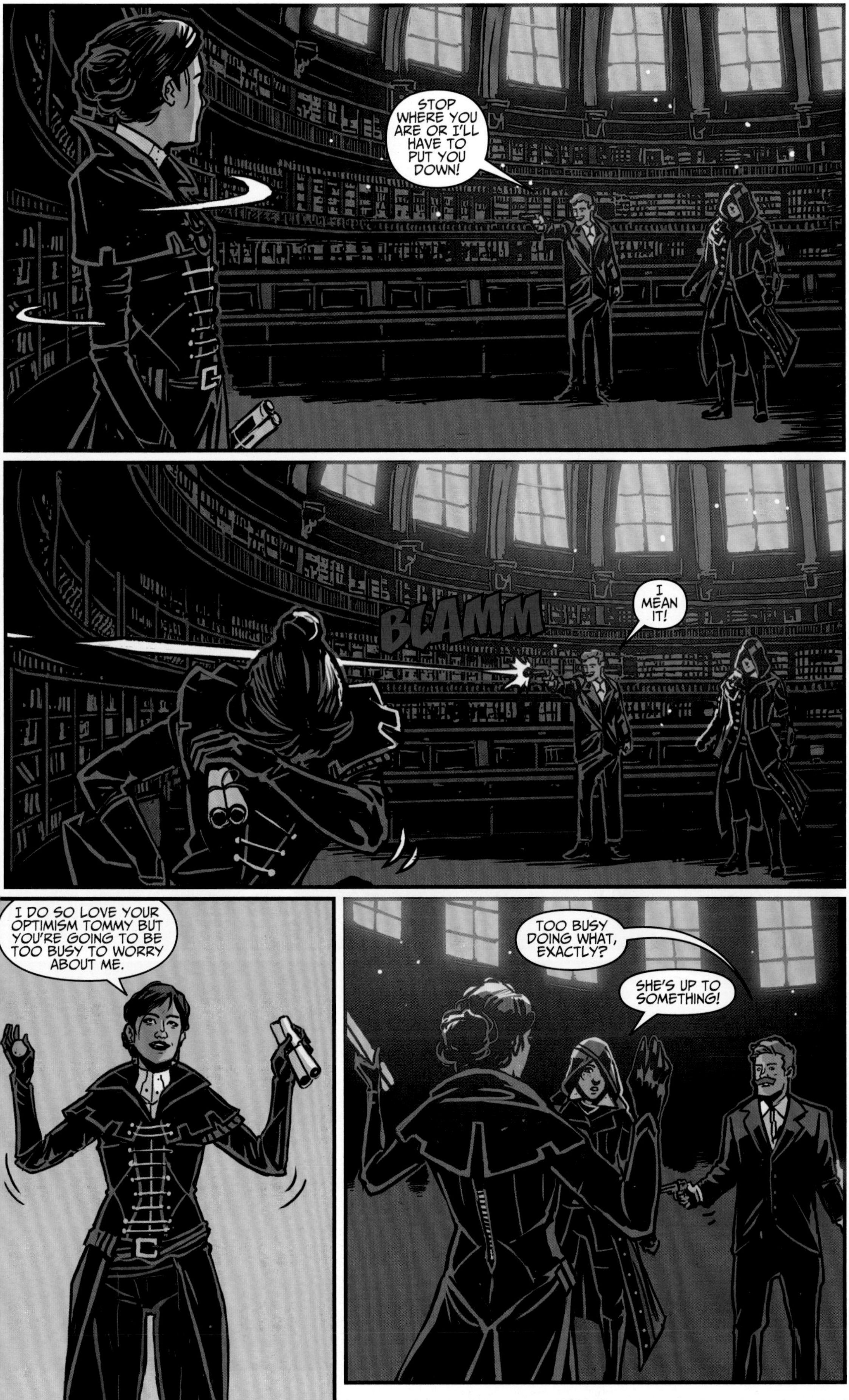
STOP WHERE YOU ARE OR I'LL HAVE TO PUT YOU DOWN!
BLAMM
I MEAN IT!
I DO SO LOVE YOUR OPTIMISM TOMMY BUT YOU'RE GOING TO BE TOO BUSY TO WORRY ABOUT ME.
TOO BUSY DOING WHAT, EXACTLY?
SHE'S UP TO SOMETHING!

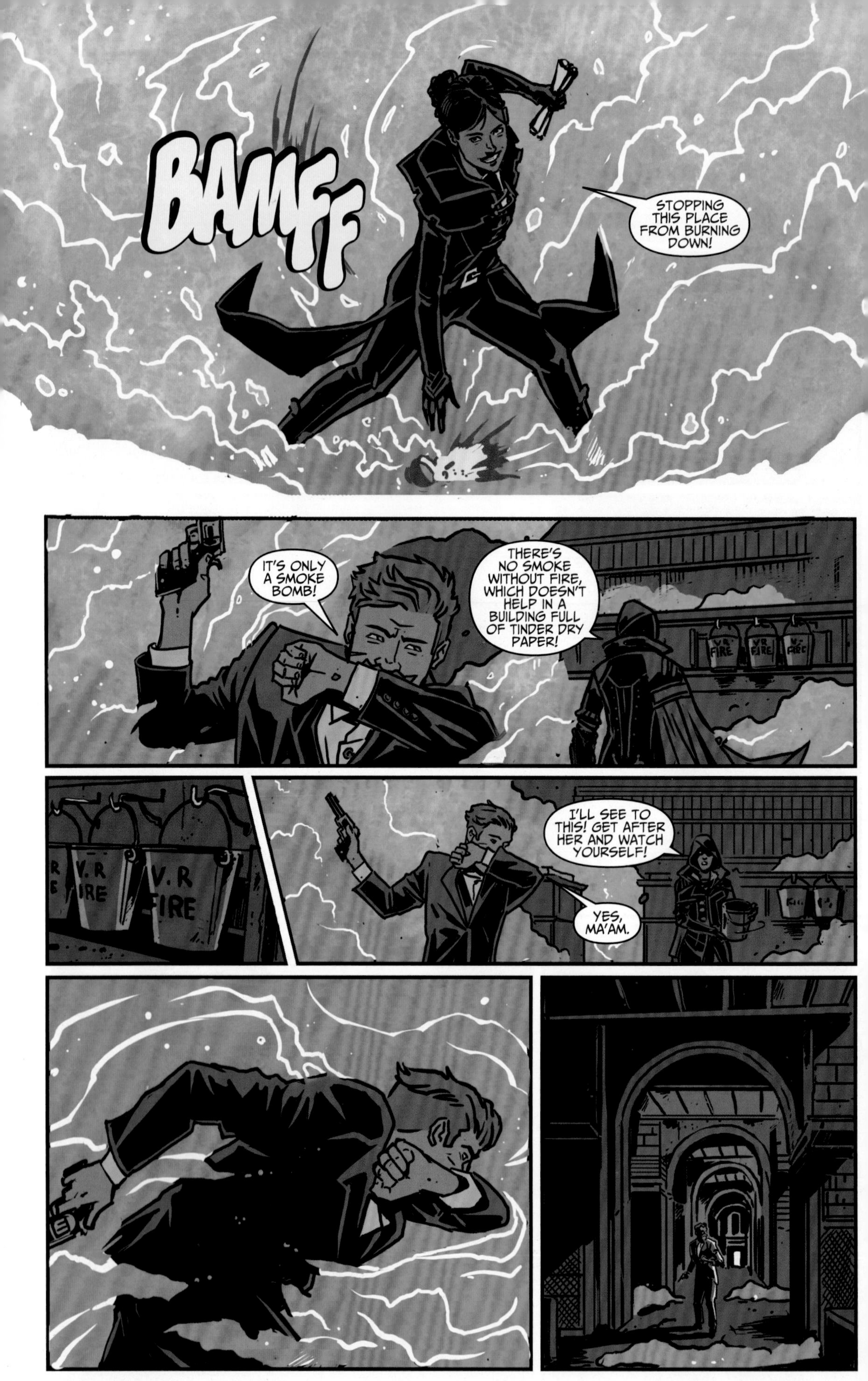
BAMFF
STOPPING THIS PLACE FROM BURNING DOWN!
IT'S ONLY A SMOKE BOMB!
THERE'S NO SMOKE WITHOUT FIRE, WHICH DOESN'T HELP IN A BUILDING FULL OF TINDER DRY PAPER!
V.R FIRE
V.R FIRE
I'LL SEE TO THIS! GET AFTER HER AND WATCH YOURSELF!
YES, MA'AM.

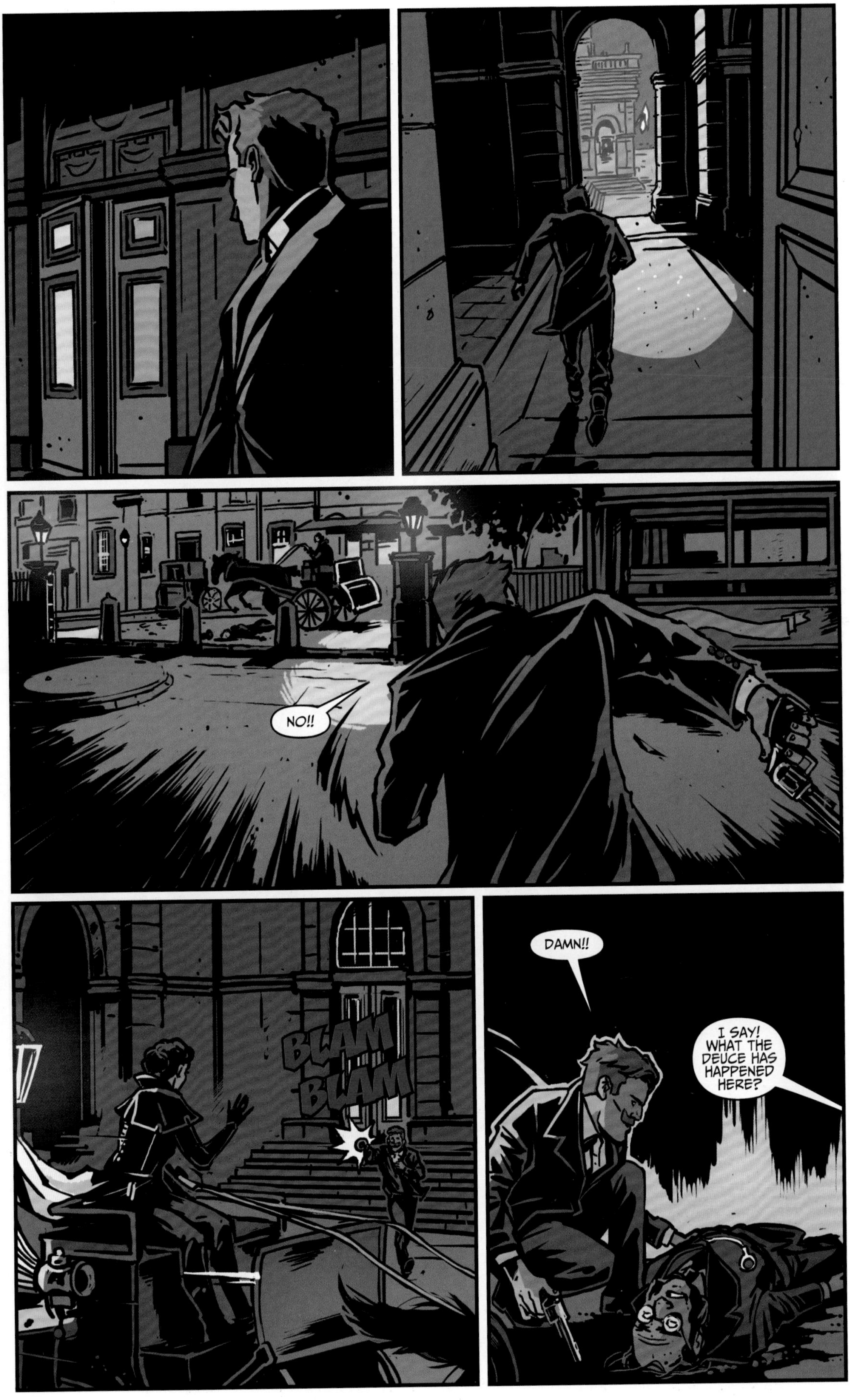
NO!!
BLAM
BLAM
DAMN!!
I SAY! WHAT THE DEUCE HAS HAPPENED HERE?

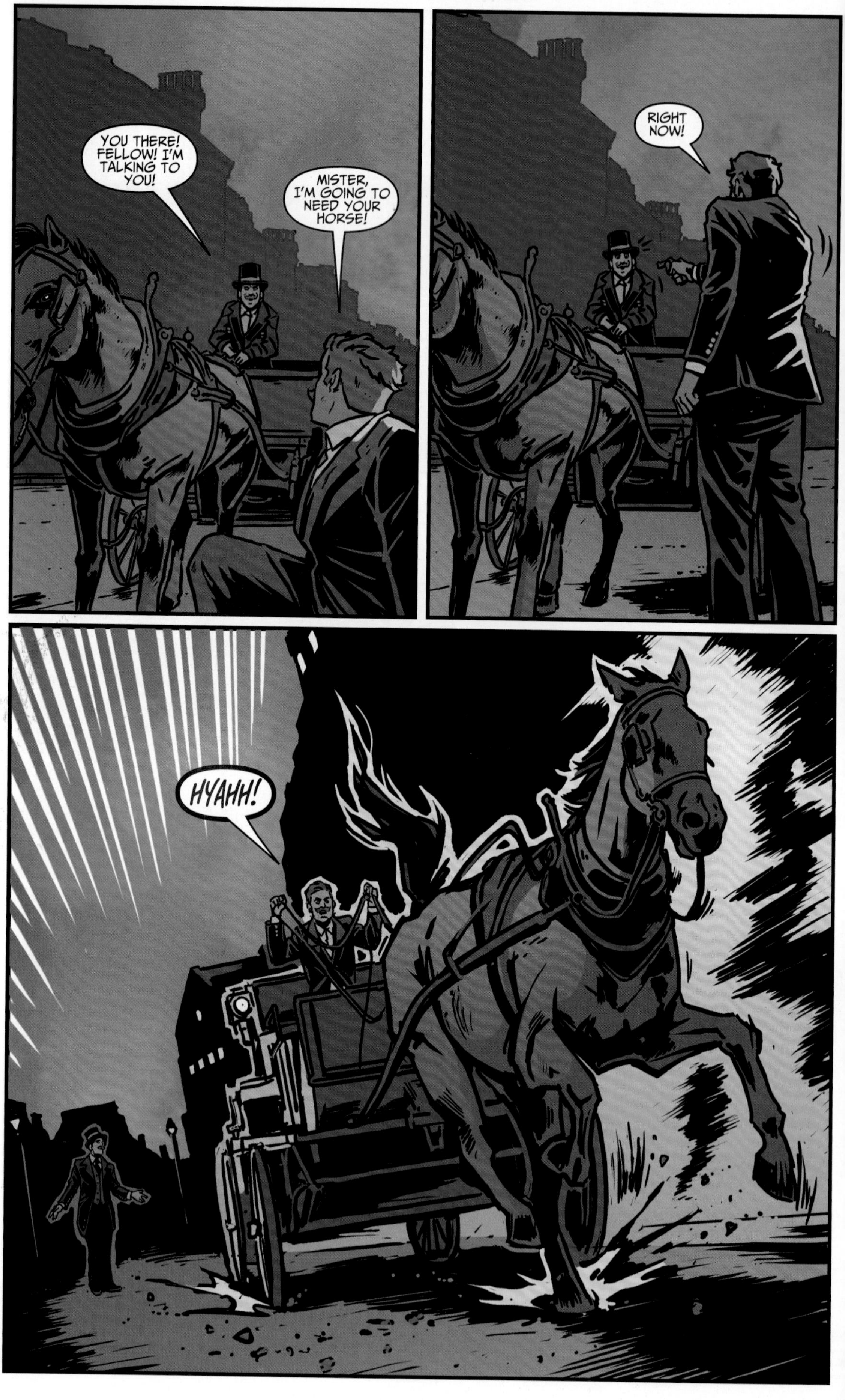
YOU THERE! FELLOW! I'M TALKING TO YOU!
MISTER, I'M GOING TO NEED YOUR HORSE!
RIGHT NOW!
HYAHH!

CHAPTER

4

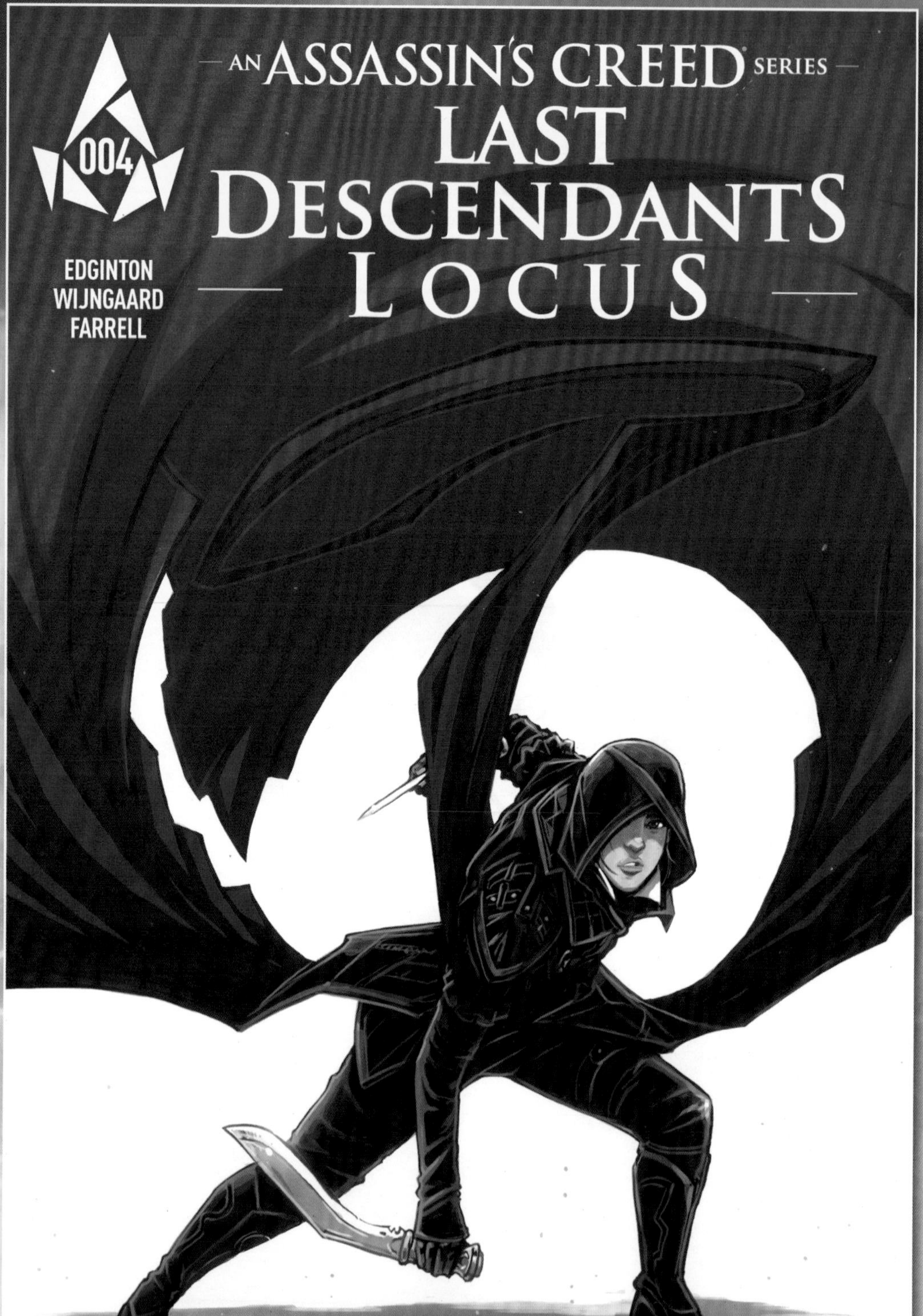
AN ASSASSIN'S CREED SERIES
LAST DESCENDANTS
LOCUS
004
EDGINTON
WIJNGAARD
FARRELL
COVER A: CASPAR WIJNGAARD

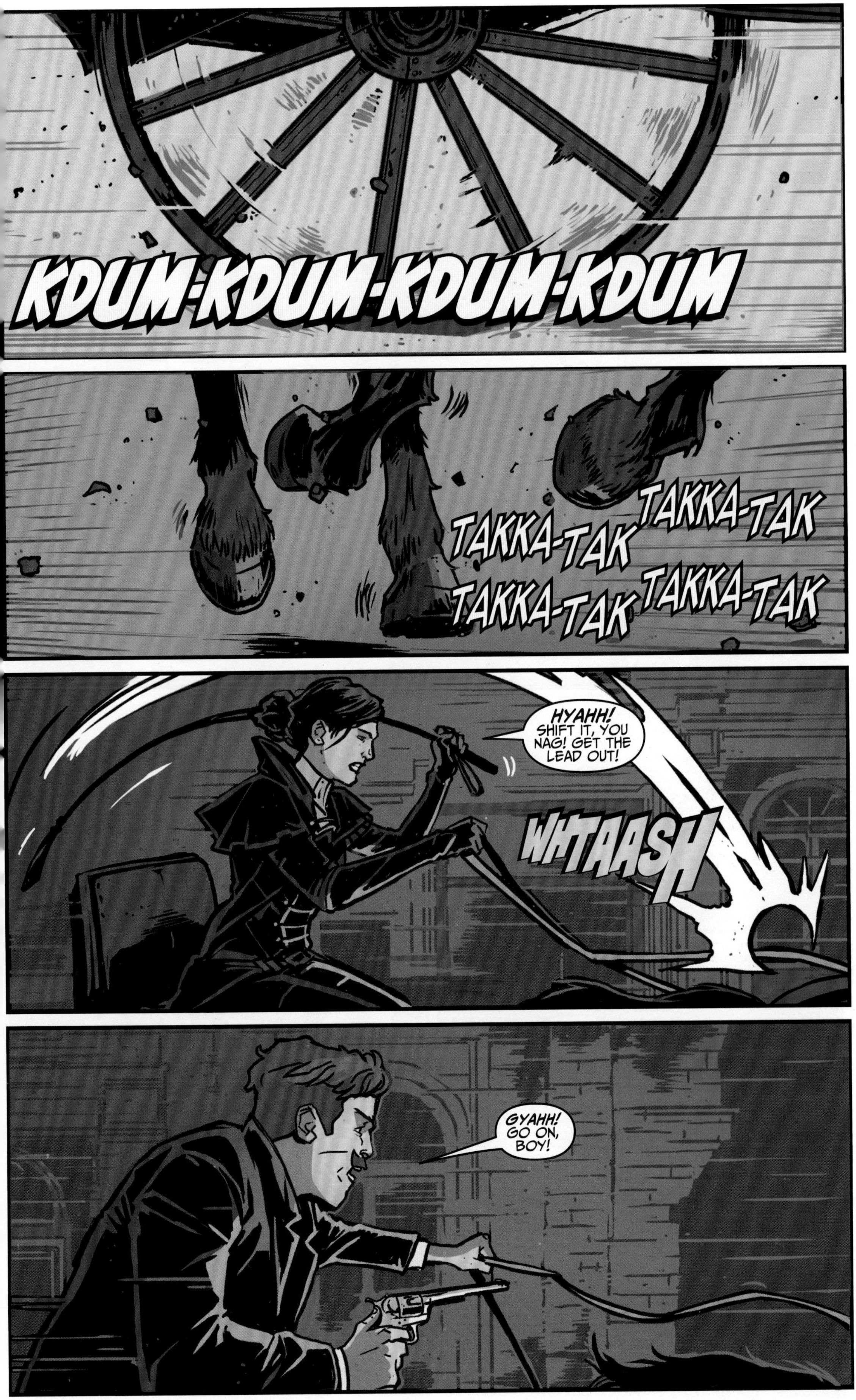
KDUM-KDUM-KDUM-KDUM
TAKKA-TAK TAKKA-TAK
TAKKA-TAK TAKKA-TAK
HYAHH! SHIFT IT, YOU NAG! GET THE LEAD OUT!
WHTAASH
GYAHH! GO ON, BOY!

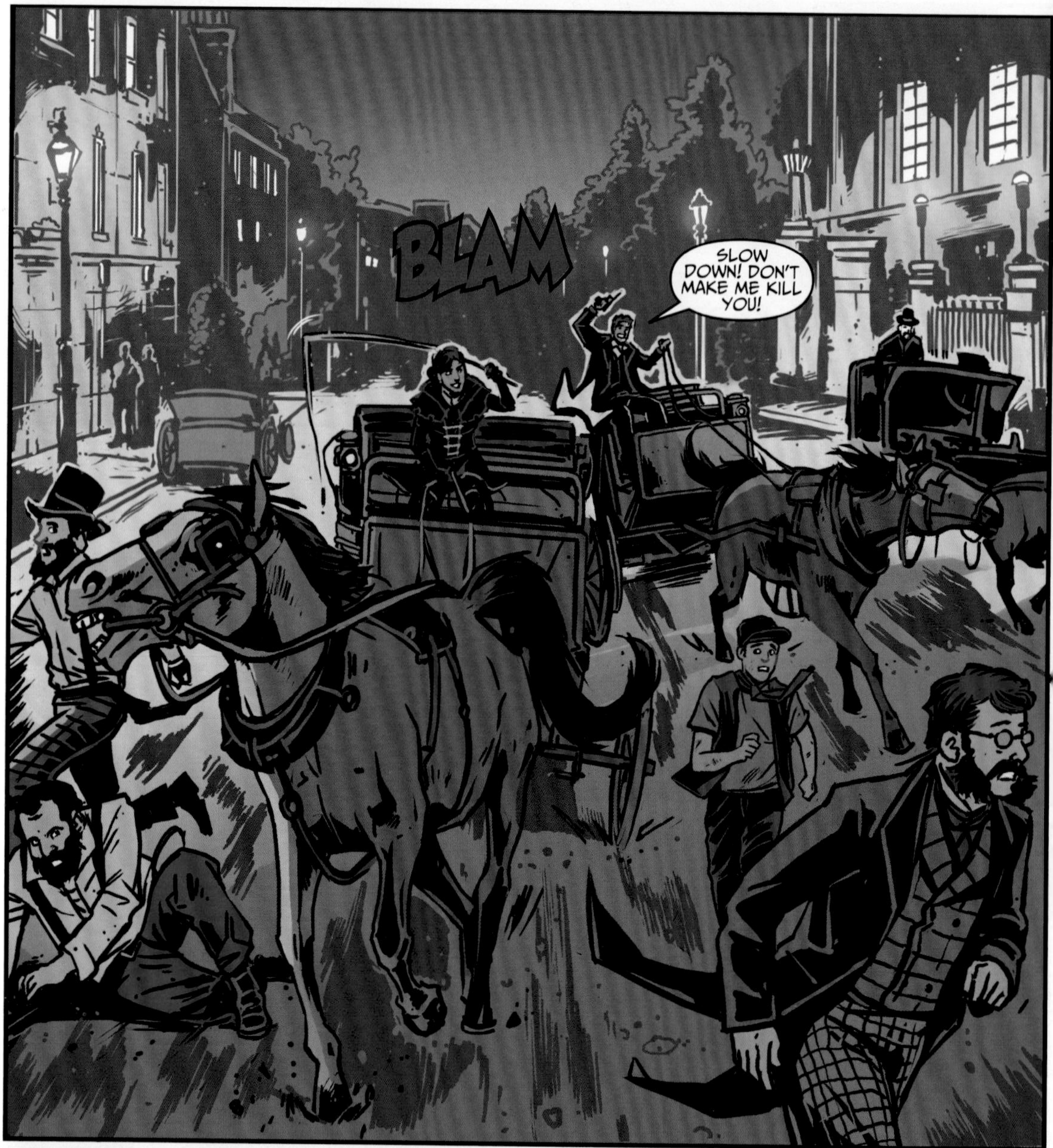
BLAM
SLOW DOWN! DON'T MAKE ME KILL YOU!

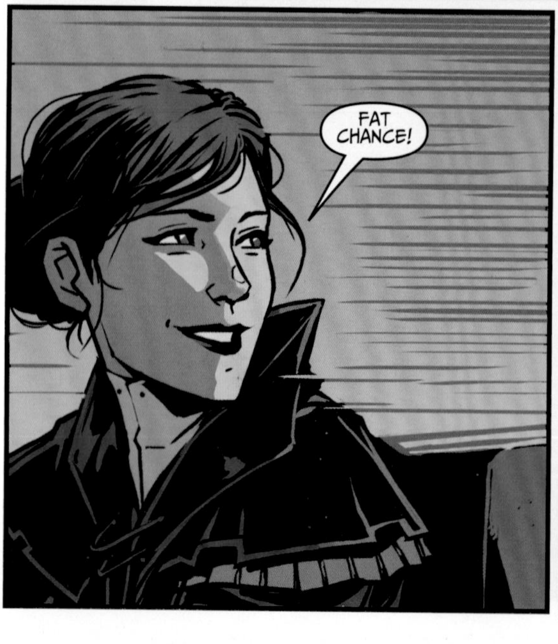
FAT CHANCE!

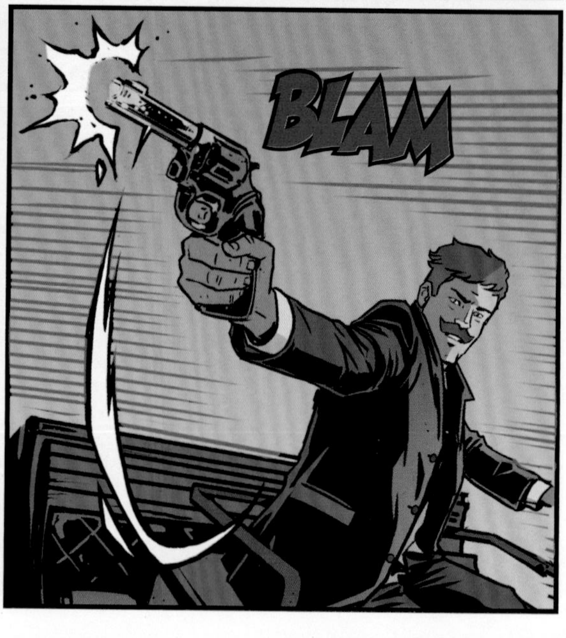
BLAM

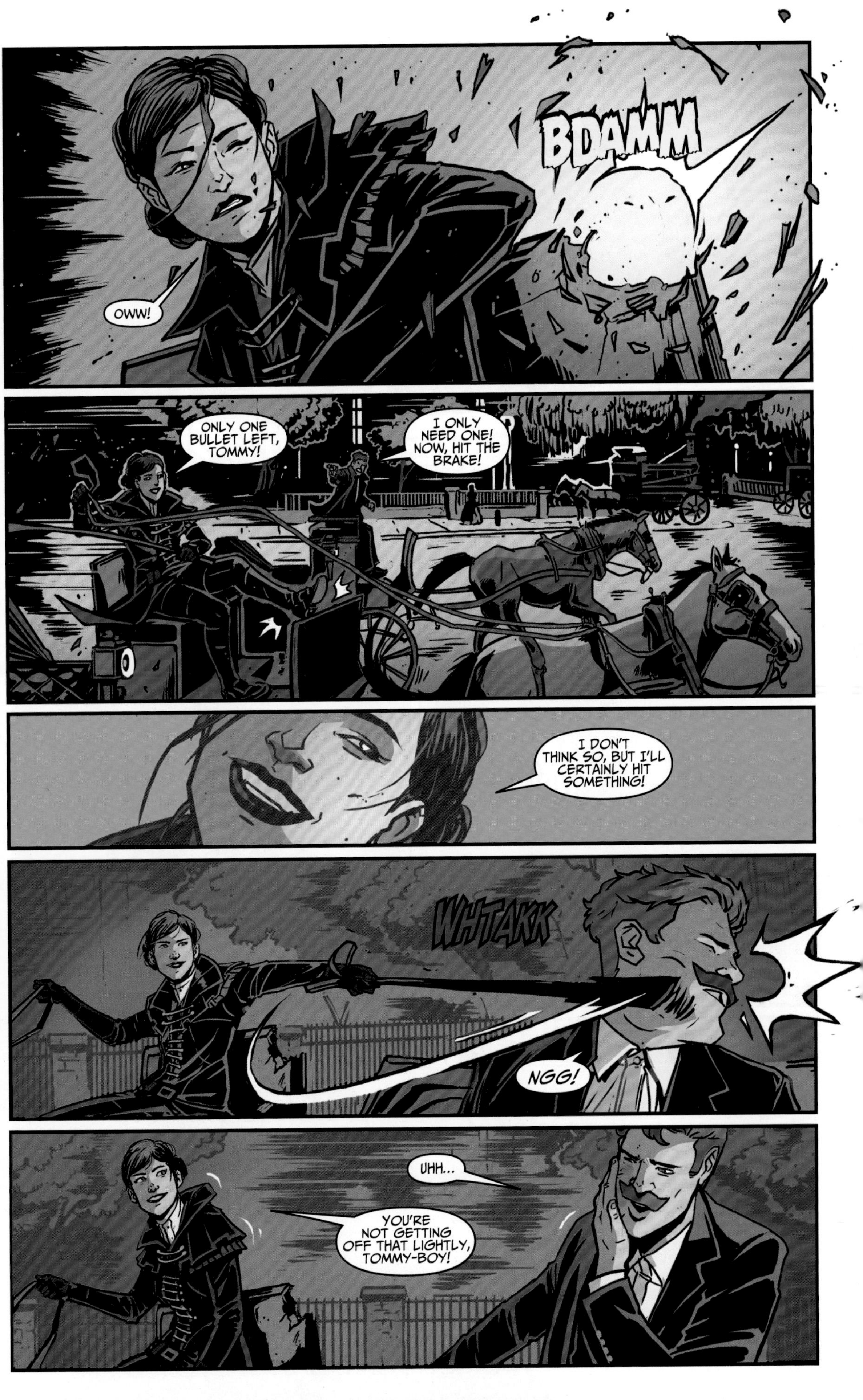
BDAMM
OWW!
ONLY ONE BULLET LEFT, TOMMY!
I ONLY NEED ONE! NOW, HIT THE BRAKE!
I DON'T THINK SO, BUT I'LL CERTAINLY HIT SOMETHING!
WHTAKK
NGG!
UHH...
YOU'RE NOT GETTING OFF THAT LIGHTLY, TOMMY-BOY!

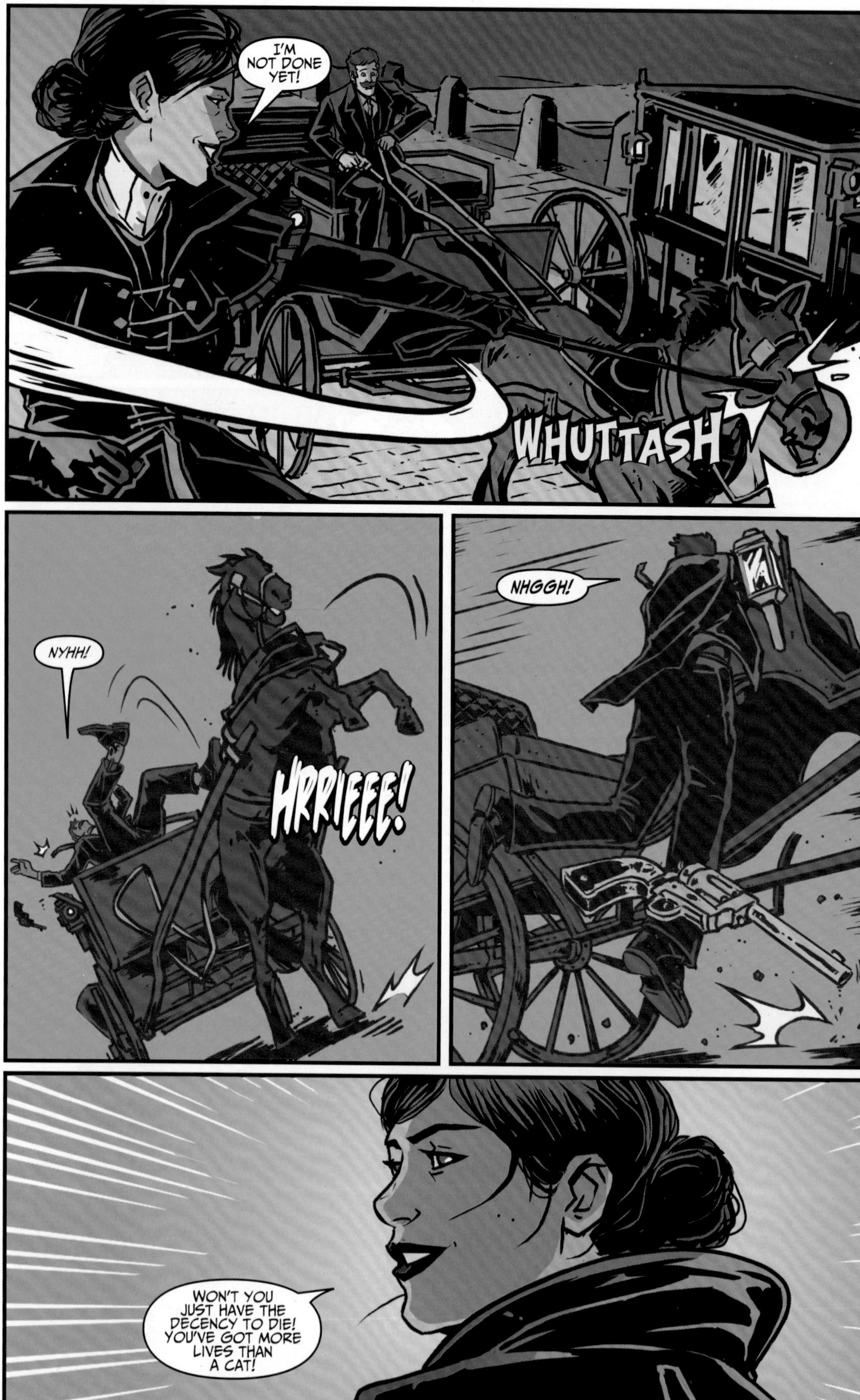
I'M NOT DONE YET!
WHUTTASH
NYHH!
HRRIEEE!
NHGGH!
WON'T YOU JUST HAVE THE DECENCY TO DIE! YOU'VE GOT MORE LIVES THAN A CAT!

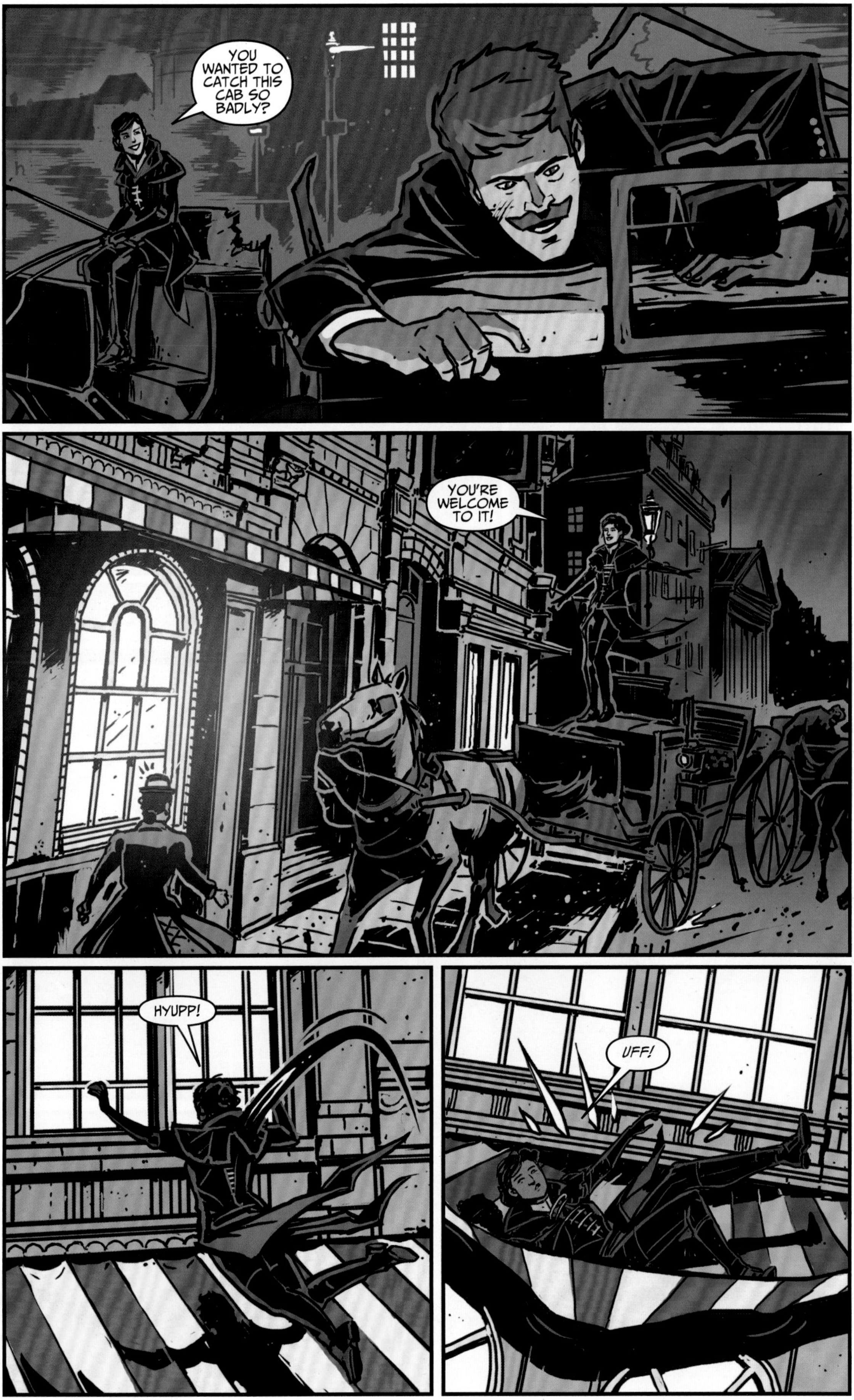
YOU WANTED TO CATCH THIS CAB SO BADLY?
YOU'RE WELCOME TO IT!
HYUPP!
UFF!

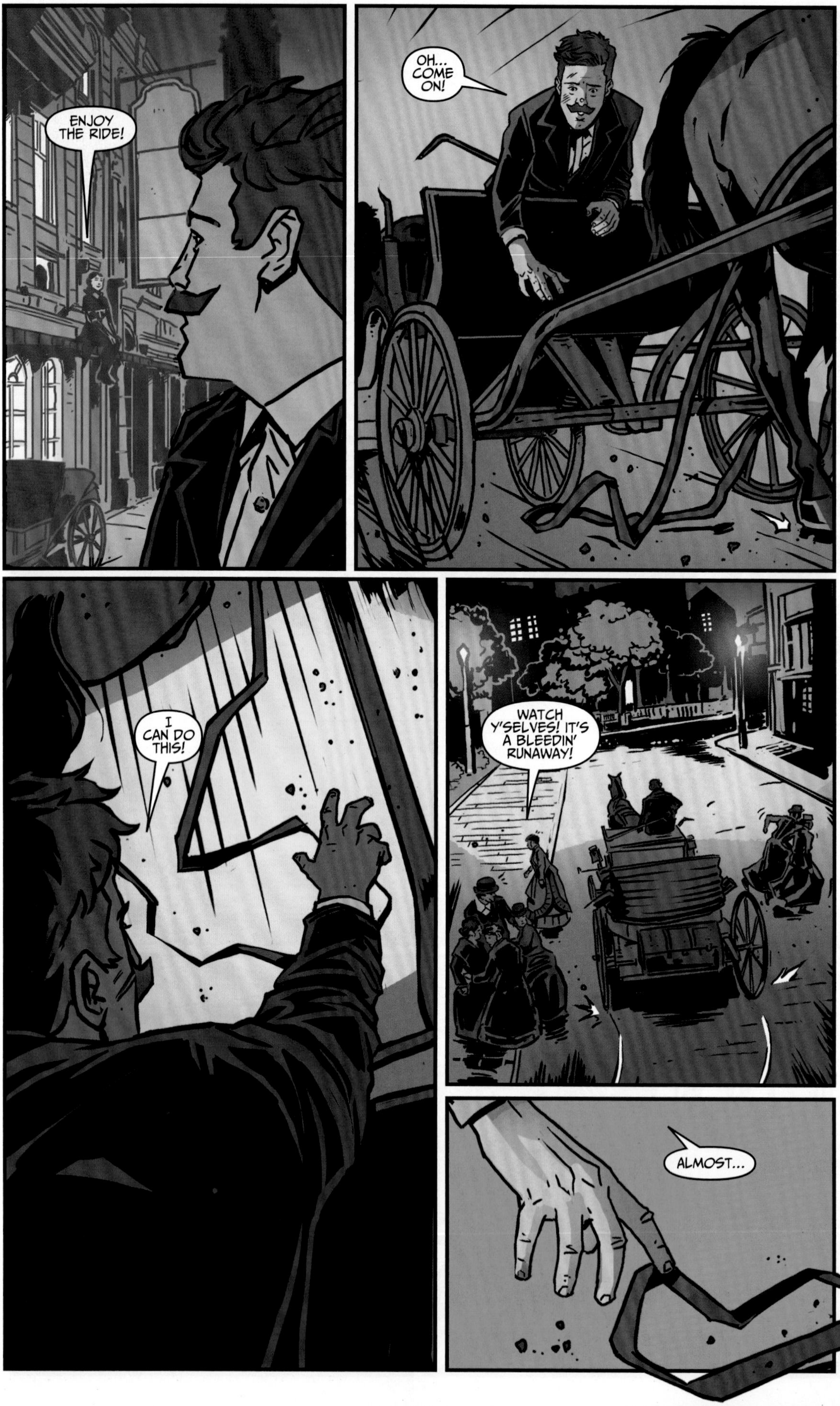
ENJOY THE RIDE!
OH... COME ON!
I CAN DO THIS!
WATCH Y'SELVES! IT'S A BLEEDIN' RUNAWAY!
ALMOST...

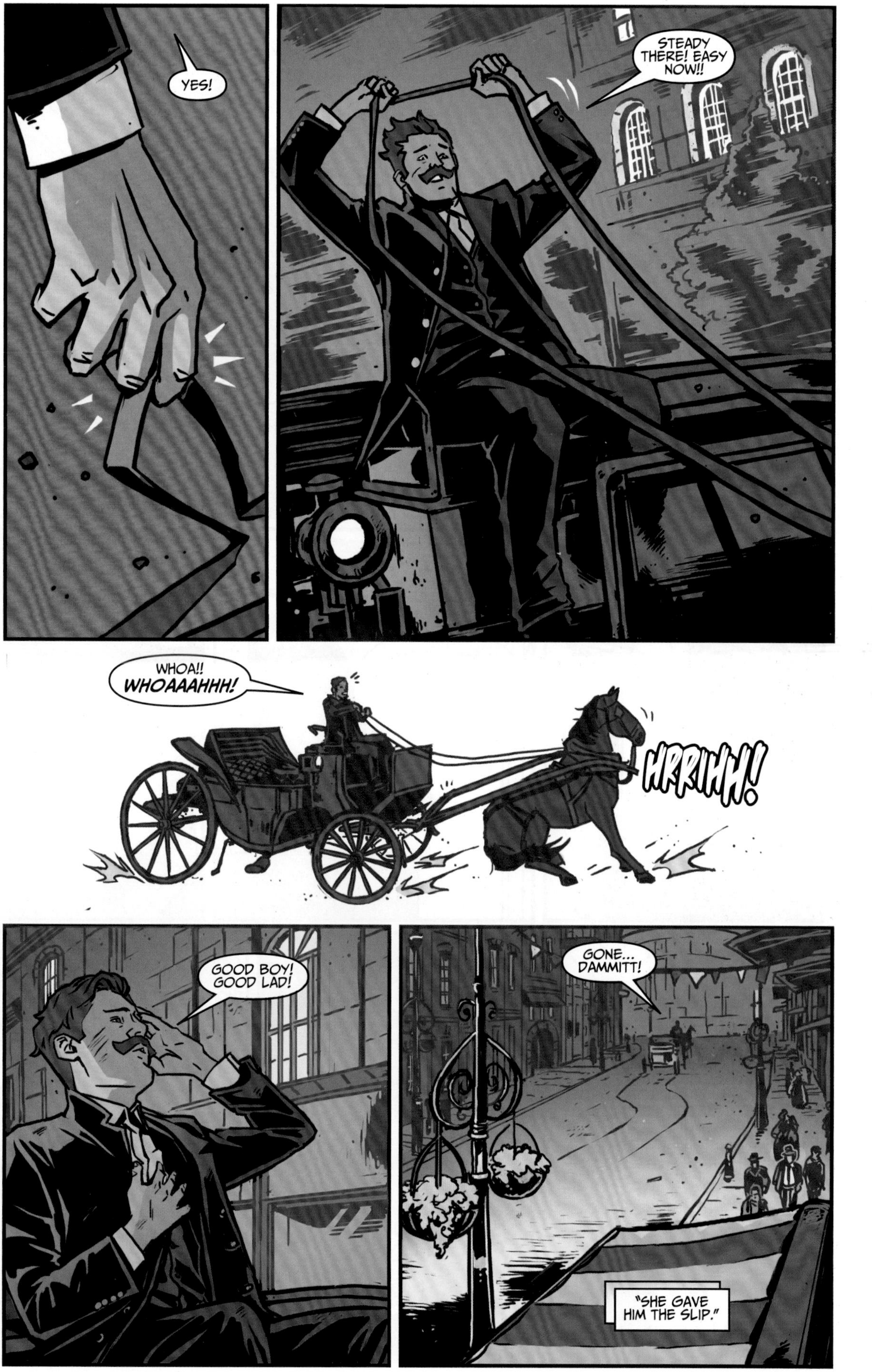
YES!
STEADY THERE! EASY NOW!!
WHOA!! WHOAAAHHH!
HRRIHH!
GOOD BOY! GOOD LAD!
GONE... DAMMITT!
"SHE GAVE HIM THE SLIP."

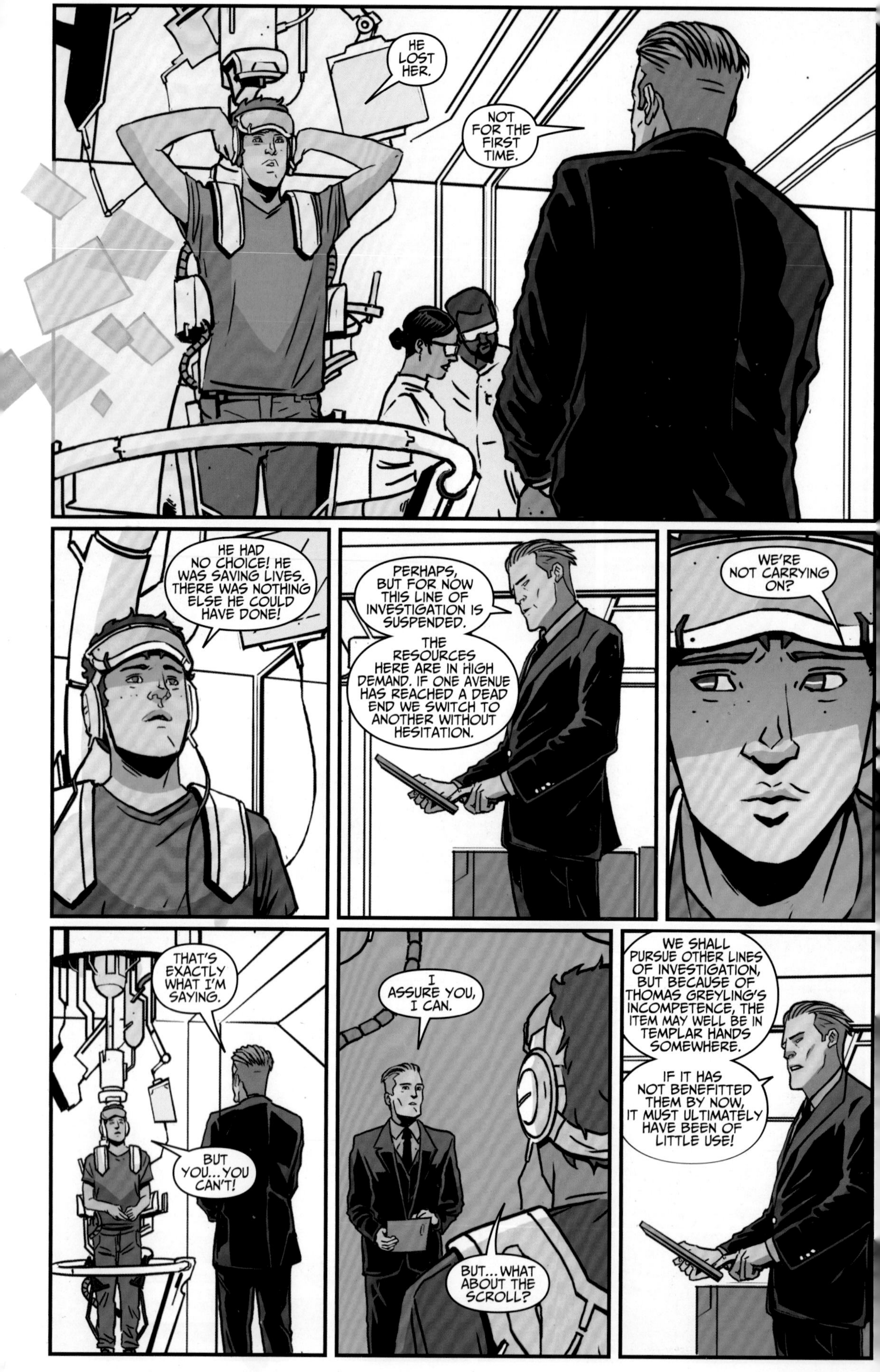
HE LOST HER.
NOT FOR THE FIRST TIME.
HE HAD NO CHOICE! HE WAS SAVING LIVES. THERE WAS NOTHING ELSE HE COULD HAVE DONE!
PERHAPS, BUT FOR NOW THIS LINE OF INVESTIGATION IS SUSPENDED.
THE RESOURCES HERE ARE IN HIGH DEMAND. IF ONE AVENUE HAS REACHED A DEAD END WE SWITCH TO ANOTHER WITHOUT HESITATION.
WE'RE NOT CARRYING ON?
THAT'S EXACTLY WHAT I'M SAYING.
BUT YOU...YOU CAN'T!
I ASSURE YOU, I CAN.
BUT...WHAT ABOUT THE SCROLL?
WE SHALL PURSUE OTHER LINES OF INVESTIGATION, BUT BECAUSE OF THOMAS GREYLING'S INCOMPETENCE, THE ITEM MAY WELL BE IN TEMPLAR HANDS SOMEWHERE.
IF IT HAS NOT BENEFITTED THEM BY NOW, IT MUST ULTIMATELY HAVE BEEN OF LITTLE USE!

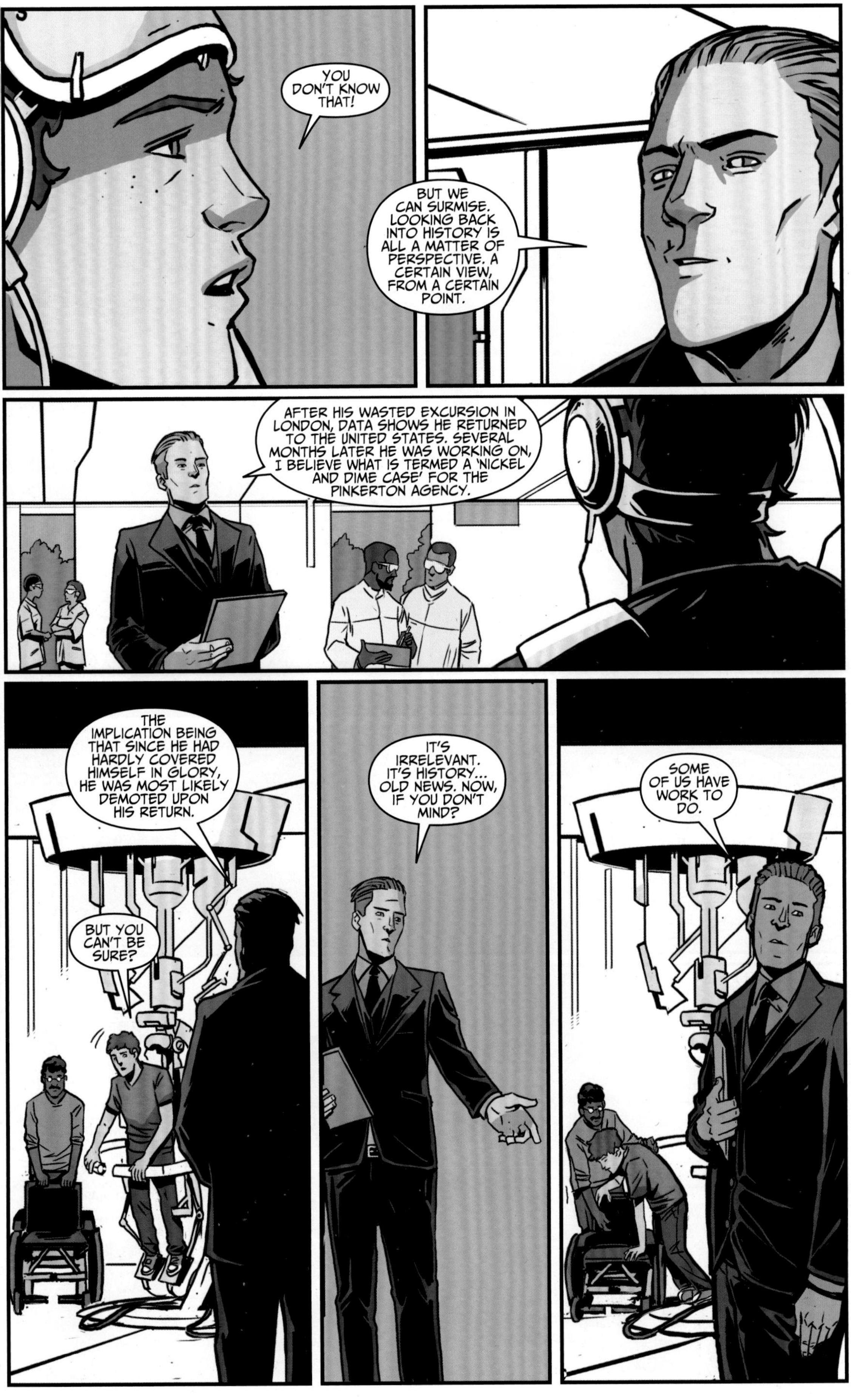
YOU DON'T KNOW THAT!
BUT WE CAN SURMISE. LOOKING BACK INTO HISTORY IS ALL A MATTER OF PERSPECTIVE. A CERTAIN VIEW, FROM A CERTAIN POINT.
AFTER HIS WASTED EXCURSION IN LONDON, DATA SHOWS HE RETURNED TO THE UNITED STATES. SEVERAL MONTHS LATER HE WAS WORKING ON, I BELIEVE WHAT IS TERMED A 'NICKEL AND DIME CASE' FOR THE PINKERTON AGENCY.
THE IMPLICATION BEING THAT SINCE HE HAD HARDLY COVERED HIMSELF IN GLORY, HE WAS MOST LIKELY DEMOTED UPON HIS RETURN.
BUT YOU CAN'T BE SURE?
IT'S IRRELEVANT. IT'S HISTORY... OLD NEWS. NOW, IF YOU DON'T MIND?
SOME OF US HAVE WORK TO DO.

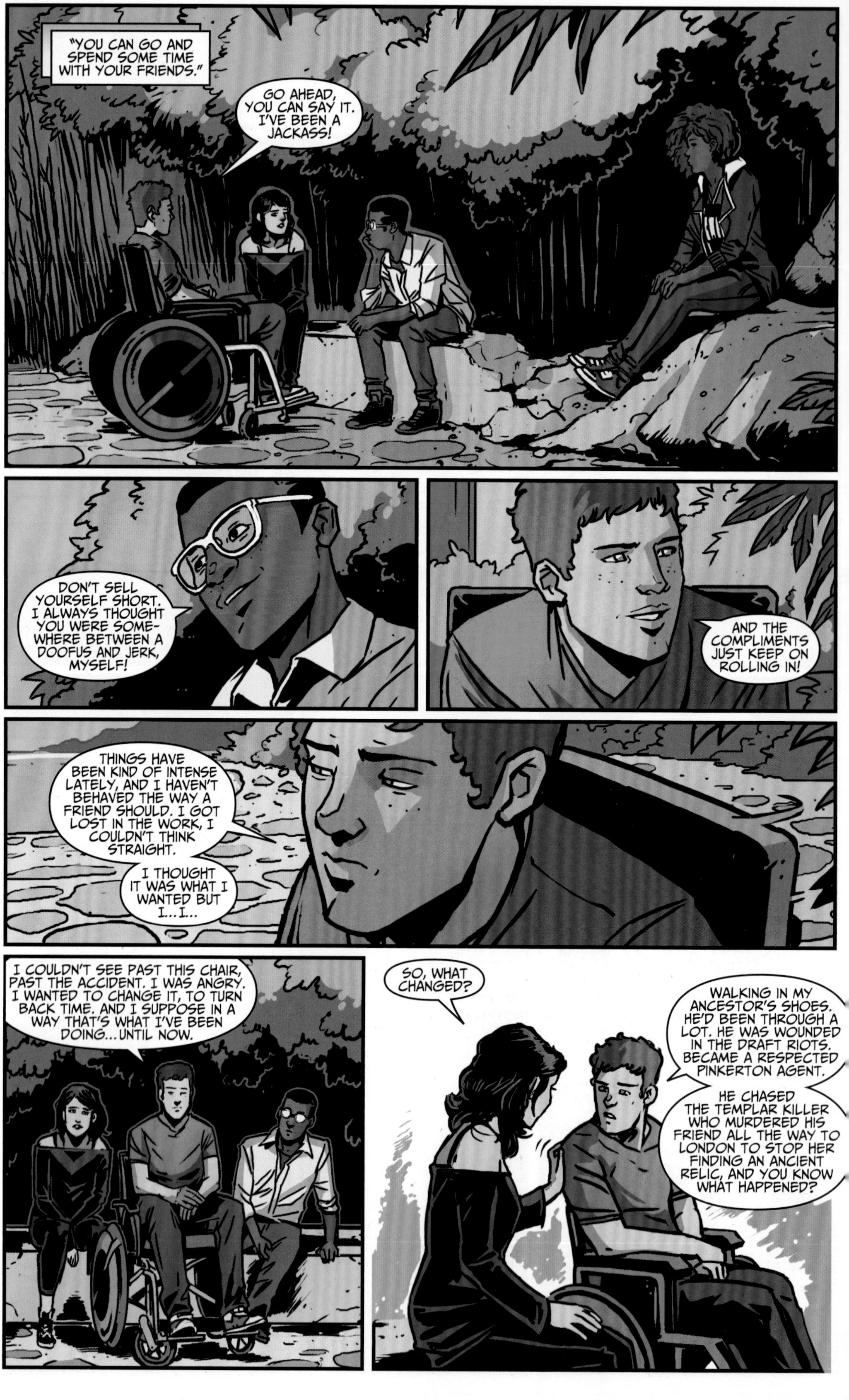
"YOU CAN GO AND SPEND SOME TIME WITH YOUR FRIENDS."
GO AHEAD, YOU CAN SAY IT. I'VE BEEN A JACKASS!
DON'T SELL YOURSELF SHORT. I ALWAYS THOUGHT YOU WERE SOME-WHERE BETWEEN A DOOFUS AND JERK, MYSELF!
AND THE COMPLIMENTS JUST KEEP ON ROLLING IN!
THINGS HAVE BEEN KIND OF INTENSE LATELY, AND I HAVEN'T BEHAVED THE WAY A FRIEND SHOULD. I GOT LOST IN THE WORK, I COULDN'T THINK STRAIGHT.
I THOUGHT IT WAS WHAT I WANTED BUT I...I...
I COULDN'T SEE PAST THIS CHAIR, PAST THE ACCIDENT. I WAS ANGRY. I WANTED TO CHANGE IT, TO TURN BACK TIME. AND I SUPPOSE IN A WAY THAT'S WHAT I'VE BEEN DOING...UNTIL NOW.
SO, WHAT CHANGED?
WALKING IN MY ANCESTOR'S SHOES. HE'D BEEN THROUGH A LOT. HE WAS WOUNDED IN THE DRAFT RIOTS. BECAME A RESPECTED PINKERTON AGENT.
HE CHASED THE TEMPLAR KILLER WHO MURDERED HIS FRIEND ALL THE WAY TO LONDON TO STOP HER FINDING AN ANCIENT RELIC, AND YOU KNOW WHAT HAPPENED?

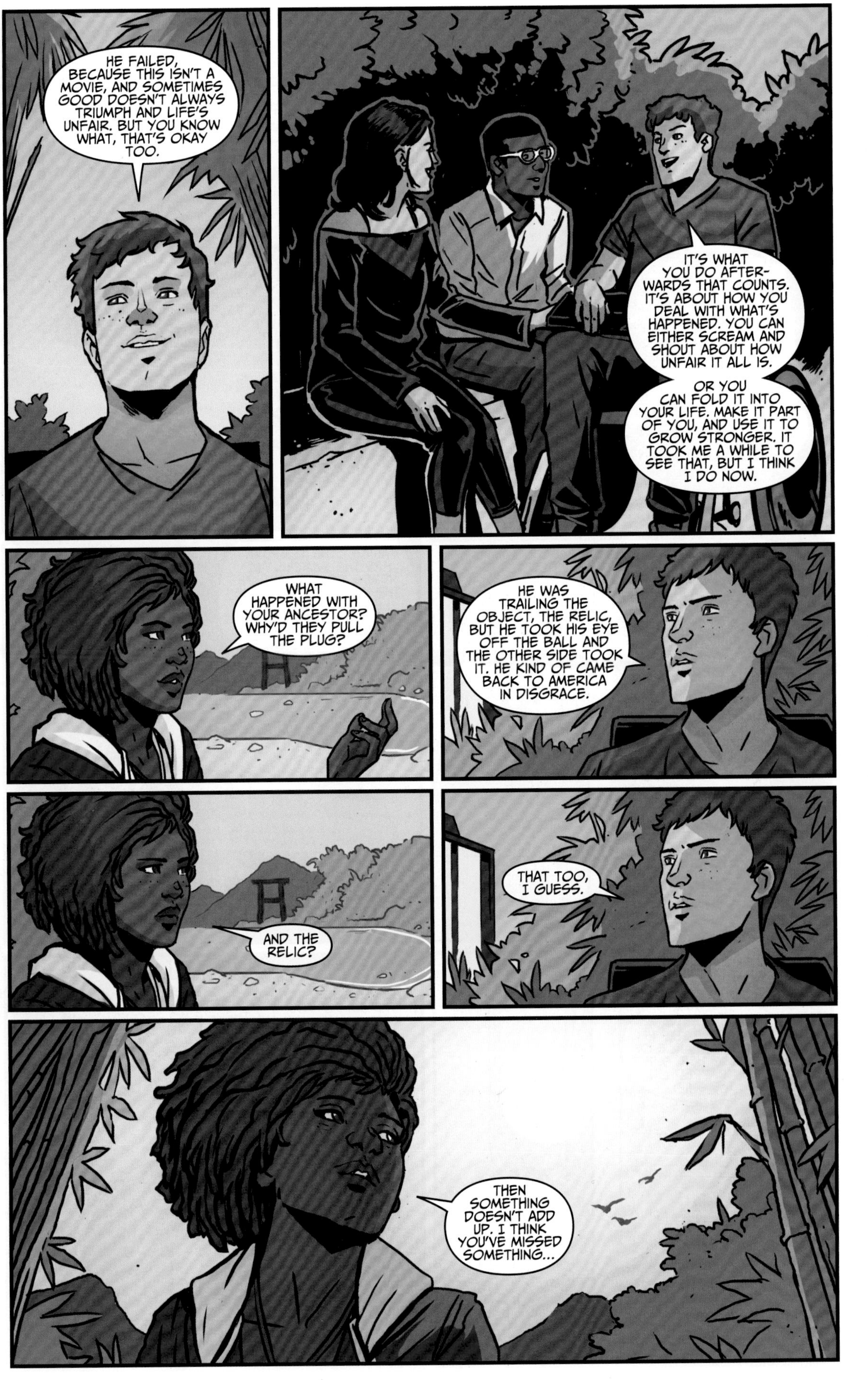
HE FAILED, BECAUSE THIS ISN'T A MOVIE, AND SOMETIMES GOOD DOESN'T ALWAYS TRIUMPH AND LIFE'S UNFAIR. BUT YOU KNOW WHAT, THAT'S OKAY TOO.
IT'S WHAT YOU DO AFTER-WARDS THAT COUNTS. IT'S ABOUT HOW YOU DEAL WITH WHAT'S HAPPENED. YOU CAN EITHER SCREAM AND SHOUT ABOUT HOW UNFAIR IT ALL IS.
OR YOU CAN FOLD IT INTO YOUR LIFE. MAKE IT PART OF YOU, AND USE IT TO GROW STRONGER. IT TOOK ME A WHILE TO SEE THAT, BUT I THINK I DO NOW.
WHAT HAPPENED WITH YOUR ANCESTOR? WHY'D THEY PULL THE PLUG?
HE WAS TRAILING THE OBJECT, THE RELIC, BUT HE TOOK HIS EYE OFF THE BALL AND THE OTHER SIDE TOOK IT. HE KIND OF CAME BACK TO AMERICA IN DISGRACE.
AND THE RELIC?
THAT TOO, I GUESS.
THEN SOMETHING DOESN'T ADD UP. I THINK YOU'VE MISSED SOMETHING...

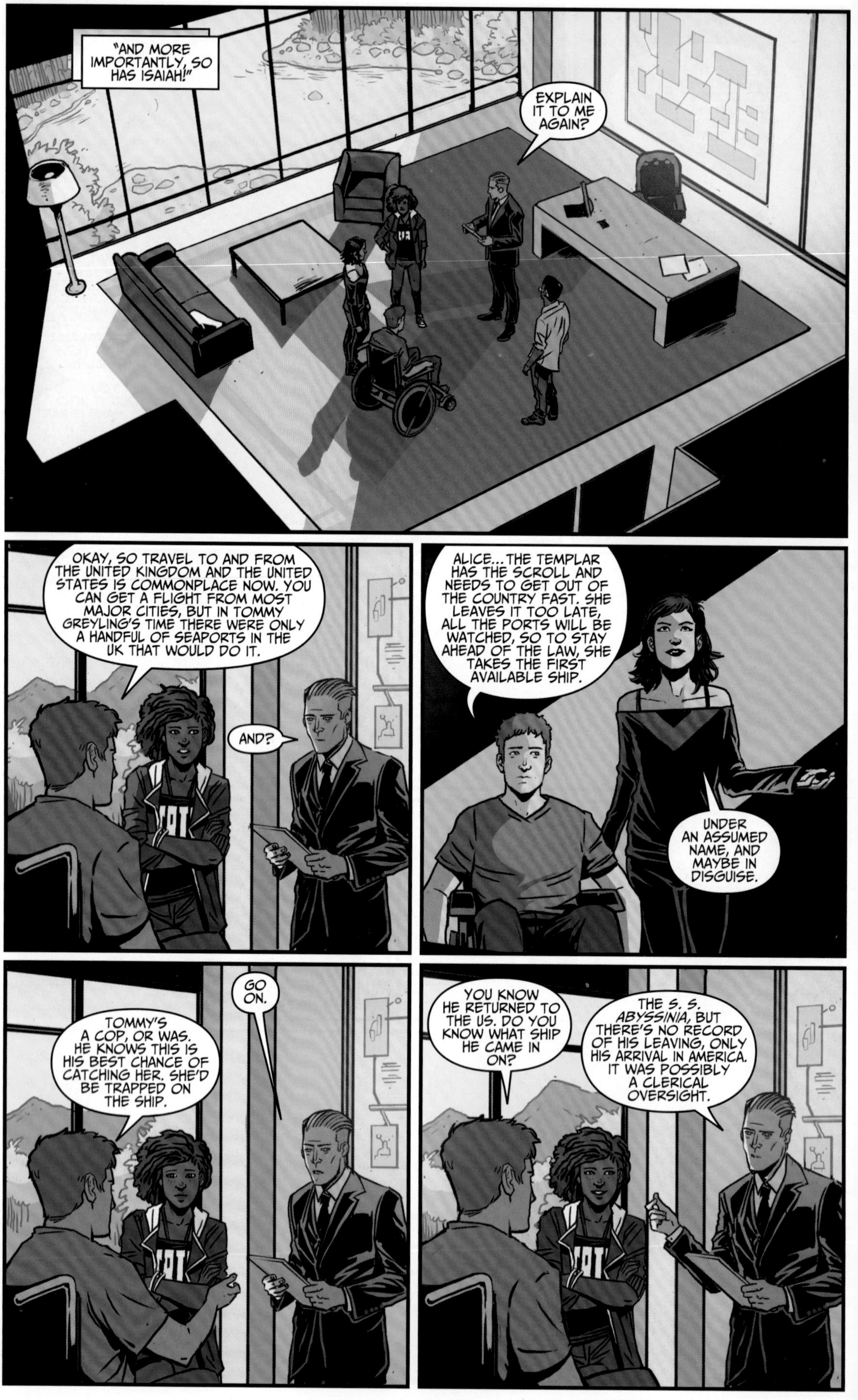
"AND MORE IMPORTANTLY, SO HAS ISAIAH!"
EXPLAIN IT TO ME AGAIN?
OKAY, SO TRAVEL TO AND FROM THE UNITED KINGDOM AND THE UNITED STATES IS COMMONPLACE NOW. YOU CAN GET A FLIGHT FROM MOST MAJOR CITIES, BUT IN TOMMY GREYLING'S TIME THERE WERE ONLY A HANDFUL OF SEAPORTS IN THE UK THAT WOULD DO IT.
AND?
ALICE...THE TEMPLAR HAS THE SCROLL AND NEEDS TO GET OUT OF THE COUNTRY FAST. SHE LEAVES IT TOO LATE, ALL THE PORTS WILL BE WATCHED, SO TO STAY AHEAD OF THE LAW, SHE TAKES THE FIRST AVAILABLE SHIP.
UNDER AN ASSUMED NAME, AND MAYBE IN DISGUISE.
TOMMY'S A COP, OR WAS. HE KNOWS THIS IS HIS BEST CHANCE OF CATCHING HER. SHE'D BE TRAPPED ON THE SHIP.
GO ON.
YOU KNOW HE RETURNED TO THE US. DO YOU KNOW WHAT SHIP HE CAME IN ON?
THE S. S. *ABYSSINIA*, BUT THERE'S NO RECORD OF HIS LEAVING, ONLY HIS ARRIVAL IN AMERICA. IT WAS POSSIBLY A CLERICAL OVERSIGHT.

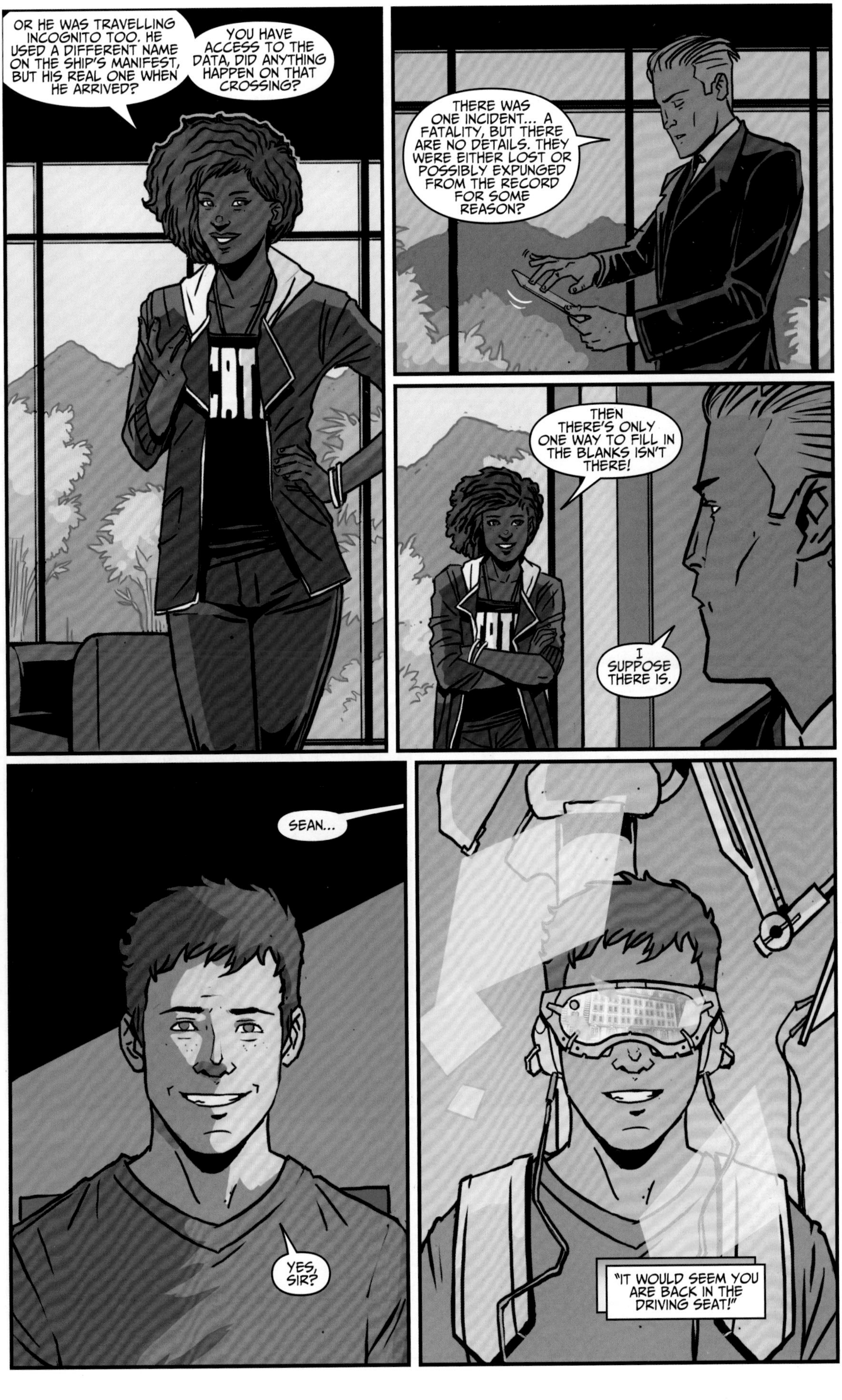
OR HE WAS TRAVELLING INCOGNITO TOO. HE USED A DIFFERENT NAME ON THE SHIP'S MANIFEST, BUT HIS REAL ONE WHEN HE ARRIVED?
YOU HAVE ACCESS TO THE DATA, DID ANYTHING HAPPEN ON THAT CROSSING?
THERE WAS ONE INCIDENT... A FATALITY, BUT THERE ARE NO DETAILS. THEY WERE EITHER LOST OR POSSIBLY EXPUNGED FROM THE RECORD FOR SOME REASON?
THEN THERE'S ONLY ONE WAY TO FILL IN THE BLANKS ISN'T THERE!
I SUPPOSE THERE IS.
SEAN...
YES, SIR?
"IT WOULD SEEM YOU ARE BACK IN THE DRIVING SEAT!"

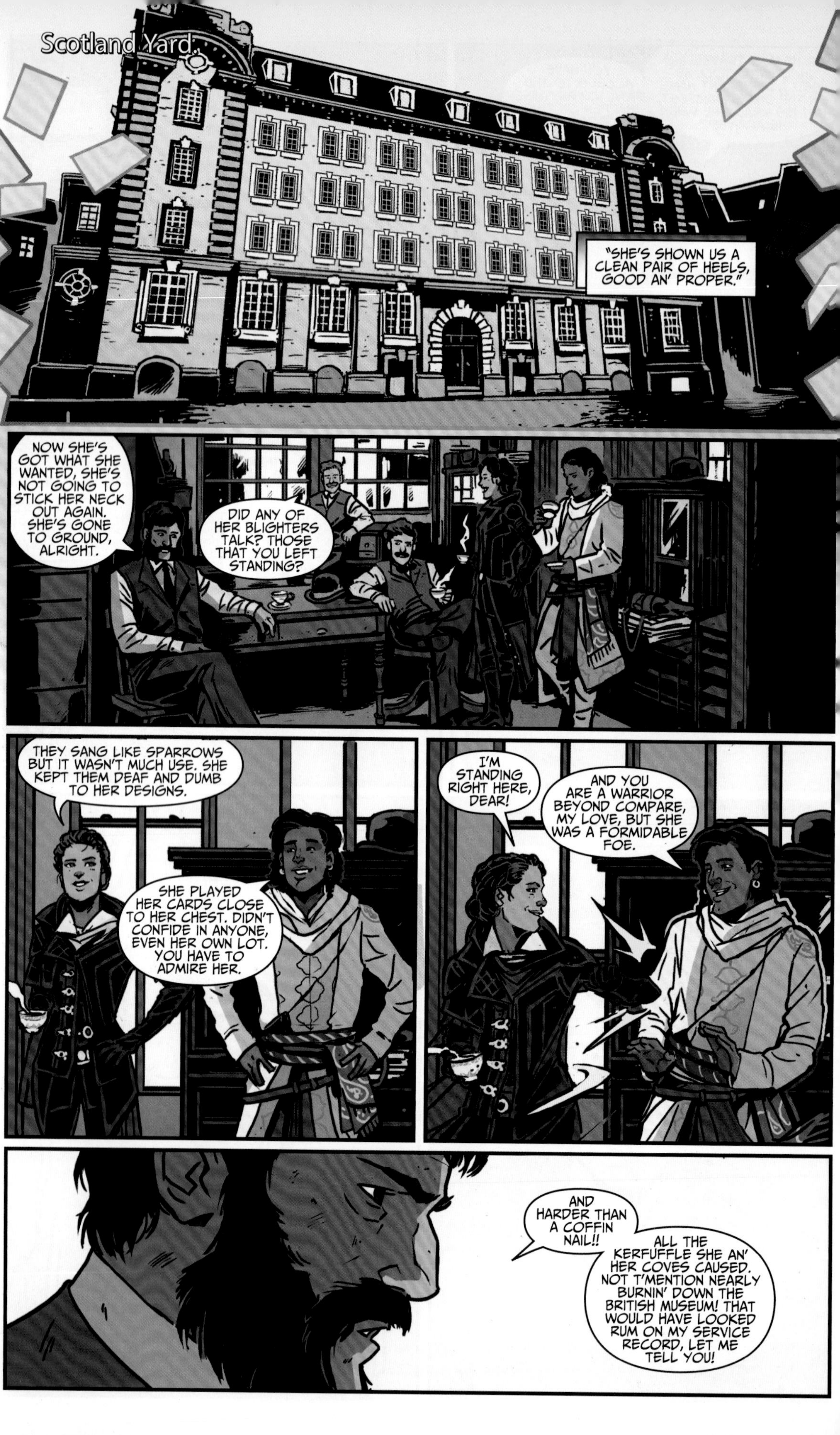
Scotland Yard.
"SHE'S SHOWN US A CLEAN PAIR OF HEELS, GOOD AN' PROPER."
NOW SHE'S GOT WHAT SHE WANTED, SHE'S NOT GOING TO STICK HER NECK OUT AGAIN. SHE'S GONE TO GROUND, ALRIGHT.
DID ANY OF HER BLIGHTERS TALK? THOSE THAT YOU LEFT STANDING?
THEY SANG LIKE SPARROWS BUT IT WASN'T MUCH USE. SHE KEPT THEM DEAF AND DUMB TO HER DESIGNS.
SHE PLAYED HER CARDS CLOSE TO HER CHEST. DIDN'T CONFIDE IN ANYONE, EVEN HER OWN LOT. YOU HAVE TO ADMIRE HER.
I'M STANDING RIGHT HERE, DEAR!
AND YOU ARE A WARRIOR BEYOND COMPARE, MY LOVE, BUT SHE WAS A FORMIDABLE FOE.
AND HARDER THAN A COFFIN NAIL!!
ALL THE KERFUFFLE SHE AN' HER COVES CAUSED. NOT T'MENTION NEARLY BURNIN' DOWN THE BRITISH MUSEUM! THAT WOULD HAVE LOOKED RUM ON MY SERVICE RECORD, LET ME TELL YOU!

SO HOW DID YOU EXPLAIN IT AWAY?

I TOOK A LEAF OUT OF YOUR BOOK, MR TWAIN, AND INDULGED IN A MODICUM OF FICTION!

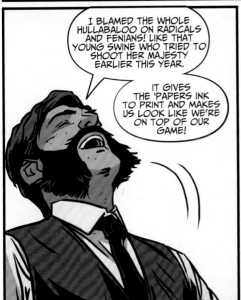

I BLAMED THE WHOLE HULLABALOO ON RADICALS AND FENIANS! LIKE THAT YOUNG SWINE WHO TRIED TO SHOOT HER MAJESTY EARLIER THIS YEAR.

IT GIVES THE 'PAPERS INK TO PRINT AND MAKES US LOOK LIKE WE'RE ON TOP OF OUR GAME!

WHAT ABOUT YOU, MR GREYLING? WHAT'RE YOUR PLANS?

THE PINKERTONS AREN'T PAYING ME BY THE HOUR, SO I'M HEADING HOME.

I'VE GOT PASSAGE BOOKED ON THE NEXT SHIP BACK TO THE UNITED STATES. IT'S THE S. S. ABYSSINIA, THE SAME SHIP WE ARRIVED ON.

WAIT A MINUTE...

WHAT IS IT?

AM I RIGHT IN THINKING THAT, BESIDES THE ABYSSINIA, THERE'S NO OTHER SHIP MAKING THE CROSSING FOR THE NEXT WEEK OR TWO?

SOUNDS ABOUT RIGHT. THERE'S FEWER THIS TIME OF YEAR, WHAT WITH THE WEATHER TURNING.

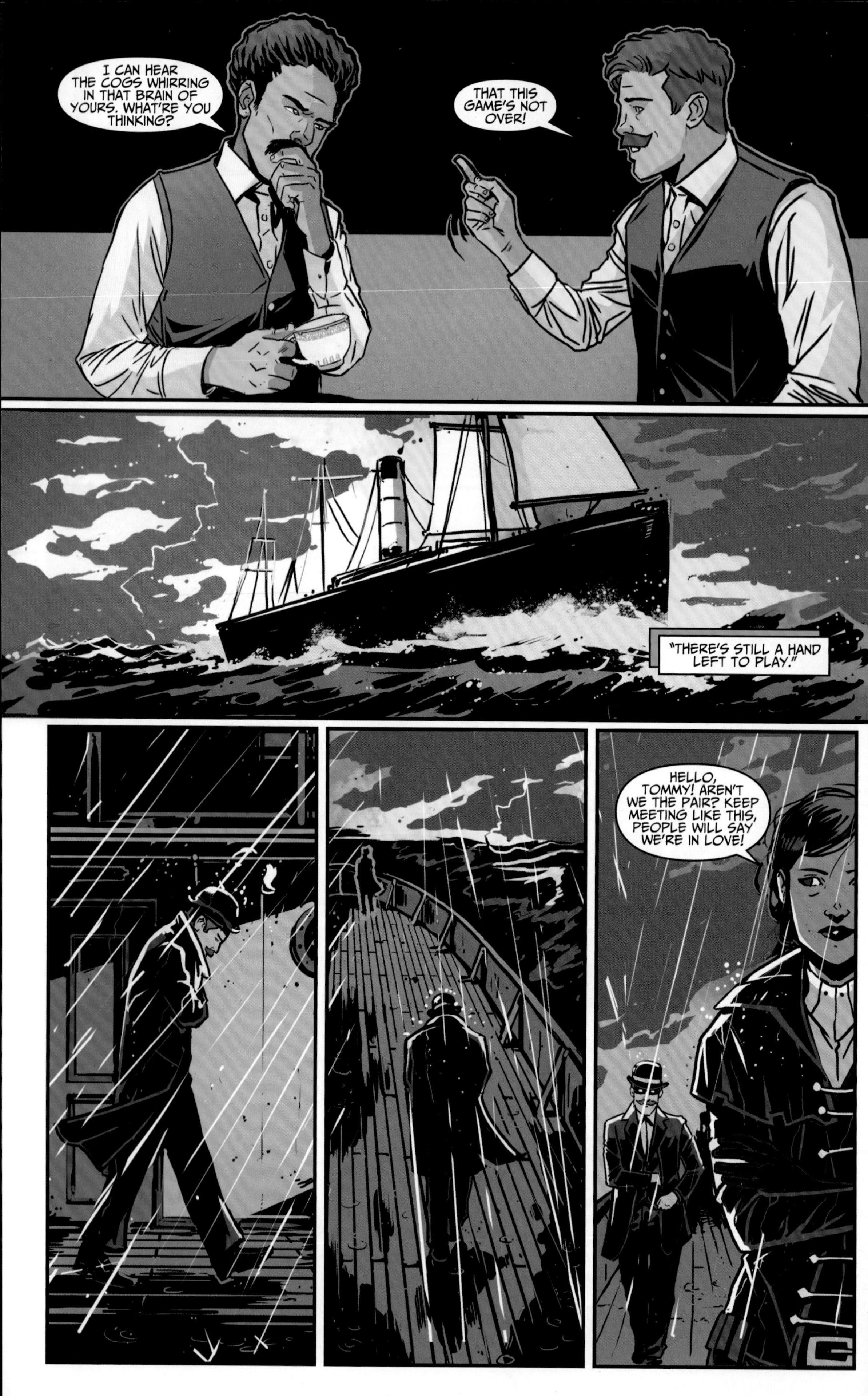
I CAN HEAR THE COGS WHIRRING IN THAT BRAIN OF YOURS. WHAT'RE YOU THINKING?
THAT THIS GAME'S NOT OVER!
"THERE'S STILL A HAND LEFT TO PLAY."
HELLO, TOMMY! AREN'T WE THE PAIR? KEEP MEETING LIKE THIS, PEOPLE WILL SAY WE'RE IN LOVE!

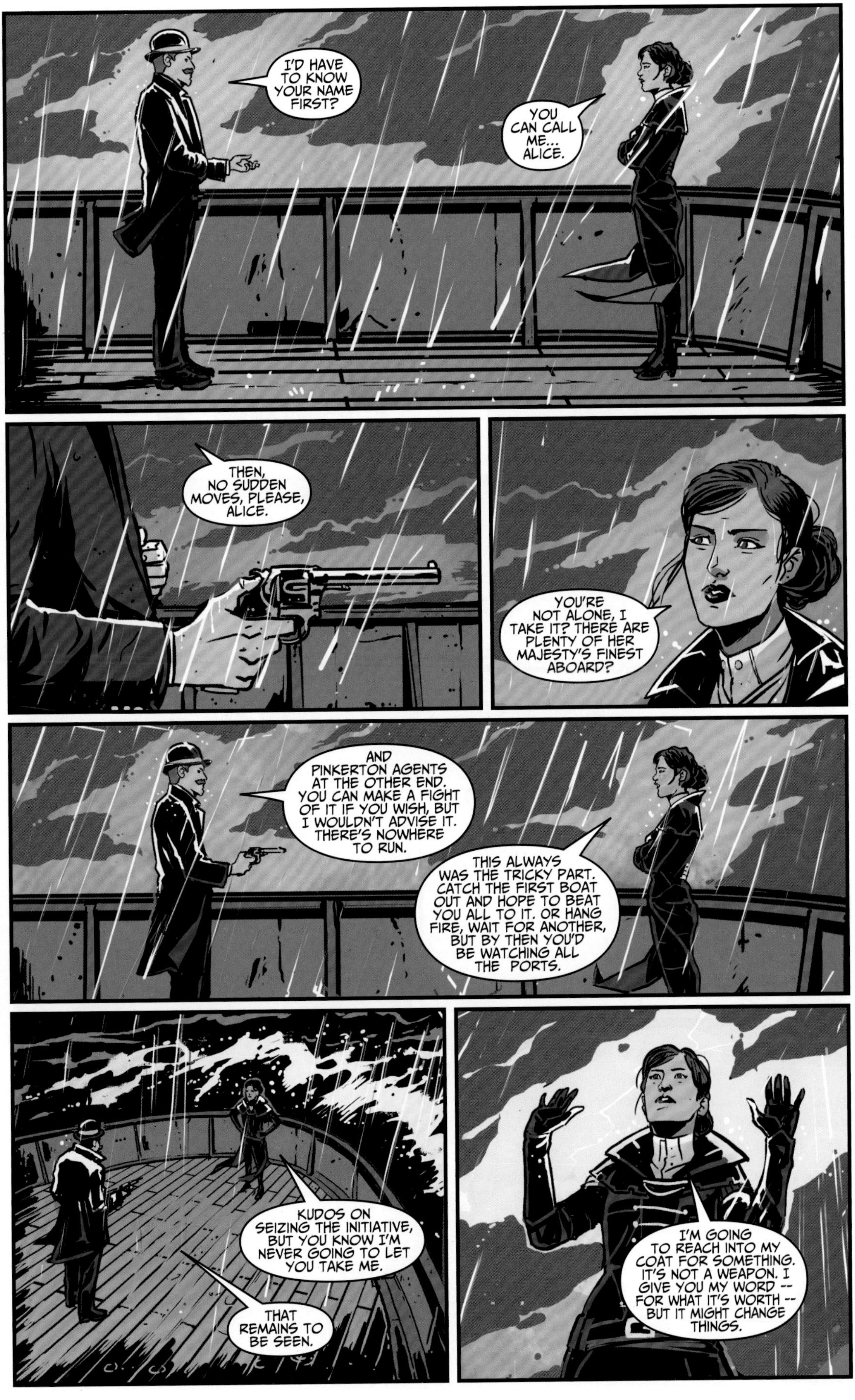
I'D HAVE TO KNOW YOUR NAME FIRST?
YOU CAN CALL ME... ALICE.
THEN, NO SUDDEN MOVES, PLEASE, ALICE.
YOU'RE NOT ALONE, I TAKE IT? THERE ARE PLENTY OF HER MAJESTY'S FINEST ABOARD?
AND PINKERTON AGENTS AT THE OTHER END. YOU CAN MAKE A FIGHT OF IT IF YOU WISH, BUT I WOULDN'T ADVISE IT. THERE'S NOWHERE TO RUN.
THIS ALWAYS WAS THE TRICKY PART. CATCH THE FIRST BOAT OUT AND HOPE TO BEAT YOU ALL TO IT. OR HANG FIRE, WAIT FOR ANOTHER, BUT BY THEN YOU'D BE WATCHING ALL THE PORTS.
KUDOS ON SEIZING THE INITIATIVE, BUT YOU KNOW I'M NEVER GOING TO LET YOU TAKE ME.
THAT REMAINS TO BE SEEN.
I'M GOING TO REACH INTO MY COAT FOR SOMETHING. IT'S NOT A WEAPON. I GIVE YOU MY WORD -- FOR WHAT IT'S WORTH -- BUT IT MIGHT CHANGE THINGS.

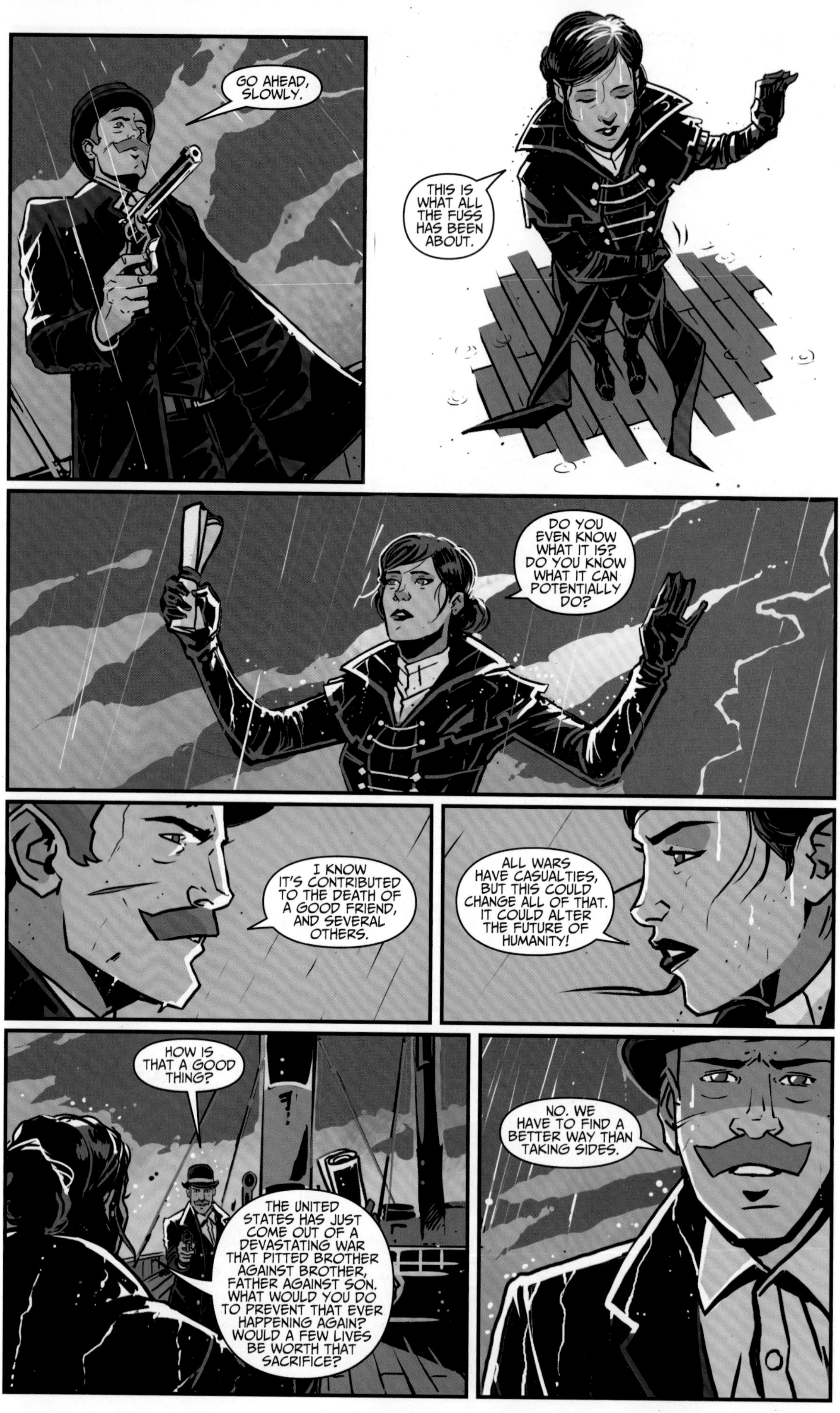

GO AHEAD, SLOWLY.
THIS IS WHAT ALL THE FUSS HAS BEEN ABOUT.
DO YOU EVEN KNOW WHAT IT IS? DO YOU KNOW WHAT IT CAN POTENTIALLY DO?
I KNOW IT'S CONTRIBUTED TO THE DEATH OF A GOOD FRIEND, AND SEVERAL OTHERS.
ALL WARS HAVE CASUALTIES, BUT THIS COULD CHANGE ALL OF THAT. IT COULD ALTER THE FUTURE OF HUMANITY!
HOW IS THAT A GOOD THING?
THE UNITED STATES HAS JUST COME OUT OF A DEVASTATING WAR THAT PITTED BROTHER AGAINST BROTHER, FATHER AGAINST SON. WHAT WOULD YOU DO TO PREVENT THAT EVER HAPPENING AGAIN? WOULD A FEW LIVES BE WORTH THAT SACRIFICE?
NO. WE HAVE TO FIND A BETTER WAY THAN TAKING SIDES.

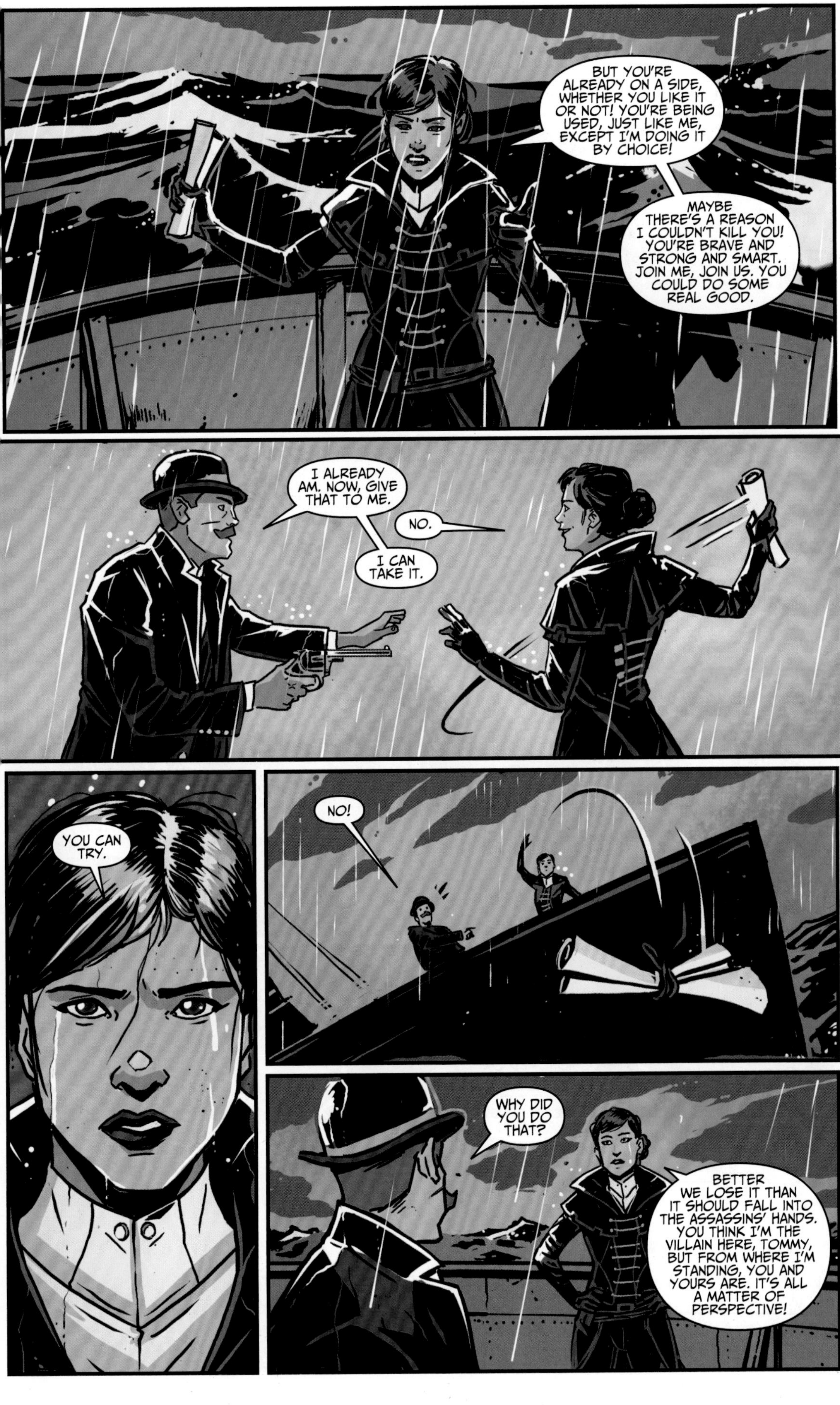
BUT YOU'RE ALREADY ON A SIDE, WHETHER YOU LIKE IT OR NOT! YOU'RE BEING USED, JUST LIKE ME, EXCEPT I'M DOING IT BY CHOICE!
MAYBE THERE'S A REASON I COULDN'T KILL YOU! YOU'RE BRAVE AND STRONG AND SMART. JOIN ME, JOIN US. YOU COULD DO SOME REAL GOOD.
I ALREADY AM. NOW, GIVE THAT TO ME.
NO.
I CAN TAKE IT.
YOU CAN TRY.
NO!
WHY DID YOU DO THAT?
BETTER WE LOSE IT THAN IT SHOULD FALL INTO THE ASSASSINS' HANDS. YOU THINK I'M THE VILLAIN HERE, TOMMY, BUT FROM WHERE I'M STANDING, YOU AND YOURS ARE. IT'S ALL A MATTER OF PERSPECTIVE!

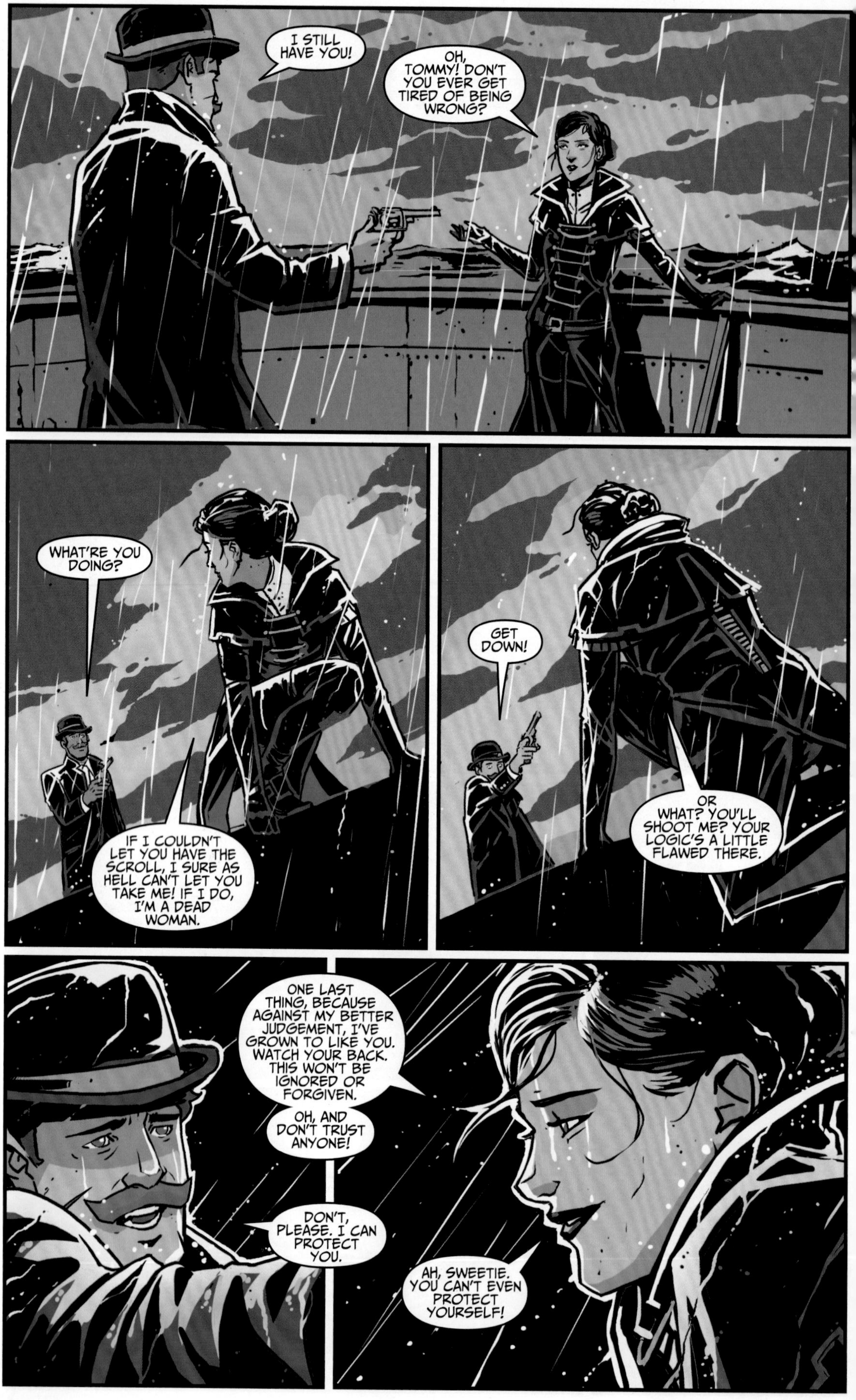
I STILL HAVE YOU!
OH, TOMMY! DON'T YOU EVER GET TIRED OF BEING WRONG?
WHAT'RE YOU DOING?
IF I COULDN'T LET YOU HAVE THE SCROLL, I SURE AS HELL CAN'T LET YOU TAKE ME! IF I DO, I'M A DEAD WOMAN.
GET DOWN!
OR WHAT? YOU'LL SHOOT ME? YOUR LOGIC'S A LITTLE FLAWED THERE.
ONE LAST THING, BECAUSE AGAINST MY BETTER JUDGEMENT, I'VE GROWN TO LIKE YOU. WATCH YOUR BACK. THIS WON'T BE IGNORED OR FORGIVEN.
OH, AND DON'T TRUST ANYONE!
DON'T, PLEASE. I CAN PROTECT YOU.
AH, SWEETIE. YOU CAN'T EVEN PROTECT YOURSELF!

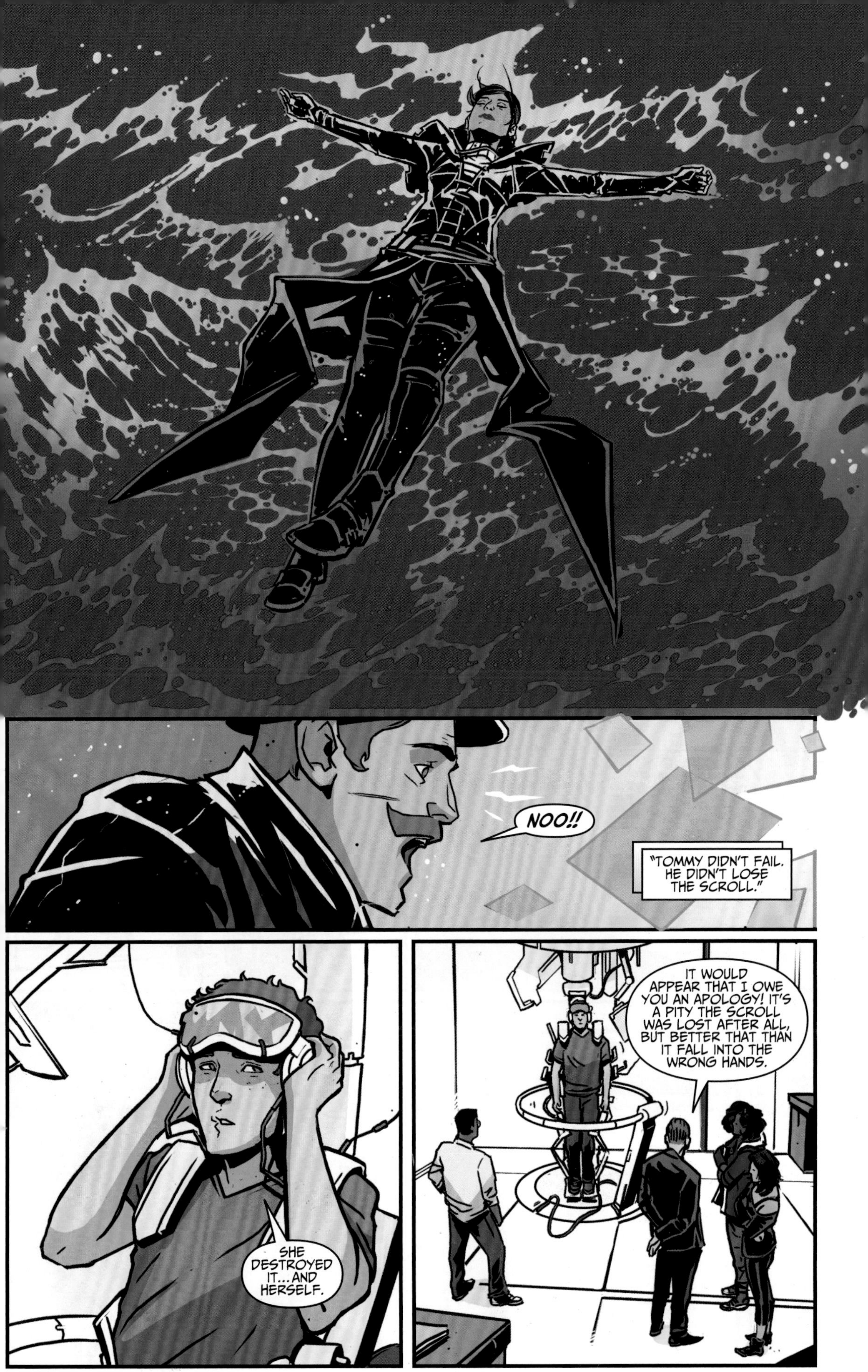
NOO!!
"TOMMY DIDN'T FAIL. HE DIDN'T LOSE THE SCROLL."
SHE DESTROYED IT...AND HERSELF.
IT WOULD APPEAR THAT I OWE YOU AN APOLOGY! IT'S A PITY THE SCROLL WAS LOST AFTER ALL, BUT BETTER THAT THAN IT FALL INTO THE WRONG HANDS.

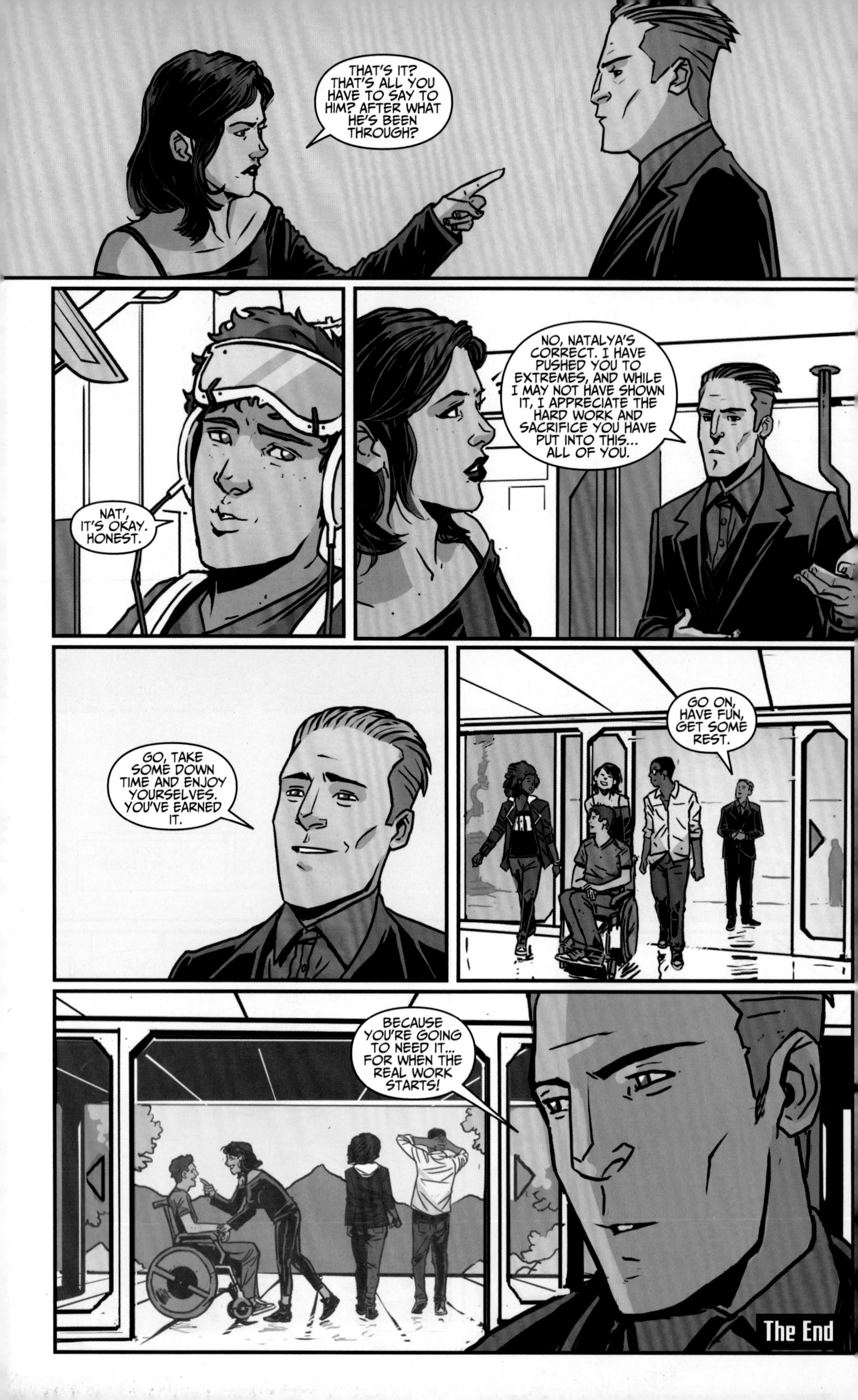
THAT'S IT? THAT'S ALL YOU HAVE TO SAY TO HIM? AFTER WHAT HE'S BEEN THROUGH?
NAT', IT'S OKAY. HONEST.
NO, NATALYA'S CORRECT. I HAVE PUSHED YOU TO EXTREMES, AND WHILE I MAY NOT HAVE SHOWN IT, I APPRECIATE THE HARD WORK AND SACRIFICE YOU HAVE PUT INTO THIS... ALL OF YOU.
GO, TAKE SOME DOWN TIME AND ENJOY YOURSELVES. YOU'VE EARNED IT.
GO ON, HAVE FUN, GET SOME REST.
BECAUSE YOU'RE GOING TO NEED IT... FOR WHEN THE REAL WORK STARTS!
The End

THE ORIGINAL PRIVATE EYES

Founded in 1850 by Allan Pinkerton – an immigrant barrel-maker turned Chicago police detective – the PINKERTON NATIONAL DETECTIVE AGENCY was one of America's most notorious crime-prevention and private security firms of the late nineteenth century.

Though Pinkerton initially specialized in train robberies and counterfeiting cases, after foiling a plot to assassinate Abraham Lincoln – who would later hire the agency as his personal 'secret service' during the American Civil War – the fledgling enterprise garnered a reputation as America's go-to office for counter-intelligence and security operations. By the early 1870s it had grown into the largest private law enforcement organization in the world.

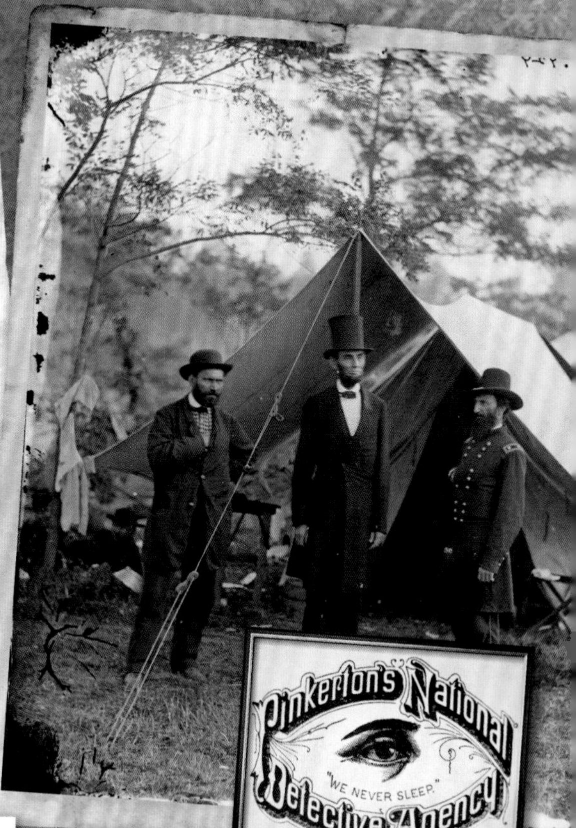

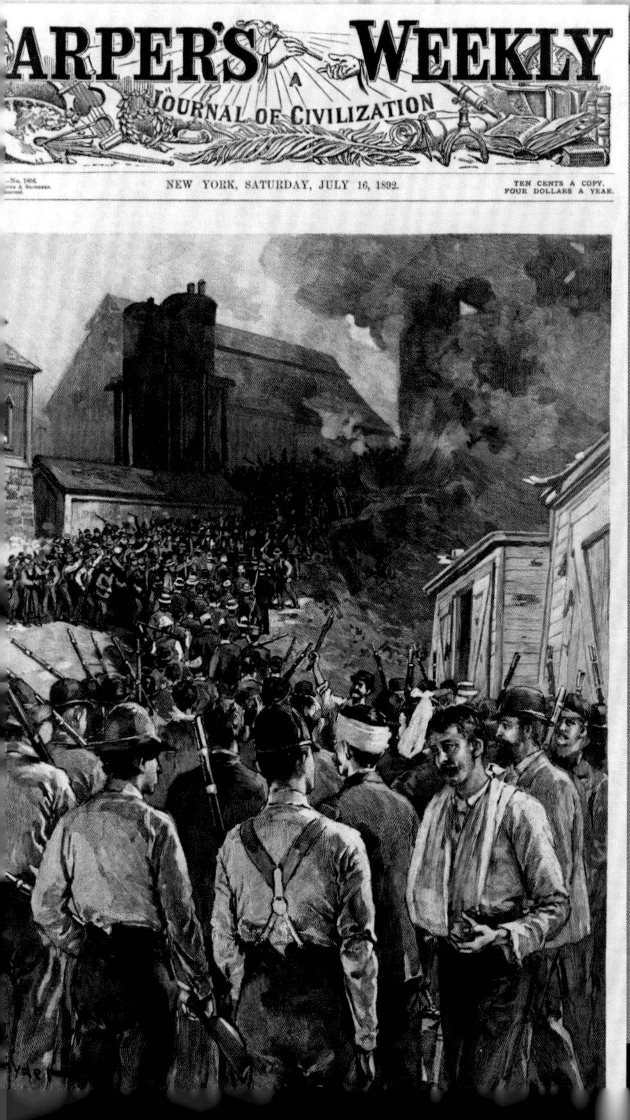
ARPER'S WEEKLY

A JOURNAL OF CIVILIZATION

NEW YORK, SATURDAY, JULY 16, 1892.

TEN CENTS A COPY.
FOUR DOLLARS A YEAR.

Adhering to a strict code of ethics and defined by its striking company logo (the supposed inspiration of the term 'private eye'), at its heyday, the Pinkerton agency had more agents under its employ than the standing US army and, using its extensive collection of mugshots, established the world's first criminal database. Frequently subcontracted for espionage operations by the US government, the agency also remained a favorite of the railroad companies, gaining legendary status for its role in the hunt and capture of outlaws like Wild Bill and Jesse James. But, as the century drew to a close and ownership passed to Allan's sons, Robert and William, the agency's public perception would take a turn for the worse.

Pinkerton's involvement with the labor strikes of the 1890s would ultimately prove their downfall. The company's past use of heavy-handed tactics, coupled with accusations of violence from union sympathisers, soon led to public outcry, culminating in the events of the Homestead Strike of 1892 when a firefight involving 300 Pinkerton agents led to the death of 16 men. Pinkerton's reputation was left in tatters and the company would spend years struggling to rebuild it.

Nevertheless, the Pinkerton agency endured, and today Pinkerton Inc. has grown into a billion dollar multinational organization, remaining one of the world's leading providers of security.

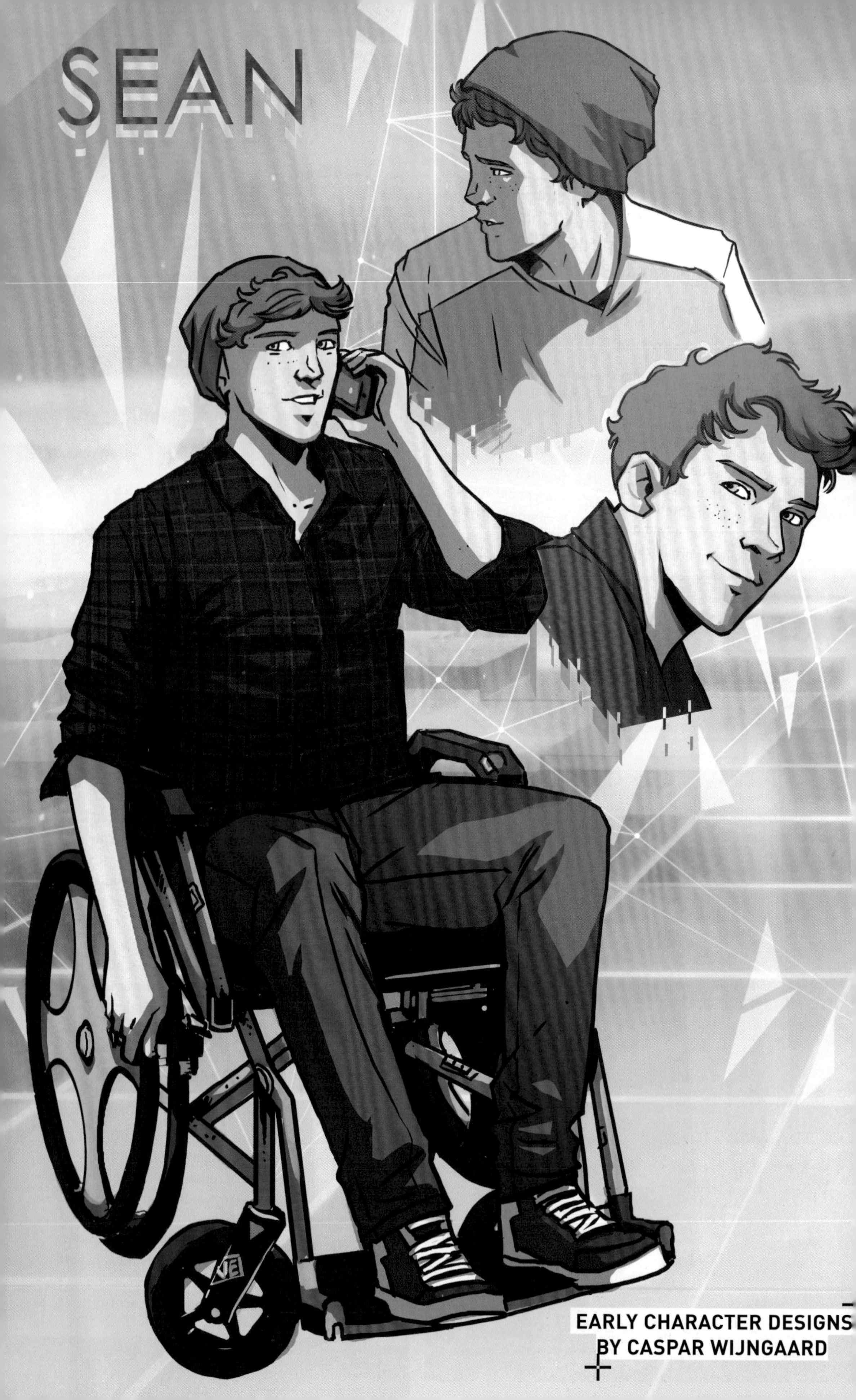
SEAN

EARLY CHARACTER DESIGNS
BY CASPAR WIJNGAARD

GRACE

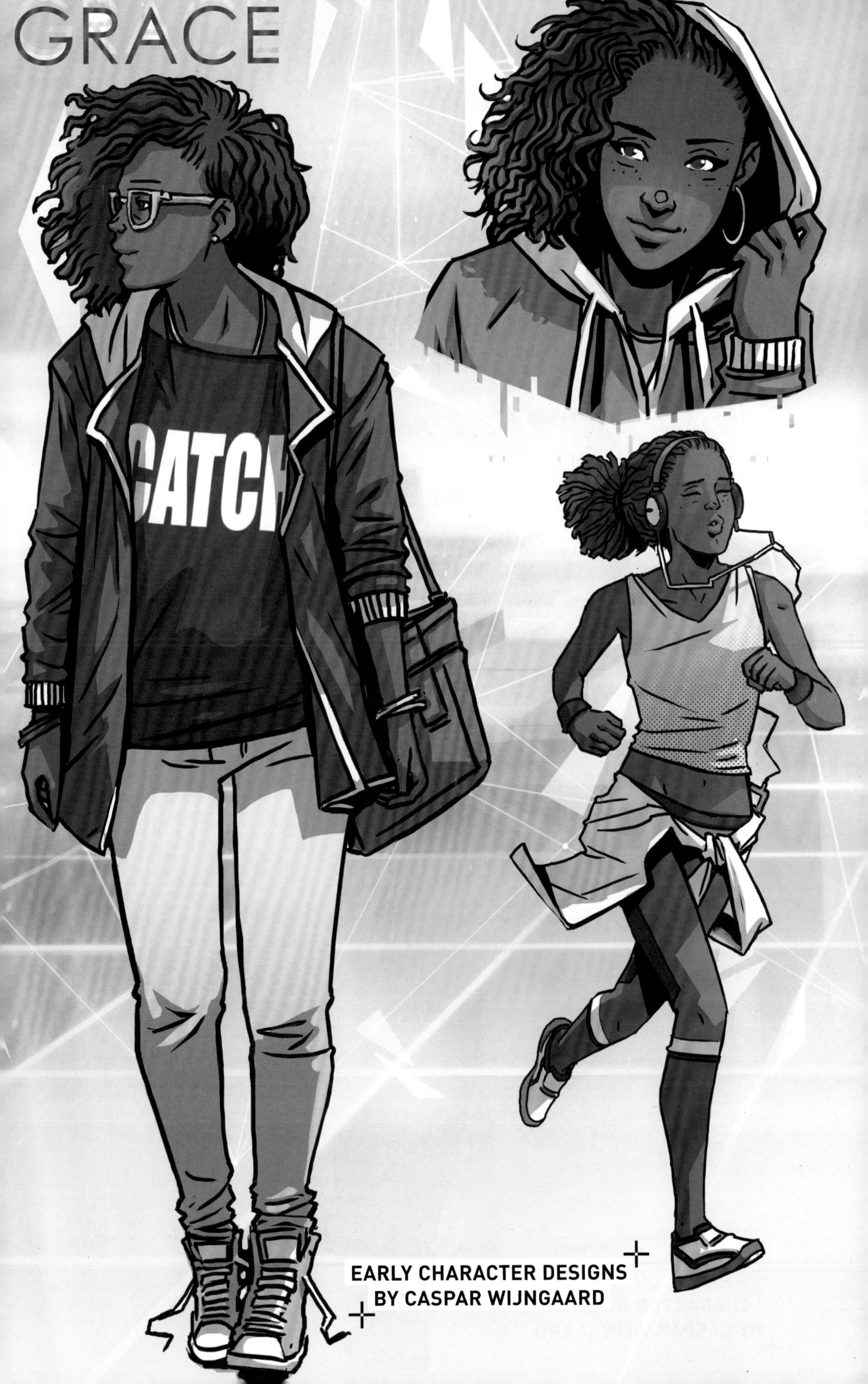

EARLY CHARACTER DESIGNS
BY CASPAR WIJNGAARD

EVIE FRYE

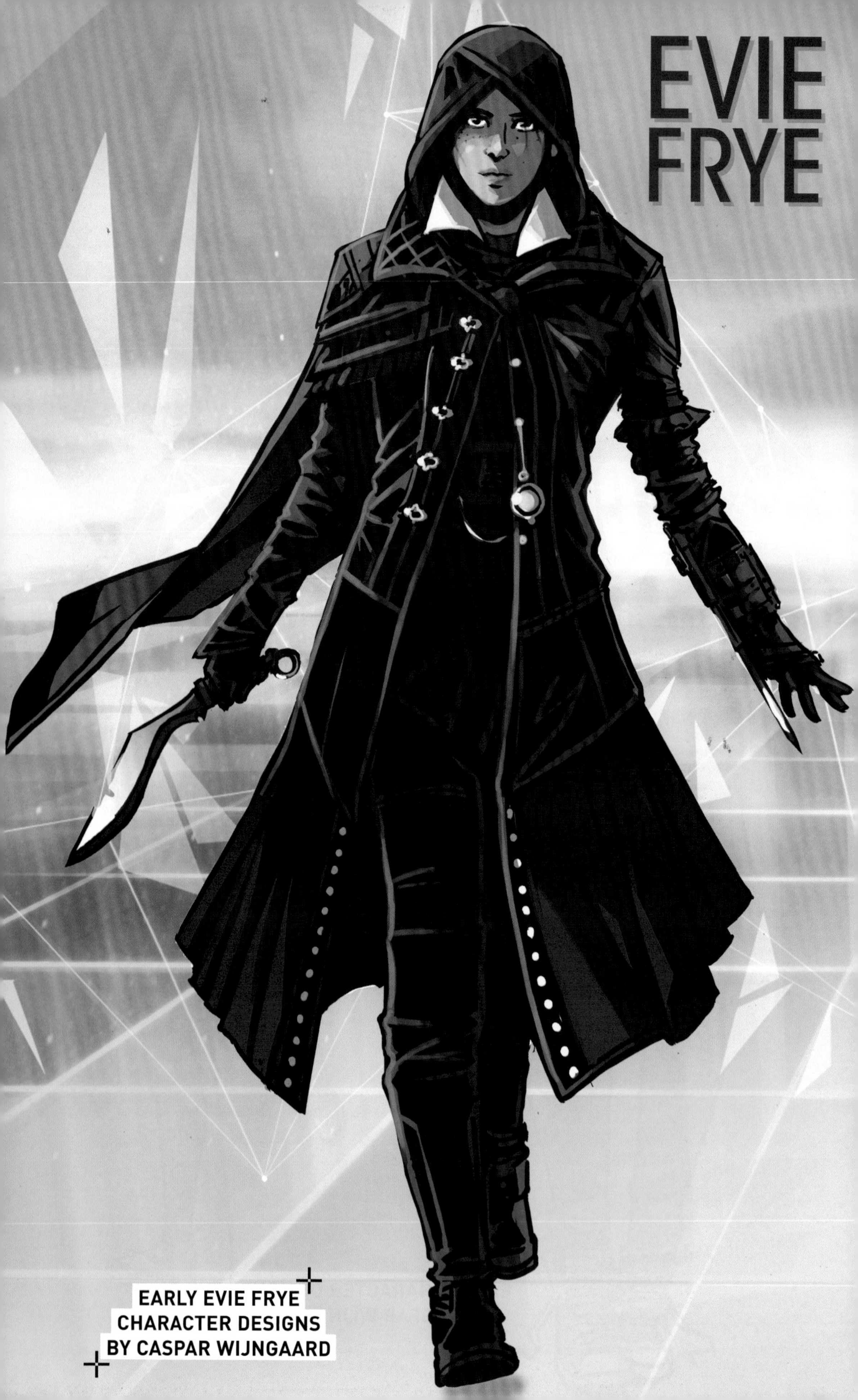

EARLY EVIE FRYE
CHARACTER DESIGNS
BY CASPAR WIJNGAARD

COVER
GALLERY

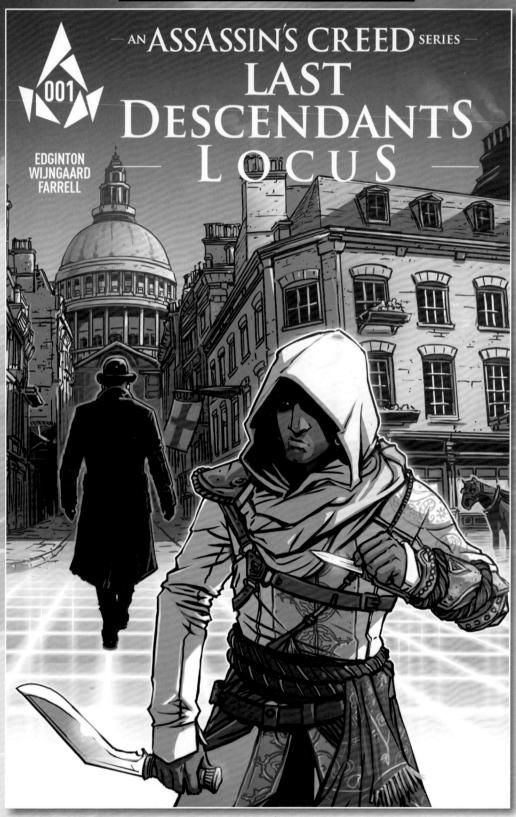

AN ASSASSIN'S CREED SERIES

LAST DESCENDANTS
LOCUS

001

EDGINTON
WIJNGAARD
FARRELL

COVER A: CASPAR WIJNGAARD

COVER B: VALERIA LUXFERA

COVER C: I.N.J. CULBARD

COVER D: VERITY GLASS

COVER E: SCHOLASTIC TIE-IN COVER

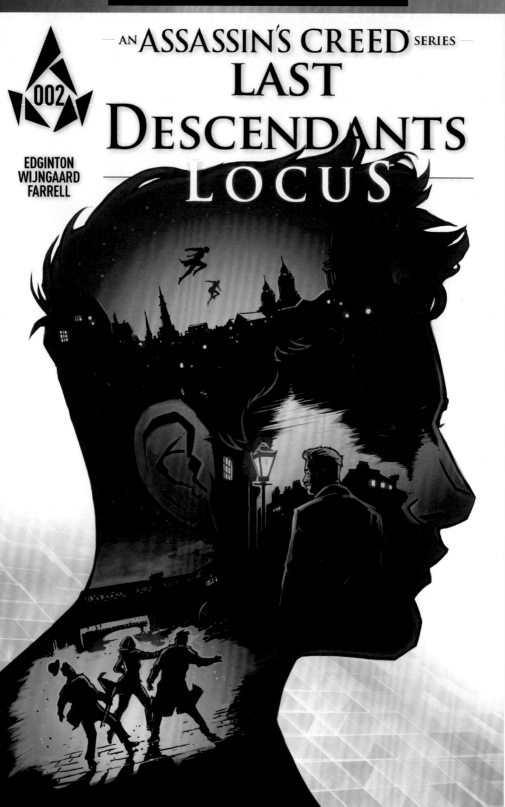

AN ASSASSIN'S CREED SERIES
LAST
DESCENDANTS
LOCUS

002

EDGINTON
WIJNGAARD
FARRELL

COVER A: CASPAR WIJNGAARD

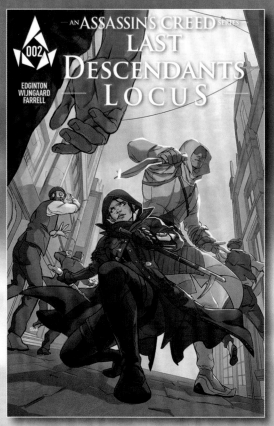

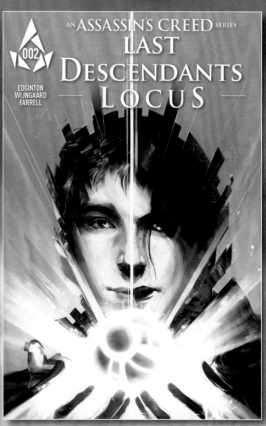

COVER B: VALERIA FAVOCCIA

COVER C: VERITY GLASS

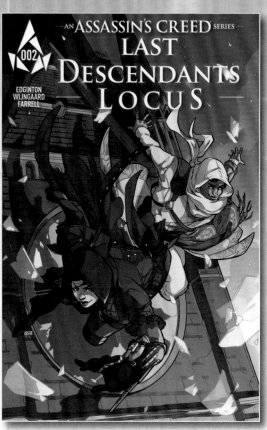

NYCC EXCLUSIVE COVER: VALERIA FAVOCCIA

AN ASSASSIN'S CREED SERIES

LAST DESCENDANTS

LOCUS

EDGINTON
WIJNGAARD
FARRELL

COVER A: CASPAR WIJNGAARD

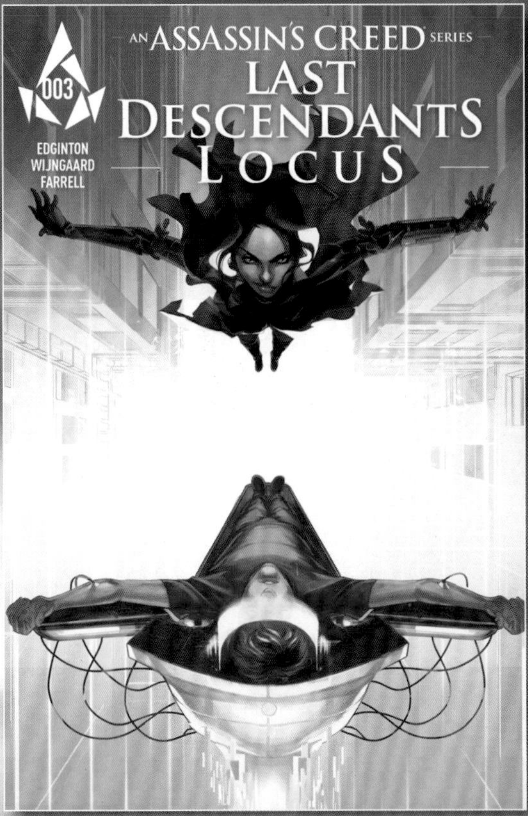
AN ASSASSIN'S CREED SERIES
LAST
DESCENDANTS
LOCUS
003
EDGINTON
WIJNGAARD
FARRELL

COVER B: VERITY GLASS

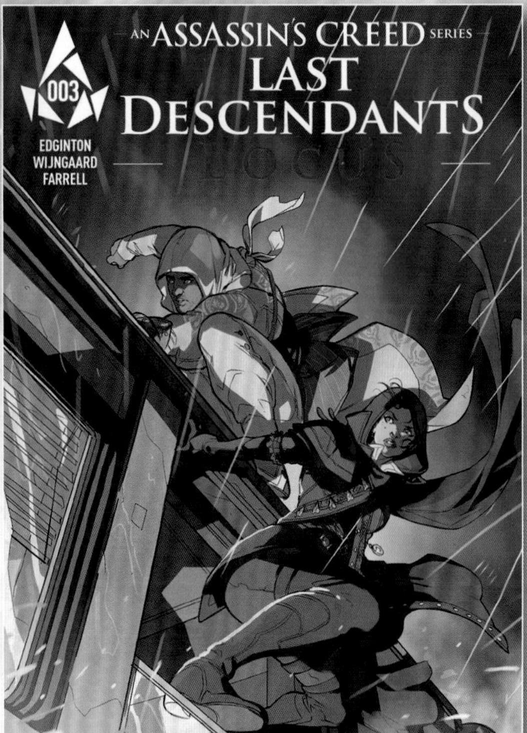
AN ASSASSIN'S CREED SERIES
LAST
DESCENDANTS
LOCUS
003
EDGINTON
WIJNGAARD
FARRELL

COVER C: VALERIA FAVOCCIA

An ASSASSIN'S CREED SERIES

LAST DESCENDANTS LOCUS

004

EDGINTON
WIJNGAARD
FARRELL

COVER A: CASPAR WIJNGAARD

AN ASSASSIN'S CREED SERIES
LAST DESCENDANTS
LOCUS
004
EDGINTON
WIJNGAARD
FARRELL

COVER B: VALERIA FAVOCCIA

AN ASSASSIN'S CREED SERIES
LAST DESCENDANTS
LOCUS
004
EDGINTON
WIJNGAARD
FARRELL

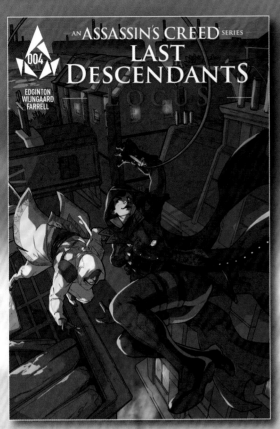

COVER C: VERITY GLASS

BIOS

WRITER
IAN EDGINTON

Ian Edginton is a British comic book writer who has worked for a variety of publishers including Marvel, DC, Dark Horse, IDW, BOOM! and many more. Best know for his collaborations with 2000AD on titles including *Stickleback*, *Leviathan*, *Red Seas*, *Ampney Crucis Investigates* and *Brass Sun*, Edginton has worked extensively on game properties like *Kane and Lynch*, *Dead Space*, *Warhammer 40K* and *The Evil Within*. Past work includes *Judge Dredd*, *Batman*, *Wolverine*, *X-Force*, *Uncanny X-Men* and *Blade*, as well as *Aliens*, *Predator*, *Terminator*, *Star Trek*, *Star Wars*, *Planet of the Apes*, *Torchwood* and *Doctor Who*.

ARTIST
CASPAR WIJNGAARD

Is a British comic artist and illustrator, who has worked for a variety of publishers including Image Comics, BOOM! and Titan, along with illustrating for companies such as the BBC, Virgin and Microsoft. His most recent series, the highly acclaimed *Limbo*, was co-created with fellow British writer Dan Watters. In addition to comics, he enjoys retro video games, bad VHS movies and resides in the English countryside with his partner and two year old daughter.

COLORIST
TRIONA FARRELL

Triona Farrell is an Irish comic artist and colorist. Branching out professionally around four years ago, Farrell has worked for BOOM!, Titan Comics and a number of independent publishers, on various titles including *Weavers* and *Big Trouble in Little China/Escape From New York*.